Out of Time

NO MATTER WHEN

NANCY ADAMS

No Matter When
ISBN # 978-0-85715-750-8
©Copyright Nancy Adams 2011
Cover Art by Lyn Taylor ©Copyright October 2011
Interior text design by Claire Siemaszkiewicz
Total-E-Bound Publishing

NO MATTER WHEN

Dedication

Thanks to my friends Kate, Rhonda, Megan and Cindy for your unconditional support and encouragement.

Prologue

Roses.

Small, red roses were hand-stitched into the sheets on the bed.

The flower was a fitting symbol.

You cannot come into contact with her, on any level. McGill's warning was still fresh in his mind.

Strands of brown hair hung across her face. The need to brush them away had the muscles in his stomach clenching and his hands squeezing into fists. Fighting the need to touch her was one battle he didn't want to win.

Damn it. Either way, he was screwed. He could destroy everything he'd worked for with a single touch to her skin...or end up torturing himself if he didn't take this opportunity.

He reached out and skimmed the tips of his fingers over her cheek in a light caress, allowing himself the brief luxury. Then, pulling his hand away, he stepped back, keeping watch over her relaxed features.

Rebellion filled his chest as his hands turned once again into fists. Knowing full well she would remember the words, he stared at her and quietly said, "You're mine, angel." The whispered declaration was barely audible. Yet he knew each word would have already been stored.

Turning away, he headed for the door. He had to go. He couldn't take any more chances. He just didn't trust himself when it came to her. With just the whisper of those three words, he might already have done irreversible damage.

He clenched his jaw and glanced back to where she slept on the bed. If that was the case and he'd screwed up, he'd find a way to undo it. Time was on his side.

Chapter One

Northern England

"You're being summoned."

With arms crossed and legs braced apart, Gabriel Sutherland watched the movement in the forest from the high walls of the keep. "How does he look?"

Stepping closer to him, Harry answered, "Like he's been sliced open wi' an axe."

Slowly turning his head, Gabe raised a single, golden eyebrow.

"How the hell do ye think he looks?" Harry crossed his thick arms and glared back. "The man is going to die, very soon." Harry sighed. "He's agitated about something. You need to get down there. I'll take care of things here."

Gabe nodded and turned back to the forest. "Go and find out who is behind this. These Scots are too well organised — they're running basic assault drills."

"Really?" Harry focused on the forest.

"Mmm. They're running *our* basic drills," Gabe clarified.

"That's interesting. Then I suppose I'll pay those boys a quick visit, while you see to Thomas."

In the shadow of the heavy wooden door, Gabe stood motionless, watching.

Shit!

Harry was right—Thomas was dying. And from what the professor had said, Thomas would be dead before midnight.

Thomas. The poor bastard had been hit from behind with an axe three days ago, and his wound had grown steadily worse since then. Gabe watched as Thomas closed his eyes and gritted his teeth. Even the simple act of breathing looked to be almost unbearable.

Squeezing his hands into fists, Gabe stared at him. This was no way for a man like Thomas to die. He was tall and strong, and a talented fighter.

The unfamiliar feeling of amazement shook him again.

Everything Professor McGill had told him was true—it had all taken place just as he'd said it would. He hadn't believed a goddamn word the little man had said until this very moment. He *still* was having a hard time believing...everything. He narrowed his eyes as he studied Thomas lying helpless on the large bed. He and Thomas were so similar in appearance it was scary. He should be used to it by now—two weeks had passed since he'd first arrived—yet it still amazed him.

When McGill had told him that Thomas was a distant relative, he'd thought the man was a mental case. Until the proof was standing in front of him.

They were roughly the same size and build and they both shared the same light brown hair, green eyes and strongly angled chin. And, from what Gabe could tell, Thomas was calm, self-assured and assessed situations before reacting, traits that made a good soldier great. And if he was anything, Thomas was a soldier.

The steady pounding against the north wall echoed inside the keep as Gabe continued to study Thomas.

Thomas smiled weakly and called out, "So the Scottish bastards are still at it?"

Gabe's deep chuckle echoed in the chamber. Shifting his weight casually, he stepped from the shadows. "Yes, they are."

Stopping a few feet away, Gabe kept his stance non-threatening as he looked Thomas over. The man was pale and clearly struggling to breathe, yet his eyes were bright and sharp as he stared back. Gabe clasped his hands tightly behind his back. This was wrong—a soldier shouldn't die like this. And even though he knew Thomas was a man of high-ranking stature—a lord, of all things—he was still a soldier.

Gabe paused and gave a slight bow as he reached the side of the man's bed.

"We are beyond that now, Gabriel." Thomas waved his hand. The slight movement seemed to take tremendous effort.

"Are we?" Gabe asked, watching the man who, to all appearances, was his uncle.

"Do you dare argue with me?" His arrogant tone made Gabe smile. "You are Edwin's son, my nephew, and soon to be Lord Sutherland."

Narrowing his eyes, Gabe studied Thomas closely. "I am the bastard son of your brother."

9

The information McGill had given him about Thomas had come in handy — all he'd had to do was plant the idea of his being Edwin's son and Thomas had latched on to it. Gabe didn't like to lie and it wasn't something he did on a regular basis, but if it made things easier, then so be it. "The King sent me to help protect your holding. I didn't come to collect a title as payment."

"Your father would have said the very same thing. Ah, Edwin! You remind me of him." Thomas' soft chuckle changed to a rough, painful-sounding cough. "I miss him." Thomas shook his head and looked up at Gabe. "I hope to see Edwin when I join Marie and my son. Though I doubt God would allow him through the gates."

Gabe frowned. "No."

Thomas smiled. "Your father was happiest when he was either in battle or in a woman's bed. *Any* woman's bed," he stressed. The chuckle that followed caused the upper half of his body to shake painfully.

Gabe's frown deepened.

"Edwin will most certainly be denied entry into paradise. Yet, it was those sins that have brought me aid. The fact that you are my brother's bastard means nothing to me. You are a Sutherland and you will be my successor."

"What about your youngest brother, Edmund?" Gabe asked. "You should choose a legitimate heir."

"Edmund would make a suitable replacement, but he is vassal to Gomfrey in the south, and his wife is expecting their firstborn. He would not be able to arrive in time. This land cannot be without protection for even one day." Thomas raised his voice, clearly agitated. "The risk of the Scots raiding further inland

is too great and that is something I will not allow."
Thomas finished on a harsh tone, his battered body
stiff.

Gabe nodded patiently, understanding Thomas's
determination to protect what belonged to him.

"If Edwin was alive today, I would have chosen him
over Edmund. Your father was unmatched in battle."

The man was dead. How good could he have been? Gabe
raised his eyebrows to show his interest but kept his
thoughts to himself.

"He was vassal to Fleming when he was killed. I
was told the battle was exceptionally brutal. It took
four men to bring Edwin down, and three didn't
survive the blows he delivered before his passing."

"Impressive," Gabe admitted, to Thomas and to
himself.

"Edwin was killed so many years ago fighting for
Fleming that I did not think to look for his kin."
Thomas shook his head sadly. "It is a mistake I sorely
regret." The man was telling the truth—Gabe would
know if he was lying.

Thomas was an easy man to like and, in Gabe's
eyes, his honesty and loyalty increased his worth as a
man. "How could you have known?" Gabe shrugged.
"From the little my mother spoke of him, he had only
one son and he died before he knew of my existence."
It was the tale McGill had made him memorise—it
also just happened to be the mirror image of his own
life—his real life.

"So, Edwin spent time with your mother?" Thomas
asked subtly.

Shrugging, he answered, "My mother never said
otherwise."

It had never bothered Gabe that his real parents hadn't been married—it was normal in his time—but here, now, it mattered a great deal.

A whisper of movement caught Gabe's attention and Harry stepped up beside him and leaned in close. "I have some interesting Intel on our visitors. They've also moved to the north wall. If we don't get a move on, there will be a big fucking hole in it by midnight."

Gabe nodded and focused his attention back on Thomas, who was staring at Harry in surprise.

Harry bowed slightly and gave the lord a wide, friendly smile. "I am sorry to interrupt, my Lord."

"Not at all, Harry. In fact I welcome your intrusion." Thomas's words ended in a cough.

Gabe frowned at Thomas's rough cough. "I must go. Your north wall is becoming a liability."

Thomas turned his green stare towards Gabe. "Not yet," he ordered. "Bring my steward in here."

Gabe held on to his patience and turned to Harry, nodding.

Harry followed Thomas' steward back into the chamber and, once the heavy, wooden door was closed, Gabe turned back towards Thomas and waited quietly.

"I will be dead soon," Thomas began, "which will leave my title and lands without a lord and my people without protection. As Gabriel is Edwin's son, and my nephew, I have chosen him as my successor." Thomas turned his sharp, green eyes on Gabe and addressed him directly. "I am giving my title and lands to you," he declared in a commanding voice. "It is a large burden to undertake and at times will not be easy. But you are Edwin's son—I have no doubt that you will be able to bear the weight of being lord of this holding and the lands that accompany it. If, however, you feel the need to pass the title over to Edmund at such time as he is able to travel north, that too is acceptable. But promise me" — Thomas stopped to catch a painful breath — "as Edwin's son and as a Sutherland, that you will not leave my land and my people unprotected after I have left this world."

Gabe studied the man. The offer was unbelievable. An entire life ready made, with a large keep, a small army to train how he saw fit, acres of land and a title to top it all off. It was the perfect set-up in which he and the others could live, at least until the time came when the professor could explain why they were here.

Gabe hesitated. It felt wrong misleading Thomas and now accepting what he freely offered. Yet all of their basic survival needs would be met…

Gabe shook his head. "I didn't come here for this. I only came to help."

Thomas smiled and Gabe couldn't help but notice the grey tinge to his mouth. "Your father would have said the same. And as I wouldn't have with him, I am not giving you a choice in the matter. I am handing the fate of my people, my land and my holding over to you. You will take care of them." It was an order.

Gabe stood looking at Thomas. This was so fucked up. All of this. His survival instincts had gone into overdrive from the second he'd arrived and now, with an ideal set-up being handed to him, he had no reason to hesitate. He would accept it — he had to. He nodded. "I accept."

Thomas sighed and relaxed his beaten body into the large bed.

Gabe stepped closer and gently laid his hand on the man's shoulder. "Try to rest now. I'm going with Harry to see the damage to the north wall. I will be back soon."

Thomas nodded, smiling weakly.

As Gabe pulled away, Thomas's hand flew out and grasped his wrist. The quick movement clearly caused the man great pain but he held tight. "Promise me, Gabe."

Gabe had been always so certain about his future but, as he'd recently found out, things change—life changes. Not knowing if it was a promise he would be able to keep, he gave Thomas what he thought was a reasonable substitute. Gently patting the man's hand, he nodded. "Your people and land will be protected as long as I am here."

As though a huge weight had been lifted from his body, Thomas sighed again and rested back on the bed.

Turning towards the door, Gabe stopped when Thomas spoke to his steward.

"Spread the word that Gabriel will be my heir and that, as of now, he should be treated accordingly."

"Yes, my Lord." David bowed, then turned to Gabe and bowed a second time.

"Also send word to my brother Edmund of my decision and that he should make his way north when he is able."

Gabe caught Thomas' stare and nodded at the dying man before leaving the room.

Walking side by side, Gabe and Harry made their way along the battlements towards the north wall.

"Did you visit our guests?" Gabe asked, focusing on the task at hand.

Harry nodded to the thick forest north of the castle. "Just a little to the right of twelve o' clock."

Gabe pulled his small thermal binoculars from his thigh pocket. They picked up dozens of heat signatures moving around in the dark forest. Two men, separate from the rest, caught Gabe's attention. "Who's the nervous pacer?"

When he switched off the thermal setting on his binoculars, Gabe's vision instantly adjusted to the dark. He watched as the tall, thin-faced blond marched around the campfire. It was clear that he was agitated but other than circling the fire, there was no other outward indication. He continually turned to face a dark-haired man who was sitting calmly on a log. Gabe fixed his attention on the second man, who seemed unaffected by the blond's anxiety and talked calmly as he stared into a fire.

"I'd like you to meet John. He seems to be the one behind this little skirmish. He was very unhappy when I was visiting and said something about the Scots being bloody useless."

"I assume you had no problems with entry?" Gabe asked, keeping his stare on the dark-haired man.

"Problems?" Harry snorted. "My only problem was I didn't get to prove not all Scots are useless. I cannae believe I didn't kill him for sayin' that."

"Well, that's what happens when you spend too much time in English territory. We've converted you into a civilised human being."

"Then I suppose it's lucky for me I met you after my basic training."

Gabe gave Harry a crooked smile as he continued to watch the dark-haired man. There was something about him that felt familiar. What was it?

"Gabe?" Harry asked, the humour in his voice gone. "What is it?"

Gabe turned to Harry. They had always worked well together—time and experience had caused them to become in tune with one another.

"Not sure," Gabe answered, shaking his head. "Seems to me John has more help than just those useless Scots."

"Mmm," Harry said, crossing his arms. "Feels like military, doesn't it?"

"Yes, it does. But from when?" Gabe asked softly.

"Good question." Harry paused for a moment. "I can tell you from my little excursion that the one with the dark hair is Eric. And Eric, too, seems to know a little about launching an attack on an enemy position."

"I bet he does." Gabe said quietly. "Too bad for him he won't get the chance."

"You, ah..." Harry paused a second time. "You want him put on the unavailable list?"

A smile tugged at Gabe's lips as he over the wall to assess the damage to the north wall. The Sutherland keep was large and built in an easily defensible area. Surrounded by a deep moat that joined with a river on both sides and with a large, heavily fortified gate and drawbridge at the front and a smaller version at the rear, it was nearly impossible to gain entrance to. The high walls and imposing towers rose high above the trees, making surveillance of the nearby forest and valleys easily managed.

Gabe considered the primitive weapons of this time laughable, but they were making quite a hole in the thick, fortified wall of the keep, which surprised him.

"I don't think that's necessary," Gabe answered Harry. "But Eric and his friend John will find it difficult to attack without their weapons."

"No problem," said Harry. "Should I use current methods?"

"If you can."

"Does this mean you finally believe?"

With his feet planted apart, Gabe crossed his arms and stared out into the dark forest. "I'm not sure what to believe. This could all be some fucked up dream I'm having."

"Dead men don't dream. And ye, my friend, are not dead."

"I should be." He shifted his eyes to Harry. "So should you." Gabe shook his head, trying to shake this new, medieval reality out of his mind.

Harry rested a big hand on his shoulder. "But we're not. It's difficult to adjust at first, but you have me to steer you through the proper procedures. It's the least I can do for the future Lord Sutherland." The humour was back in Harry's thick burr.

"*You* are going to show me the proper procedures for what?" Gabe asked sceptically. "Living in the year 1503?"

"Yes, Captain Sutherland, as a matter of fact I am." Harry gave him a wide smile.

Gabe chuckled, then mumbled under his breath, "Why am I not comforted by that thought?"

Chapter Two

It was rush hour, but the bike path that led into downtown was all but empty, so it was easy for Lilly to keep up a steady pace. This was her favourite part about working the evening shift, the ride into work, and at the rate she was going, she would arrive earlier than expected. Gliding down a small hill, she looked to her right at the lake and took a deep breath. The June air was clear by Toronto standards. She would enjoy it while she could, because once July hit this clear air would be replaced by humidity, thanks to Lake Ontario.

Smiling, Lilly lifted her face into the wind. She still couldn't believe her luck. It had been a total surprise when Stacey had told her all purchasing for the CN Tower would be in the evenings—something about deliveries being easier to receive at night, when the tower was closed to the public. And because she was the only part-time buyer, Lilly had been 'volunteered' to work the new evening shift. Who cared what the reasons were? She was happy with the change. She had never liked working during the day, when there were so many people around the tower, talking, yelling and laughing as they stared up at the mammoth structure. Besides, dealing with the other employees wasn't exactly her strong point. It wasn't that she didn't like them — they were all very nice. She just liked being alone. She worked better alone. She *was* better alone.

Working evenings would free up enough time for her to add another class to her schedule at school, which would mean she could complete her Master's in medieval studies sooner than expected. She loved her classes, loved studying the past — specifically the medieval era. There was something so romantic about it — kings and queens, battles, grand castles, and knights rescuing damsels in distress. Although she knew in reality the time had been plagued with death, destruction and disease — it amazed her that humans had not only survived in that time, but had thrived.

Reaching the main offices of the tower, Lilly glided to a stop, hopping off her bike.

"Hey, Lilly," Stacey greeted her. "How was the ride?"

"Stress-free, thanks." She lifted her back wheel into the bike rack and asked, "Busy today?"

"Yup. The schools are rushing to get in a few extra field trips. There were kids everywhere. Want to go back to days?" Stacey teased.

A light gust of wind pulled at Stacey's black hair, fanning it over her shoulder.

Lilly laughed, focusing on locking up her bike. "No way. I love working evenings."

Stacey grabbed the handlebars and held the bike steady as Lilly locked up the back wheel. "I know," she said softly.

Lilly smiled. Stacey was one of those few people she could truly call a friend. She was funny, smart, and she had accepted Lilly for who she was.

"What are you up to tonight?"

"Not much." Stacey shrugged. "Go home, feed the cat, maybe feed the husband. Watch some reality trash."

"You should go for a walk. It's beautiful by the lake."

"Of course you'd say that. Unlike you, some of us don't belong outdoors." Stacey scratched at her throat. "I think it's an allergy."

Lilly laughed. "Fresh air is good for you."

"Yes, dear." Stacey rolled her eyes.

"Okay, then, what am *I* up to tonight?" Lilly asked, as the light breeze turned into a sudden rush of wind that tugged at her. She looked down to see dust and leaves swirling around her feet in a perfect circle. Feeling uneasy, she stepped slightly to the right, out of the spinning air.

"Normal orders. It'll be a quiet night. Actually, knowing you, it will only take you an hour to finish. You should ditch work and come and have dinner with Ted and me."

"A boss doesn't tell her employee to ditch work. You're not setting a good example," Lilly scolded playfully.

"Yeah, you're probably right." Stacey waved her hand. "You're fired."

"Okay, but without me you'll have to order all those miniature souvenirs of the tower yourself," Lilly teased, then frowned as she felt the wind spin around her legs and feet once again. She stepped back and to the left, away from it.

"I hate those things," Stacey groaned. "They give me nightmares. You're un-fired. Oh! Here comes my bus. I'll call you later." Stacey unexpectedly gave Lilly a quick hug.

Startled by the show of affection, it took Lilly a second to recover. "Okay."

Stacey ran for her bus. Boarding, she returned Lilly's wave, then disappeared inside the bus as it pulled away from the kerb.

A terrible sense of dread caused Lilly's stomach to lurch. It was so sudden and so strong, she placed her hand to her middle. She had a strange sense that was the last time she would ever see Stacey's smiling face. She jumped when a horn sounded and the bus driver shook his fist at the driver of a dark blue SUV parked in the bus lane.

The wind suddenly picked up. Lilly looked down, puzzled to see dirt and leaves spinning around her again. The mini whirlwind of dust had grown and was now at thigh-height, covering her black capris in dirt. She attempted to step out of the spinning debris, but it moved with her, keeping her in its centre.

"Weird," she whispered to herself and unsnapped her bike helmet.

She felt the ground tremble as a strong vibration shot through her body. It was followed by an ear-shattering explosion from above. Her head flew up, just in time to see bright orange flames shooting out of the main observation deck. Shards of glass and chunks of light grey concrete began to fall from the sky.

Struggling to move, Lilly stared up as the city around her became eerily quiet. The top of the tower swayed in the wind, tilting from one side to the other. There was a loud crunching noise as a large chunk of cement broke free. Watching in horrified slow motion, Lilly sucked in a breath as the space deck and antenna tipped gracefully to the side and slid from the top of the tower. Even as she watched, frozen, Lilly knew the top of the tower was going to land right where she was standing. Right on top of her. It had a little over a kilometre to fall before it reached her. She was a good runner, but not fast enough to outrun gravity, even if she could move. But she couldn't move. She felt weighed down, as though an unseen force was keeping her locked in place.

A large chunk of concrete landed only a few feet away from her, exploding. She tried to turn away from the flying debris, but she just couldn't. She had lost control over her own body.

Smaller fragments had been caught up in the vortex spinning around her, scratching her arms and legs and stinging her face and neck. The largest of the fragments hit her forehead just below her hairline, causing her vision to narrow and grow dark. She blinked hard, trying to focus, feeling her own blood slide down the side of her face.

Every muscle in her body was frozen as she listened to the rush of the wind whipping around her, the crunching of stone as it fell to the ground and the screams of people racing to get out of the path of destruction. Frozen moments passed like hours.

The shadow of the falling space deck grew as it raced towards her. She was going to die. But her life didn't flash before her eyes, not that she would have expected it to. She hadn't really lived so there would have been little to see. Oddly enough, a sense of peace came over her. She was ready. Ready to see her mom. Ready to be with someone she loved. God, she had really missed that.

As she stood in the shadow of the falling deck, the vortex closed over the top of her head, and she closed her eyes against the dust and dirt spinning around her. A feeling of weightlessness enveloped her as she sucked in another breath...and fell.

She connected with the soft, uneven ground with such force that her knees buckled and her body flew back, slamming her to the earth. The air was forced from her lungs and her head bounced off the ground. Blinking back the pain, she felt the vortex pull at her until she began to slide.

Panic rose even as the wind whipping around her slowed, but she continued to slide. Then, as quickly as it had claimed her, the strange, paralysing wind released her and she could suddenly move her arms and legs. Confused and disoriented, she flipped over onto her stomach and began to claw at the earth until she caught hold of a root sticking out of the ground and she was jarred to a halt. The sudden turning and stopping caused her throbbing head to spin even more and darkness closed over her.

Resting her forehead in the soft dirt, she breathed heavily as she struggled to maintain her hold—on the root, and on consciousness. The urge to let go was so strong—her hand ached and her arm was shaking uncontrollably as the pounding in her head seem to increase. The ground began to vibrate under her, as if something was hammering from beneath the dirt. She fought to keep her eyes open. She just couldn't do it—she felt so sluggish, so tired. Her eyelids drooped and her body began to relax. The hand clinging to the root became limp and she began to slide.

An instant later, a deep voice cursed at the same time a strong grip locked around her wrist, pulling at her. With her face in the cool dirt, Lilly finally conceded, allowing the darkness to sweep over her.

* * * *

"Come on, wake up." The voice was deep, quiet, like a whisper in her head.

Lilly felt her body shake, but she hadn't willed the movement and when she tried to open her eyes she couldn't seem to lift her lids.

"Open your eyes for me." His soft, accented words seemed to pull at her. "Just once and I'll be happy." The way he was calling to her, she could hear the need in his voice, yet he sounded calm.

A warm hand gently smoothed her hair back from her face; fingertips brushed her ear. The deep voice spoke again. "Come on, angel, just once, so I know you're okay."

The lure of his voice was so tempting Lilly felt compelled to do as he asked. Her lashes fluttered as she slowly opened her eyes. Her head was pounding and the edges of her vision were dark. Still, she wanted to see who was calling to her.

"That's it," the deep voice urged.

Lilly looked up, trying to focus on his face, but could only see intense, green eyes staring back before the dark edges closed in, turning her world black.

His hand smoothed her hair once again, as he whispered, "Hello, Lilly."

Chapter Three

"Christ almighty." Lilly woke to a heavily accented voice. "Look at the bloody state of her, will you?" The harsh whisper sounded Scottish.

She winced. Her head was throbbing, there was a lump on the back of her head and she could feel the pressure and the pain wrapped over her skull, down her neck and to her temples. She didn't have to move a muscle to know she had taken a beating.

A gentle touch to her shoulder made her tense, and she remained that way as the hands poked and prodded her arms, then ran the length of each leg.

"I don't feel anything broken." This was a different voice. It, too, was accented, but not thickly like the Scottish brogue—this voice was English.

Not the same voice that had coaxed her to open her eyes. *That* voice had come with a pair of beautiful, green eyes, sharply focused yet soft with concern. They flashed behind her closed lids.

"I'll need you two to turn her so I can feel her back and spine. If she landed as hard as you say, she could have a compression fracture," said the Englishman.

"Landed hard? She slammed into the ground, and right on the edge of the gulley! What the hell is the matter wi' him? She could have been killed." The Scottish whisper was harsh, unlike the gentle hands that slowly turned her onto her side. A dull pain ran though her upper back and shoulders, her head spun and her stomach turned. She did her best not to groan, and exhaled slowly instead as skilled fingers probed her spine.

"He can't control where we land, you know that, Harry," said a much younger voice.

"But he *is* able to control the velocity at which we travel," said another voice, soft and deep.

Lilly held her breath, listening. Green eyes. That was it, the voice that had called to her, told her to open her eyes. The voice that had called her...angel.

"He'll have a few questions to answer when he decides to show up." The soft words were overshadowed by the menacing edge.

Lilly sucked in a breath as they rolled her gently onto her back again. Lying quietly, she waited for the voices to continue. Where was she? Who were these men?

The room remained quiet as the edge of the bed shifted and the person sitting next to her placed a hand on her shoulder.

"Lilly?" He paused. "I'm sorry if we hurt you, it was necessary."

"Is she okay?" the Scottish voice asked.

"Oh, I think so. She landed on her back, so her shoulders and upper back might bruise and she will be tender for the next few days. She also has quite a few scratches on her arms, neck and face, but they're superficial and will heal quickly enough. Edna is making a herbal lotion for her cuts and bruises and a tea for the headache she is going to have. I do, however, want to double check and see if there are any signs of a concussion. Which means, young lady" — his suddenly firm tone caught her off guard — "you'll have to open your eyes so I can check to see if your pupils are reacting normally."

They knew she was awake! She didn't move. *What was going on?* She felt her heart pound and her palms become damp. One minute she'd been about to be squashed by the CN Tower, the next she was lying in some bed, God knows where, with at least four men surrounding her. And how in the *hell* did they know her name?

"Lilly." Even with her lids closed, she could see the beautiful, green eyes, staring at her. "We are not going to harm you. George is a doctor and wants to help you, so there is no need for you to be afraid. Open your eyes." Green Eyes used that compelling tone on her, and again she felt the need to do as he asked.

* * * *

Gabe stood back, watching, as Lilly opened her eyes. She looked so small and fragile lying in the big bed. Her face and neck had light bruises and scratches, and there was a deep cut along her hairline that George had already stitched closed. All thanks to McGill. He fought to keep his displeasure under control. The professor had better be prepared to answer for this. Harry was right — if they hadn't got there in time to pull her up, she would have slid right down the side of the gulley and into the river.

Gabe stood quietly, watching her. She was scared — it radiated from her, but she gave no outward reaction. Her eyes slowly moved to each of the men, studying them intently, as if she was locking their faces into her memory. When her eyes slid to his, there was a slight widening, as of recognition. He had wondered if she would remember him. It was a good sign she hadn't suffered any serious damage from the blows to her head.

She looked at him as she had the others, as though memorising his face, and he did the same with hers. Even in the candlelit room, his vision was clear. None of her features were hidden from him. Her dark brown hair lay on her shoulders, tangled with bits of dirt and leaves from her fall. Thick lashes framed her brown eyes, which curved up slightly at the outer edges, giving her an exotic look. Yet the numerous scratches she had received, mixed with a scattering of freckles, gave her an innocent appearance that he found sweet and very appealing.

With his gaze still locked on her face, he noticed her mouth tremble slightly, drawing attention to an old scar on her light pink lower lip. Gabe felt unexpectedly sorry for her. She hadn't had the best start to her new life and it would get worse before it got better.

Deliberately keeping his tone soft, he asked, "How do you feel, Lilly?"

She blinked up at him and swallowed, then answered his question with one of her own. "How do you know my name? You said my name earlier, too, when you stopped me from sliding." Her voice was low and a little shaky.

Gabe found himself smiling down at her. He liked the fact that even though she was scared it didn't stop her from asking questions, and he liked the fact that she remembered a little of what had been going on around her after she had hit her head. He looked at Harry and motioned to him.

"We found this clipped to the inside of yer bag," said the Scotsman

* * * *

Lilly stared up at the giant of a man as he stepped forward, holding out his hand. He looked mean, with rough-looking features hidden behind a thick beard. His eyes were black, with dark brows slashing above them, and his dark hair was unruly, hanging past his shoulders.

Turning her attention to his outstretched hand, she saw the metal clip of her employee ID badge resting in his large palm. She looked up at him and he gave her a wide, friendly smile, drawing attention to a wicked-looking scar close to the corner of his mouth. It cut deep into his cheek and ran along the side of his face to stop just below his ear. Her quick look clearly didn't bother him and his black eyes sparkled as he gave her a wink and placed her ID badge in her hand.

"So that was how." She looked at the badge, feeling a little stupid.

"Just so you know" — the giant held up his hands — "it wasnae my idea to go through your bag. Gabe decided we should give you a name, and that you would probably prefer the one you already have."

Lilly smiled again, her face a little hot. "I appreciate that. What name did you give yourself?" The words came out before she had time to censor them.

"Ah, she's a wee bit sassy." He nodded approvingly at Green Eyes, "I like that. Harry York. Although I'd be happy to change that. Can't say I'm happy being named after a king."

"There's nothing wrong with being named after royalty. My parents named me after George," the doctor said, a hint of pride in his voice. George Redding." He nodded at her. "It's a pleasure to meet you, Lilly."

She smiled back. He looked to be the oldest of the men, with a rounder frame and thinning hair, and his muted blue eyes held a bit of sadness in them.

"Which one? Weren't there five of them?" the youngest of the men asked from the end of the bed. He was very obviously the youngest, and probably younger than she was. He was quite good-looking, with brown eyes and spiky, blond hair that was styled like something out of the eighties. He was quite thin and a bit pale, giving Lilly the impression he spent most of his time indoors.

"I'm not sure. Which one caused the least amount of trouble?"

"Like I would know that!" the younger man said sarcastically, shaking his head. "Marc Kelly. My likes include numbers and anything that has to do with engineering. My dislikes? The outdoors and history, which means I'm, like, totally screwed." He talked like something out of the eighties, too.

Lilly nodded uncertainly, not completely understanding what he meant. "Okay."

He smiled. "So, what year did you come from, good-lookin'?"

"Pardon?" Lilly raised her brow.

"What year did you come from?" Marc enunciated each word.

Lilly looked at Marc. "What year?" He nodded.

With George's help, she slowly pulled herself upright and asked, "Is that a trick question?"

"No, it's a simple question. What year are you from?"

"Do you mean what year was I born?"

"Ahhh! No." He huffed. "But that's a start."

Lilly looked around at the four men, ending up with the man she guessed was Gabe. This was weird. All four men were waiting, apparently fascinated, to hear what year she'd been born in. "I was born in '86."

"What '86?" Marc gave an irritated sigh. "1886? 1986? 2086?"

Lilly's eyes flew back to Marc. "Are you kidding?"

Marc sighed loudly. "No, I'm not. What century?"

Century? Lilly stopped and looked at the young man, Marc—really looked at him. He was wearing a white cotton shirt that opened into a V at his neck, a brown leather vest, brown pants...wait, were those capris? She blinked hard and pulled the information free.

Breeches. He was wearing woollen breeches and stockings. Slowly shifting her eyes, she studied each of the men again. They were all wearing similar clothing, except Gabe. His clothing looked...rich. She was sure his white shirt was silk, and his black breeches were cotton.

A sudden lump appeared in her throat, while her mind considered the new intake of information.

Silk shirts. Breeches. Stockings.

It was a perfect example of Tudor fashion. Why would they be wearing clothing from the Tudor period? Did they know she was taking medieval history at school? Was this some weird joke? Maybe they were the cast of a play that was in town. Taking a breath, she blurted out, "1986." She reached for the blanket resting on her legs and drew it close to her, as a nervous feeling clawed away at her stomach. This wasn't right. The sudden need to get out of the room became very strong.

"That's enough, Marc." Green Eyes' voice was firm and Lilly slid her gaze to meet his as he stepped to the side of the bed and sat facing her. Lilly had taken in every detail of his face but, once again, she found herself staring at him. He looked perfect—too perfect.

His light brown hair was thick and hung neatly down the back of his neck. It looked very soft, with gold streaks running through it. His sharp, green eyes stood out in his tanned face and the few days' worth of stubble accented his sharply angled chin and muscled jaw. His body looked lean and strong, with well-developed chest and shoulder muscles under his silk shirt and his arms looked hard and unyielding, with a faint tracing of scars on his exposed forearms. And that voice. That deep voice, combined with his accent, was just too perfect.

"Gabe," she whispered to herself, staring into his green eyes. Not realising he had heard.

He nodded, staring back. "Gabriel Sutherland," he confirmed softly—a whisper, really. She grabbed the edge of the blanket and toyed nervously with it.

"How old are you, Lilly?"

"I'm..." She hesitated, looking at the other men and then back to Gabe. "I'm twenty-six. Why?"

Gabe continued to stare as he asked, "Marc?"

"It was 2012." Marc's reply was instantaneous.

Gabe nodded, directing another question at her. "What month is it right now?"

Lilly slowly drew her knees up to her chest and shook her head. This was getting creepy. "You don't know what month it is?" Her heart started to race. How could they not know what month it was? What weirdness had she been caught in the middle of?

Looking around the room, she saw only one door, the only exit. Fighting her stiff muscles, she slipped her legs out from under the warm blanket. She didn't want anything slowing her down if the time came and she had to make a run for it. She placed her hands on either side of her for stability and asked slowly, "Where am I?"

Gabe's hand was warm as he slid it over hers, holding her firmly in place. "I know how confused you must feel, Lilly." He curled his fingers around the back of her hand and she could feel the rough texture of his fingers on her palm. "But I won't allow you to do something reckless that might cause you to injure yourself further. Please" — his voice dropped, drawing attention to his accent even more — "answer our questions. It might help us work out why you are here." He squeezed her hand reassuringly. "The month, Lilly, please."

She blinked, trying to process three different sensations at once. The warm, comforting touch of his hand, the idea that someone was actually concerned for her physical well-being, and the terrifying thought that these men had no idea why she was here, either—wherever *here* was. She opened her mouth, then hesitated. Gabe smiled softly at her, and she found she couldn't help but tell him what he wanted to know.

"It's June. June 12th."

"That date ring any bells, Harry?" Gabe looked back over his shoulder.

"Sorry, nothing's coming to mind," Harry responded.

Gabe sighed.

Why had he asked Harry that question, rather than any of the others? Wait—why had he asked the question in the first place? *What was going on here?* Lilly eyed Gabe cautiously as George drew her attention.

"Lilly, are you American or Canadian?" he asked politely.

"Canadian."

"And what city do you live in?"

Okay, this was too much. They didn't know what year it was, they didn't know what month it was, and now they had no idea what city they were in. How could they not? There was only one CN Tower. It was the building that had been crashing down on her. They could hardly have missed it—

She stopped in mid-thought. How *had* she got away? Had one of these men—or maybe all of them— saved her? Where was she, anyway? The nervous feeling clawing at her stomach became almost painful. This all seemed just *too* bizarre. She didn't know where she was or who these people were, but she did know something was not right.

Feeling the need to move, she quickly swung her legs off the side of the bed and slowly stood. The movement sent pain shooting through her head and she closed her eyes, struggling to fight off the accompanying waves of nausea. As her head spun, she felt a pair of warm hands grip her waist, keeping her steady.

* * * *

Gabe tightened his hold as she swayed. She looked up at him with a dazed expression, her eyes looking very dark in contrast to her pale complexion. She was so damn white, he was worried she was going to black out again. She lowered her eyes, giving him only a glimpse of her fear and confusion.

"I'm okay." She pulled back and, despite his instinct, he let her go. She stepped past him slowly, moving around the small room, studying it intently. The small window, the hearth, the floor and bed. Close behind her, Gabe followed her gaze but saw nothing out of the ordinary. It wasn't a large room, but it was clean and comfortable with a good-sized hearth.

Reaching out, she hesitated before she gently touched a stone in the wall. "Where am I?"

"England," he answered honestly. There was no reason to hide the truth from her. This was her life, now.

She turned to face him and wavered when she saw how close he was. "England?" She shook her head. "That can't be."

Gabe frowned. Did she really have *no* idea where she was? Maybe she'd hit her head harder than he'd thought. Something in his chest tightened along with the muscles in his neck, and he studied her closely, watching for any other signs of trauma.

"Why can't it be?" George asked, stepping up next to him.

"Because... I had just gotten to work..." She shook her head again. She was obviously having a hard time absorbing the information she was getting. They all had, but none of them had landed the way she had, and none of them had sustained injuries like she had. And by the look of her, she had received some of those cuts before she'd arrived. Which made Gabe wonder what had been going on around her when she'd been taken.

* * * *

She was dead! She had to be — or maybe in another dimension, or some place where areas of your real life mixed with your fantasies. Because this room, with its stone walls, large fireplace and very small window with its roughly-made glass pane, was just what she pictured while studying medieval architecture. The clothes — they were Tudor, too. She should know — she must have read and studied every book in existence on the subject, and locked every single word into her memory, whether she wanted to or not. Her special ability — a blessing and a curse.

If that was the case, though, and she had died, then why were they asking her all these questions? Shouldn't they already know the answers? Maybe she hadn't died, and she was in a dream-like state caused by getting your head crushed in by a giant antenna. Maybe they didn't know the answers because *she* didn't, and they were just phantoms she had invented to help her cope. She frowned, not comforted by that thought any more than the other.

Whatever the explanation was, she didn't care — she just needed to get away and go...somewhere.

She looked at the door and contemplated what might be on the other side and if she would be able to make it out. She couldn't care less if she got hurt — she might already be dead.

Even before she thought about bolting for the door, Gabe was in front of her. He reached for her hand, once again holding it securely in his.

"Why can't it be, Lilly? Where did you work?"

"This is so..." She stopped, looking at him, then relented, shaking her head. "I work at the CN Tower."

"The CN Tower? What's th—?"

"Holy shit!" Marc choked out. All heads turned to the young man. "Toronto." He paused and looked at Gabe. "He took her from Canada!"

Chapter Four

"Canada!" Gabe turned to Lilly. "Is that true? Are you from Canada?"

She nodded. The gnawing feeling in her stomach grew even stronger.

"Can he do that?" Harry demanded.

"I have no idea." Gabe continued to stare down at her as he rubbed his chin. "He never mentioned that he could. Then again, I never thought to ask."

"A better question is why did he take *her*? Why not someone from here?" Marc asked, appalled.

Gabe locked his green eyes on the younger man. "Lilly," he said quietly. "Her name is Lilly Marten." His voice was as soft as ever but there was an underlying warning to his words.

Marc stepped back, holding up his hands. "I know. I apologise," he said quickly. "I just meant it must be easier to take someone from the same country. But Lilly was taken from an entirely different *continent*.

From what little the professor has told me, it seems like a long process. It must have taken him quite a while to bring her" — Marc hastily corrected himself — "I mean *Lilly*...here."

Marc stared nervously at Gabe, until Gabe shook his head. The young man exhaled and visibly relaxed.

Lilly glanced up at Gabe, stunned. Never, not once, had a man defended her in any way. Not even her father. Her stomach flipped over just as a knock sounded at the door.

All four men went quiet and looked to Gabe. He gave Harry a curt nod. Without a sound the giant moved to the door and paused, looking back to Gabe again. Gabe slid his arm around Lilly's waist and pressed his body close to hers. "Wait until I have her back in bed."

Gabe quickly ushered her over to the bed and pulled the blankets over her.

"What's going on?"

He sat on the bed next to her and reached for her hand, then looked over his shoulder to Harry, who opened the door.

Gabe turned quickly to Lilly and murmured, "You have a lot of questions and I will answer as many as I can, but first I want George to give you a good once-over and check for any serious damage."

A high laugh caught her attention and Lilly glanced at the door.

"The woman at the door is my cook, Edna. George has asked her to mix up a natural remedy to help heal your cuts and bruises."

Lilly nodded, looking back at the door, where a plump woman with red hair stood in the doorway, smiling at George. Her clothes, they were... She leaned to the side to get a better view and blinked several times. The woman was wearing a long, light-coloured... Lilly paused and pulled the name of the garment from her mind. *Chemise.* Edna was wearing a chemise, with a green kirtle layered on top of it. Sitting back Lilly blinked. Then leaned to the side to look at the woman again, just to make sure she wasn't going crazy. She studied the garment. It *was* a kirtle. A green, linen kirtle. It laced down over her breasts and to her waist, where the material split open down to her feet to reveal the chemise underneath. Her mind went into overdrive and her heart jumped.

Still confused, she began rambling, her mind pulling up pieces of information from her books, in an attempt to make sense of this woman. "She makes her own salves, and ointments with medicinal herbs." The healing properties of herbs were widely known and extensively used in medieval times.

Medieval times? The clothes, the room, and now the use of herbs for healing... Could it possibly be true?

"She'll use what she has available to her," she continued absent-mindedly. "Lavender, sage, maybe goldenrod and rosemary and St John's wart." She rambled off the different herbs she knew would heal her specific injuries. "Each herb helps with cuts, bruising, pain..."

"How do you know that?" She turned at the sound of Gabe's voice, her face heating.

Blinking, she said the first thing that came to mind. "I...read it. In a book. I like to read."

His green eyes narrowed, searching her face.

She wasn't lying — she really did like to read. She had read every book she could get her hands on about herbs and the use of them — the only thing was she had read each book just once and retained *every* word on *every* page. She could recite them back in the order in which she read them three years ago. Perfectly. But she couldn't tell him that. He would think she was a freak, just like the others had.

She shrugged a second time, "I really do like to read, a lot."

A slight smile touched his perfectly formed lips, giving the impression he knew she wasn't telling him the complete truth.

The door closed and George came to her side and placed a tray on the bed. Gabe looked up. "What's all this?"

"It would seem," Harry called out in a merry tone, "word has got out about the young *Lady* here."

"Harry..." Gabe sighed, keeping his temper in check. He didn't want to scare Lilly any more than she already was. He would deal with her reaction to her new position here later, but right now she needed medical attention. "Take Marc out of here. Lilly needs to rest."

"Yes, sir," Harry said cheerfully and motioned to Marc. "Come on, you. Let's go and eat."

Harry looked at Lilly. "Goodnight, Lilly." He winked. "See you tomorrow." He bowed slightly. Gabe raised an eyebrow, annoyed at Harry's attempt to stir the pot a little more.

"'Night, Lilly," Marc said and leaned against the doorframe, trying to be suave. "If you need anything, and I mean *anything*" — he winked — "I'm four doors down on the left..." Harry cuffed him on the back of the head. "Ouch! What was that for?"

"For being an arse!"

"I was just offering my services —"

"Out!" Harry ordered and shoved the younger man out of the door, exiting behind him.

George chuckled as they left.

"Well, George?" Gabe prompted.

"Right." George cleared his throat. "Edna has made up an ointment to help speed the healing of your cuts and bruises." He pointed to a small bowl with a thick, dark green paste. "It's truly remarkable stuff—I'm still amazed how well it works."

Gabe glanced at Lilly, tilting his head slightly. "Did she say what was in it?" He asked the question while staring straight at her, taking note of how her shoulder muscles became stiff.

"As a matter of fact, I did ask," George confirmed. "It's nothing more than a variety of common plants and herbs, nothing unusual."

Gabe watched Lilly's cheeks become pink as George repeated the very same herbs she had mentioned. Reading a lot was one thing. Knowing the specific uses for medicinal herbs in medieval England could be something different. What exactly had she done at this CN Tower?

Gabe turned back to the tray and pointed to a cup. "And that?" Despite his misgivings, he still wanted Lilly to know what everything was, so she knew they weren't trying to deceive her in any way. He needed to have her trust, and she needed to know he was trustworthy and that he would always see to her safety. How could he not? He had done it for the others, and would do no less for her.

"A tea, of sorts," George answered. "It helps with headaches and it will also help her to sleep. And of course some food. Edna thought the new lady..."

George stopped abruptly and smiled at Lilly. "She thought you might be hungry."

She nodded at the doctor, her thin brows pressing together.

"Now," George continued, "I'd like to put some of this ointment on your cuts and have a closer look at that bump on the back of your head. Your neck and shoulders are sore, too?"

Silently, Lilly nodded.

"Anything else?"

"My upper back...it feels stiff." She reached for her opposite shoulder and massaged the muscle.

"I'll have a look. Then you may have your tea and something to eat, if you like."

Lilly flushed as her dark brown eyes shifted from Gabe to George and back to Gabe.

Watching her, Gabe pulled air into his lungs.

Fear. Sweat. Confusion. She was nervous. Of both of them.

He was about to reassure her again, but George spoke first. "Now, now. There is nothing to be embarrassed about. I've seen it all. I was a medic with the Royal Army for two years before completing medical school. Then I worked in London's largest hospital for another sixteen years, and another four years during—" He shook his head and smiled. "Another four years after that. So that's over twenty years' experience."

Lilly nodded again, quietly studying them both, then asked, "How do I know you're a real doctor? You seem to know what you're talking about—I haven't read a lot in the medical field, but you *sound* like a doctor. I just don't *know*."

Gabe looked at George and asked seriously, "Where did you attend medical school?"

George sat up straighter. "I attended Cambridge University." His pride was unmistakeable. "It was one of the top schools in my time."

Lilly frowned, "Isn't it still?"

"Of course," George said, quickly waving off her question. "Now, will you let me help you?"

She nodded. Her dark eyes looked warily from George to Gabe, her cheeks flushing again. Was it him? Was it because he was there? He started to rise. "I can leave if you want me to."

"No!" She sat forward, staring at him. Gabe immediately responded to the fear in her eyes and sat back down. Obviously embarrassed, she looked away, shaking her head. "I just... I don't... I'm not sure what to make of all this. Of what to think."

"Let George fix you up." Gabe made sure to keep his voice low. "And afterwards, you can ask me whatever you like."

Nodding, she looked at Gabe with her dark eyes and he felt somewhat relieved that she didn't want him to go. Though he was honest enough with himself to know he wouldn't have left anyway.

George asked Lilly a number of questions and thoroughly examined her neck, shoulders and upper back. Gabe frowned when he saw the bruises beginning to darken on her pale skin.

"It looks worse than it is," George said.

His opinion was quite different. His guts tightened when he saw the purple bruises forming mostly on her upper back and shoulders. It looked extremely painful, but Lilly didn't make a sound as George gently applied the ointment. When he'd finished, she sat back and watched George intently as he applied the ointment to the scratches on her forearms and face.

Gabe concentrated on her face. She was studying George's actions as she had the room. It was as if she was absorbing every tiny detail. She seemed observant almost to an extreme.

"Now," George said. "I want you to drink all of Edna's tea and eat if you can. And you" — the older man turned to face Gabe — "don't keep her up all night."

Gabe raised his eyebrows, surprised and somewhat insulted. He didn't like being ordered not to do something he hadn't intended.

Ignoring Gabe's look, George stood. "I've put a chamber pot here, next to your bed. If you have need of me, tell Gabe and he'll come and wake me." He smiled down at her. "You'll be just fine. Nothing a little time won't heal. Goodnight, Lilly." Turning, he nodded. "Gabe."

* * * *

"Thank you," Lilly called as George reached for the door.

"You are most welcome." He smiled, then gently closed the door behind him — leaving Lilly alone with one perfect man and a million questions.

Passing on the food, Lilly reached for the tea, not knowing what to ask first. She had so many questions about all the different things she had heard and seen.

"Start with the basics," Gabe offered. "Like, where are we?"

Lilly shook her head. "I already know that answer. How about *when*? *When* are we?"

Gabe's sharp eyes focused on her face. "1503."

Exhaling slowly, Lilly blinked rapidly, her mind absorbing the new information. "1503," she repeated, her heart pounding.

He gave her one clear nod as he watched her reaction.

The last hour was recent memory, so she pulled it easily from her mind, studying it like she would a book. She listened again to each word every person in the room had said. Watched every movement they had made. There was nothing to suggest that what she had witnessed wasn't real. Yet the doubt was there, sitting in her stomach, heavy and nauseating.

Although her body's reaction was to rebel against the new information, her mind would not allow her to block anything out. Her mind went through everything that had transpired since she'd awoken and, as crazy as it seemed, being in 1503 would explain everything. The herbs, the walls, the clothing and, most importantly, it would explain why the CN Tower hadn't squashed her. Or would it?

She took a sip of the tea—her head was beginning to throb again with the mere idea of being back in the past. *If* this was really...real, she had hundreds of other questions.

She blinked, her vision clearing. "Now that I know the *where* and *when*, I'll ask about the *how*. How did I get here?"

Gabe's golden eyebrows pushed together. He clasped his hands together, sighing. "I can tell you how you got here in general terms, but not the mechanics of it. I don't fully understand how he's able to do it."

Lilly took in the details of his handsome face and knew from his intense stare that not a single detail would slip past him, that he was aware of everything that surrounded him.

"You were brought here by a Time Shifting Interval System."

"What's a Time Shifting Interval System?"

"Basically, it's a fancy name for a time machine. You felt the wind, didn't you? The mini twister?"

She sat up straighter, her eyes widening. "Yeah!"

He nodded. "That's the TSIS. From what I understand, it produces the whirlwind. It's that whirlwind that tracks and locates a target—in this case, you. Once you're inside, it locks you into place so you can't slip out of it, then pulls you from one time to another."

"So that was why I couldn't get away from it. Every time I moved, it followed me."

He nodded. "I was told it locks you in place to read your genetic structure, so it can put you back together in the right order at your destination point." He paused, then cocked his head a little to the side. "It took you while you were at work?"

She took another sip of tea and swallowed. "I had just gotten there and was talking to my frie—To my manager," she corrected herself. Looking into the cup, she remembered the overwhelming feeling she'd had as Stacey left. Had it been coincidence, or part of this time shifting thing?

Time shifting? She frowned. *Do I actually believe this man?* The impossible question flew around her head. She wasn't sure—things weren't clear. She touched her temple, feeling the swollen edge of a cut on her forehead. Slowly, she traced its outline with the tips of her fingers, taking note of each stitch.

"I have seven stitches." The large chunk of cement that hit her while she was waiting for the tower to crush her. She remembered the feeling of her blood as it had slid down her face. Of course she remembered — she remembered everything. Not even shifting through time could change that.

Gabe nudged the cup in her hands and, without thinking, she took another swallow.

"What was going on around you when you were taken?"

Looking into the cup, she thought about work, about how the tower had begun to fall. Watching it back in her head now, everything seemed to be in slow motion, like it had been at the time. The antenna sliding gracefully to the side, the slow way it had begun to fall.

A thick, painful lump formed in her throat. What if there had been people trapped inside? The evening rush hour wasn't the busiest time for customers, but there was always someone walking around. And Stacey had mentioned that schools were booking last minute tours. She sucked in a breath, keeping her eyes down. What if there had been children, trapped... The idea made her sick. She closed her eyes, thinking of all the death and destruction. How horrible.

She felt such sadness for those people, it felt like she was being crushed by it. But she also felt sorry for herself. If what Gabe said was true, if she was back in 1503 and this wasn't some weird dream, then she wasn't dead. And she had been *ready* to die. She had accepted her death as she'd watched the tower falling towards her, accepted her death like she'd accepted everything else in her life — without question. With all the times in her life things hadn't worked out in her favour, she'd thought at least her death was a certainty. Now that, too, had been taken from her.

Shaking her head, Lilly looked directly into Gabe's eyes. If she shared her true feelings with him, he would probably think she was out of her mind, which at this point wasn't far off the mark.

He nodded, not pushing her on the subject. There was understanding in those light green eyes and she was grateful for that.

Instead, she cleared her throat and asked abruptly, "Where in England are we?"

He sat back, looking at her. "Northern England, about ten kilometres from the Scottish border."

"The year is 1503 and we are ten kilometres from the Scottish border," she repeated. "How often do you deal with Scottish reivers?"

He narrowed his eyes. "Enough to keep things interesting."

"Oh." She drank the last of her tea and leant back against the pillow. The pounding in her head was all but gone, her limbs felt heavy and her mind... It felt calm, almost at rest. Weird.

"What did you do at this CN Tower?" Gabe asked. He wanted to know how she knew about the reivers and the herbs and why she was so observant, and he needed the answers quickly. Edna's brew was beginning to take effect.

She placed a hand over her mouth as she yawned, displaying the light sprinkling of freckles trailing their way up her arm, "I'm a part-time buyer. I order everything for the tower—flowers, building materials, food for the kitchens and all types of souvenirs and little knick-knacks for people to buy."

Gabe nodded as he listened to her answer, knowing he had no reason to be suspicious. His gut told him Lilly wasn't anyone to be alarmed about. She was simply a woman McGill had shifted. Yet years of intense training had taken his unusually cautious nature and honed it to a fine point. So, instinctively, he pushed her for more intel.

"Part-time?" he asked casually. "What else did you do?" There was something more to her—there had to be. McGill had taken her for a reason. *What reason?*

Each of them offered something to their survival in this new time. George was a doctor. Marc was genius when it came to numbers but he was also a structural engineer. Harry was not only a highly trained and specialised soldier but he had been born and raised in the Scottish territory. Gabe, too, was a soldier like Harry, serving with him in the United Battle Force—and he was also a descendant of Thomas Sutherland, which had put him in the position to take over the role of lord when Thomas had died of his wounds. All four of them had something to contribute and, knowing McGill, Lilly would have something to give as well.

"I went to school." He took the cup from her hand as she rested her head back and closed her eyes, sighing. "I was just about finished, too. One more semester and I would have completed my Master's. That sucks—I was really looking forward to my last class. I enjoyed listening to Professor McGill. He's this little, weird guy with glasses. I sometimes feel sorry for him. I think he has some form of attention disorder, because he never sits still, but he is so passionate when he speaks."

Gabe froze, stunned by her admission. *No!* It couldn't be him. The odds were just too damn high for it to be him. But he had to ask, "What was your professor teaching you that he was so passionate about?"

She yawned again. "Medieval studies."

Hiding his surprise, Gabe placed the cup on the tray. McGill had sent them one of his students! His nostrils flared as he looked down at Lilly lying peacefully in the big bed. What had that crazy bastard done?

McGill had sent an angel capable of steering them though the sixteenth century for the rest of their lives, that's what he'd done. Did she even belong here? Had he followed his normal pattern and pulled her away just as she was about to die? He'd find out as soon as she was ready to share the details — or if he got his hands on McGill first. The last thought caused the centres of his palms to itch.

The room was dark and quiet. Gabe stared at Lilly for a long time, listening to her slow, even breaths as she drifted off. Her dark lashes twitched and she licked her lips slowly before softly asking, "I'm not dead, am I?"

Gabe stilled. The muscles in his back and neck grew tight. Her face had a peaceful glow — it was the hint of disappointment to her words that unnerved him. How could someone so young have regrets about living?

"Gabe?" she whispered.

"No, you're not dead." Flickers of light from the candles crossed her face, accenting her high cheekbones and small nose. She was sexy but seemed to be unaware of her appeal, which made her all that more appealing to him.

"Is this all a dream?" She turned towards him, keeping her eyes closed.

Reaching forward, he gently brushed her dark hair away from the stitches on her forehead. "No, angel, it's not a dream."

Chapter Five

Gabe opened the door to Lilly's room before the knock came.

"I could really use that particular talent of yours!" Harry said, crossing his arms over his barrel chest.

Gabe slipped out into the hallway and silently closed the heavy door.

"It wasn't like I had a bloody choice in the matter." He had been born with exceptionally acute hearing. So had Harry, for that matter. Harry's just wasn't quite as heightened as Gabe's.

The truth was, not a single soul in the entire Kingdom had been given a choice. Not since the Genetic Purification Act of 2040 had been put into effect under King Harry.

Gabe had grown up in a time when all humans were genetically superior, and he'd been among a rare few that exceeded a very high norm. It was because of this he'd been selected to be an officer with a special operational unit in the military.

Gabe looked at Harry. "Any problems last night?"

"No. How is she?"

"Sleeping." Gabe crossed his arms, narrowing his eyes.

Harry frowned. "You need to tell me something."

"She knows McGill."

"Yes. I just found that out," Harry revealed with disdain. Gabe raised an eyebrow, mirroring Harry's disapproval of the new information.

"When did he get here?"

"About an hour ago. He said he wants to see her right away."

"He can wait," Gabe snapped.

Harry stared him in the eye. "Am I going to have to come with you to make sure you don't kill him?"

Gabe ignored the Scotsman. "Where is he?"

"Gabe," Harry warned. "I know you're pissed off, but you cannae kill him. He is the only one who can explain all this."

Gabe narrowed his green eyes on Harry. "Where?"

Harry shook his head. "The alcove off the main battlements."

Gabe nodded again and quietly ordered, "Send word if she wakes."

* * * *

Gabe could hear the sound of McGill's continuous pacing before he reached the stairs to the battlements. As he began his climb, he frowned, looking briefly down the hall towards Lilly's door. The natural instinct to protect Lilly had come without any thought and it was strong. Very strong, and very unusual. Protecting wasn't something new for him — he protected the backs of fellow teammates, as they did for him. But that feeling was based on years of training and a sense of detached survival. The need to protect Lilly was different — it affected him emotionally. He wasn't altogether sure which emotion it roused in him — he hadn't used them very often. Hell, for all he knew, it could be all of them.

Taking the steps two at a time, he reached the top without exerting any energy and stepped out into the cool morning air. He waited patiently as McGill approached him. The professor always seemed nervous when they were alone and normally Gabe made a conscious effort to put him at ease. But things had changed the moment Lilly had come to them and, nervous or not, nothing would prevent Gabe from getting what he wanted — answers.

"Gabriel." McGill nodded, pulling his grey cloak protectively around his shoulders.

"Why Lilly?" Gabe asked calmly.

"She would have died in her own time if I hadn't." The man looked at the ground, shaking his head. "I couldn't let that happen. It would have been a waste of a remarkable mind."

Gabe listened to the man, studied his words. There was genuine conviction in his voice...and something else.

"How did you find her?"

"Not too long ago" — McGill turned and looked out into the bailey — "we had been given orders to visit new locations. And since Canada had refused to join the Kingdom, I was selected to visit Toronto in 2012. I decided that a school campus would be a good place to start and with my…appearance, I would be a good fit as a teacher."

"She was your student."

"Found that out already, did you?"

Gabe looked him in the eye.

"Of course you did." McGill smiled. "The school was in need of a professor for their medieval studies programme and I was hoping to gain a bit more insight into that particular time, so I took the position. I met Lilly on the first day of class. I did not have a large class but she stood out from the others. There was something intriguing about the way she listened and watched me. She seemed to be absorbing every word I said and, in a few instances, she repeated back to me full paragraphs of my lectures — word for word."

"So, you're telling me she's smart. What you're not telling me is why she's here. What… What would have happened to her?" He needed to know, to hear the reason why McGill had taken her, and it had better be more then the fact that she was taking medieval history in school. No matter how much her knowledge would help them, in Gabe's mind that was no justification for stealing her away from her own time.

"I told you." McGill turned to face him. "She would have died if I hadn't shifted her. Terrorists attacked the Canadian National Tower in June of 2012. Ten people died in the attack and one person was declared missing, presumed dead. Lilly Marten. Eyewitness accounts said the top of the tower landed right where she had been standing. If I hadn't shifted her, she would have been crushed. I didn't go searching for her, and I didn't influence the situation. But I wasn't about to let her die, either."

Something still wasn't right. The idea gnawed at Gabe, and the frustration of the situation was beginning to take over. He crossed his arms. "Why haven't I heard of the CN Tower or the attack on it?"

McGill stared thoughtfully up at him. "Canadians are a funny sort—very similar to us as a people. After the attack, the country as a whole seemed to pull together—cleaned up the mess, aided the families who had lost loved ones, and moved on. You have to remember, Gabe—the Kingdom cut all ties with Canada when its governing body decided against becoming a United Territory. Canadian history was removed from our education system. So I'm not surprised you haven't heard about it."

The only thing Gabe could do was nod—he had to take the professor's words as the truth until Lilly told him her version of events. "Then you checked into Lilly's future, just like you did with the rest of us?"

McGill began to fidget as he answered, "Yes."

Gabe narrowed his eyes, watching the man shift awkwardly back and forth. That was the one thing Gabe didn't like knowing—that this man had been researching his life before the day he was supposed to die. But the tone of McGill's words held something else when he spoke of Lilly. A grey area between fascination and infatuation. Had it truly been dispassionate research with Lilly, or something else? Regardless, the idea of him researching her, looking into her life, watching her without her knowledge, was enough to make him want to reach out and squeeze the little freak's neck.

Gabe lowered his voice and made certain the professor could hear the threatening edge. "Why Lilly, McGill?"

"I told you, there was something I found intriguing about her. But I couldn't put my finger on it, so I did a little digging." McGill spoke quickly, taking a few steps backwards.

Gabe wanted to laugh at the futile attempt. "Backing away won't help, and you know it." McGill was fully aware that Gabe could clear the distance in one move. McGill's mentors were the ones who had created him. "And what did you find?" he asked coolly.

"She was a normal kid with normal habits. Her life was normal, until she was twelve and she and her mother were in a car accident. The mother died and Lilly sustained a concussion." Gabe scowled, bothered by the choice of words. *The mother*. The man was so bloody scientific it made him cringe.

McGill began pacing around in circles. "A few months afterwards, her habits changed. She became withdrawn and introverted, where before she had been outgoing. Her grades in school went from average to above normal and, by the time she was fourteen and entered high school, she was studying at a college level. Gabe," the professor stressed, "Lilly is not just a smart, or even gifted, woman. She has the ability to retain any information she reads, hears, or even sees. And she will never lose or forget the knowledge she has gained over time like you and I will."

Gabe frowned. "You're saying she has a photographic memory?"

"More than that. She has perfect recall—*perfect*. And I believe the concussion she suffered during the accident was the trigger point."

Gabe's frown deepened. The skills he had, he'd had from the moment he was born. He'd never had to learn to adapt to them. Whereas Lilly had received her extraordinary skills after twelve years of a normal life, had received them while dealing with the death of her mother. Bloody hell. He wasn't altogether sure if he would really like to have her talent—there were some things, no doubt, she would choose not to remember.

"I want to see her, Gabe. I need to explain how and why she is here. She deserves that much."

"Yes, she does," Gabe agreed coolly. "I've explained as much as I could. As for the whys, you will have to explain it to all of us, together. Unless you plan on bringing someone else into our little group?"

"No. Lilly was unexpected, but she was the last."

Gabe nodded. "She's still sleeping. Go to the hall and have something to eat. Once she's awake and has had a chance to eat and get cleaned up, I'll send Harry to get you."

"I should really speak to her right—"

Gabe put up his hand, silencing the professor. "When she is awake and ready."

"I don't have much time."

"That's too bad. We, on the other hand, seem to have a great deal of time. Wait in the hall." Gabe turned and walked away.

A gut feeling made him stop and turn back to McGill. From inside the dark alcove, Gabe watched as McGill, a good twelve feet away, played nervously with his cloak. Tensing his muscles, Gabe cleared the distance without a sound, landing directly in front of McGill. He ignored the professor's shocked expression as he held out his hand. "Give it to me."

"I beg your pardon?"

Gabe fixed his sights on the professor. "The TSIS. Give me your tracker." Covered with sweat, McGill reached into his grey cloak and hesitated.

"Now!" Gabe barked.

McGill jumped at the sharp command but followed the order. He pulled the tracking device off his belt and placed it in Gabe's hand.

"Thank you," Gabe said politely. "I try to trust you, professor, but sometimes I find it difficult." He waved the tracker in front of the man's face. "You'll get this back once we've had our group discussion."

He had begun to turn again when he remembered. "And one other thing. The next time you decide to shift someone, make sure they land on solid ground."

"I'm sorry?" McGill asked nervously.

"Lilly landed on the side of a ravine." Pinning McGill to the spot with his glare, Gabe lowered his voice. "She almost fell into the river." He shook his head when McGill opened his mouth to defend himself. "Don't do it again."

Dismissing the professor, Gabe turned and headed back into the keep with one thought—Lilly.

Chapter Six

"You didn't kill him, did you?" Harry asked, keeping his voice low.

"I've decided to wait until after he gives us some answers."

Harry raised his thick, black brows in surprise. "You're not getting soft in your old age, are yeh?"

The two men turned out of Lilly's room and into the hall.

"Who'd you leave to watch him?" Harry asked.

"No one," Gabe answered honestly.

Harry eyed him suspiciously, "You do know that if you scared him, that little prat will go back to his own time and we won't find out a fucking thing?" he growled.

Curling his mouth into an evil smile, Gabe held out the TSIS tracker for his friend to see. "He isn't going anywhere."

Harry burst out laughing and slapped Gabe on the back. "I think I've become a bad influence on you."

* * * *

Lilly listened as the two men whispered to each other. Who was Gabe going to kill? What were the questions he wanted answers to? The door closed, leaving Lilly in the dark with nothing but her breathing to fill the void. A booming laugh made her jump and she turned her head towards the door, wondering what Harry was laughing at.

She had been awake for some time now, just lying on the soft bed, running the events of the day before over and over in her head and silently praying what Gabe had told her was not true.

How *could* it be true? The idea seemed impossible, yet here she was in a huge bed covered on all four sides with heavy material, and she knew that if she pulled the material closed she would be protected from the cold. And the mattress. She was lying on a mattress filled with feathers. Not foam or springs, but real feathers. She could even feel the pin-hairs of the feathers poking through the linen. She remembered the feel of the cool stone of the wall when she had touched it yesterday. Then there were the clothes and the herbal tea and ointment...and unless this was some elaborate hoax, she was back in 1503.

Gabe was telling her the truth—she was sure of it and she wanted to believe him. It was just that part about the Time Shifting Interval System and shifting through time she was having a problem with. How was it possible, and why had she been chosen? Her schooling seemed the most logical answer. She had studied medieval history, and now she was apparently back in medieval England. Why? What purpose could she possibly serve in this time? She'd been born in the eighties and grown up in the nineties, in Canada of all places. She had never even been to England.

The light groan of the door interrupted her mind-numbing questions and she held her breath, listening.

* * * *

As Gabe reached for the door, Harry said, "She's awake, by the way."

"When did she wake?"

"A little while ago."

Gabe looked at the door and, for the first time in his life, he hesitated. His chest tightened as he thought about Lilly lying in that bed, with her dark eyes and innocent face. Would she be able to handle what she was about to be told? Would any of them?

Inhaling, he pushed aside the doubt. He didn't have a choice, and he couldn't let the others have a choice either. He would *make* them accept it, and that included Lilly—he couldn't afford not to.

"Can you ask Edna to make up a tray of food for Lilly? And also ask her to boil some water for a bath."

"A bath for the Lady of—" Harry stopped when he saw Gabe's glare. He held up his hands. "You'd better tell her before one of the others lets it slip or she hears it from your servants."

"You're one of my servants," Gabe reminded him ruthlessly.

Harry laughed as he walked away. "You know, I was taught to expect that from officers during basic."

Gabe chuckled as he opened the door and stepped into the room.

His eyes adjusted instantly to the dark. He could easily make out Lilly's form covered by blankets on the bed. To all appearances she was sleeping, but her breathing told him the truth.

Moving silently to the side of the bed, he looked down at her. One hand was resting on her breasts, the other on her stomach. Her face still wore that angelic look, the same look she had had all night. Gabe frowned as the fierce need to protect her hardened the muscles in his chest. Why was this need to protect so strong with Lilly and not the others? They were all going through the same thing. What was it about Lilly that made her different?

As he sat on the edge of the bed, trying to piece together the reasons for his unusual behaviour, he kept a close watch on her face for any reaction to his proximity. When none came, he sighed. "Lilly, I know you're awake."

Even in the dark, he was able to see her eyes open and try to focus on him. A few seconds passed with them staring at each other. He could see her but he knew she couldn't see him—the room was too dark. There was dried dirt just below her bottom lip, close to her scar. Without so much as a thought, he lifted his hand, with the intent of wiping the dirt away just so he could feel that delicate little scar, but his hand stopped and he covered her hand instead. He ran his fingers over the back of her hand. "How do you feel?"

He watched her eyes dart around at the sound of his voice, searching for his face. Then she raised her head, struggling to see where his hand was resting on hers.

"Not bad." She lowered her head, a slight smile pulling at her pink lips. She turned her head, her eyes continuing to search for his face in the dark. "Yesterday I felt as though I'd been run over by a truck. But today, it feels more like a moped."

He smiled, confused by her words. *What was a moped?*

He continued to scan her face. She was beautiful — the cuts and bruises couldn't hide it. She wasn't 'perfect' like the women of his own time, but she was pure, natural and unaltered. Out of nowhere, the muscles in his belly tightened with arousal. He released her hand and quickly stood. He walked over to the small window and opened the shutters, letting in the early morning light.

* * * *

The light almost blinded her when Gabe opened the shutters. She sat up slowly, keeping her hand over her eyes, giving them time to adjust. When they had, Gabe was next to the window staring at her, his sharp green eyes focused on her.

"Edna is making you up some food, and water is being boiled for you to have a bath." He paused. "Would you like to have a bath?"

Lilly blinked, confused. She wasn't sure how to react. Again, he had thought about her feelings, about what she might want or need. It was something she wasn't used to. She found it strange to have someone putting her needs first. Her heart jumped in her chest. Looking down, she agreed right away when she saw the dirt on the backs of her hands, caked under her nails. "Yes, I would like to have a bath. Thank you."

He walked across the room to the end of the bed, a frown on his face. He reached down and pulled up a bag. She glanced at the bag and smiled. Her knapsack!

Placing the bag on the end of the bed, he continued to frown. "I had to take the more high-tech items out of your bag in case someone from this time saw them, as well as your purse. If you need them for any reason, tell me and I'll take you to them."

His jaw was set and his arms were crossed. There was no room for an argument, that much was clear, and she understood why he had hidden her belongings—but why not just destroy them? Unless, for some reason, she might need them again. Doubt crept into her mind. Was any of this real?

"If you're worried that someone might see them, why didn't you... Why not just destroy them?" she asked.

The white silk of his shirt pulled tight across his chest when he shrugged his broad shoulders. "They're your belongings, not mine. If you want me to destroy them, I will. But to be honest, I don't think you should. They're a part of your past, like photographs. Wouldn't you like to keep them as a reminder of your old life?"

Old life. Jeez, that sounded so permanent...and kind of daunting. A lump formed in her throat. *Old life.*

What in the world would her new life bring? She had studied everything she could get her hands on, but reading and studying about life was completely different from experiencing it firsthand. *If*—and that was a big if—all this was real.

She eyed him. "I guess."

"Everything else is as you left it. Let Harry know if there is anything you might need for your bath. I have a trunk full of dresses and other clothes—I'll have it brought in. They're yours if you want them. If not, I'm sure we can figure something out." He turned and, without a sound, walked to the door.

How was it possible for a man his size to move that way? Only the air had stirred. He backed out of the room. His voice dropped, emphasising his deep English accent as his gaze burnt into hers. "I hope you understand that, no matter what happens, I'm... *We* are here for you."

Stunned, all Lilly could do was stare at him.

"Call if you need me. I'll hear you." He paused briefly, then stressed," No matter where I am." He closed the heavy door.

Unaware she had been holding her breath, she let out a long sigh and closed her eyes, rubbing the back of the hand Gabe had touched. Behind her eyelids, she could still see his green eyes looking at her, looking into her, seeing all of her. She had felt completely exposed to him even though the blankets covered her from neck to toes.

I will hear you, no matter where I am. The words replayed in her head, and for some reason she believed he would, too. How could that be? She raised her head slowly and looked around the room. Hidden microphones, or maybe cameras. Was Gabe able to hear her anywhere because he was listening in on her, or watching her from some other room on a monitor? She pulled off the covers and stood with the intent of studying the room more closely, but the door opened and Harry walked in with a tray of food.

"Good morning, Lilly." His thick brogue echoed in the little room.

"Good morning." She sat back down and looked at the tray he put on the end of the bed. She wasn't normally a breakfast person, and it only consisted of a type of white bread—*Manchet*, the name appeared instantly in her mind—along with a hard-looking piece of cheese, something that appeared to be dried fish and a cup filled with...tea?

She stared at the brew. She knew teas were introduced from the east and coffee and chocolate from the west, but not until later in the Tudor era. She looked up at Harry, eyeing him. "Is this another headache tea?"

"No, just a blend Edna makes for us." He shrugged. "There's no coffee yet, so this is our substitute. George suggested it. Apparently, England survived the war on tea. It doesnae have the same kick, but it's still nice to have in the morning."

She reached for the cup and, crossing her legs, brought the brew to her nose and sniffed. It had a fresh, lively scent, maybe lemon balm and something she couldn't put her finger on. She took a sip and sighed.

"Not bad, eh?"

"Not bad at all." She smiled up at Harry. "What war?"

"Excuse me?"

"You said George suggested it, and apparently England survived on tea during the war. Which war?"

Harry crossed his arms over his chest and spread his legs wide. "World War Two."

"Oh!" Her voice sounded high to her own ears. "I really wasn't expecting that answer." She paused, quickly replaying the conversation from the night before. "He was a doctor during World War Two," she blurted out. "In London." Harry's confirmation was a curt nod.

That was why he had stopped in mid-sentence last night. He hadn't wanted to upset her more than she already was. "He's from the 1940s."

"That's right." Harry cocked his head slightly to the side, studying her.

"How did he come to be here?"

Harry shook his head, "That's for George to tell, not me. If you ask him, he'll tell you. We all will—we have nothing to hide."

Her face heated as she toyed with her cup. "Of course. I'm sorry—"

"Don't," Harry cut her off. "There's nothing to be sorry about. I didnae mean it to come across so harsh. I have a hard time letting go of my old life."

She continued to stare at him. "What was your old life?"

He shrugged his massive shoulders. "I was a soldier with UBF."

"UBF? What's that?"

"United Battle Force. It's a Special Forces unit."

Lilly nodded. "I don't know much about Special Forces, but I know I've never heard that name before. It's a Scottish unit?"

Harry laughed, a deep, rich laugh that was so contagious, Lilly found herself smiling. "I'd hope you haven't heard of it. The unit was formed in 2055."

The smiled dropped from her face. Harry laughed again, but this time it was at her.

"You're from the year...2055?"

"No, that was the year the UBF was formed. I didn't join until 2058."

Her jaw dropped open. "2058."

"That was the year I joined, not the year I was shifted." He smiled.

"The year you were shifted," she repeated. "Right!" Shocked, she shook her head, trying to make sense out of this new information. "How did you get here?"

"Well," he began, and came around to her side of the bed and leaned casually against the bedpost. "My squadron was tasked with guarding King Harry—"

"King Harry?" She said it a little too loudly—he had surprised her again. "William's younger brother?"

"That's him."

"What about... What happened to Charles and William?"

"Charlie was in for a few years, but not long 'cause of his mum and all. And as for Willy..." he shook his head sadly. "He was shot down in the last few months of Afghanistan. He and his crew were killed. He never made it to the throne and didn't have any children, so it passed to Harry."

"Wow. I never would have thought... So that's what you meant about being named after royalty. Sorry"—she waved her hand—"you were telling me about guarding Harry."

"We were tasked with the King's protection. Recent intel had come in saying there would be an attempt on Harry's life. And there was. If the professor hadn't intervened when he did, I would have been shot. Actually, I did get shot at, but it missed me because of that whirlwind the TSIS causes, and now I'm here." He turned his head and showed her the scar on the side of his face. The redness had faded, leaving a pink line on the side of his cheek that dug into his hairline and stopped just before his ear.

"Ouch! It must have been very painful."

He shrugged. "I can honestly say I've had worse. But yeah, once I landed here it hurt like hell."

She shook her head and chuckled. "Landed. It makes you sound like you're from outer space."

"It's sort of true, if you think about it. We might be on the same planet, but this century we're in, it *is* alien to us."

Holding her cup in both hands, Lilly looked up at him. It was true—if this was real and not some dream or hoax. "That's a good way to look at it. How long have you been here?"

He was watching her closely again. "About nine months."

She held his dark gaze—it wasn't something she was usually comfortable with, but there was something welcoming about Harry that invited her trust. "Did the others arrive at the same time?"

He was about to speak when a loud knock came at the door. He sauntered over and opened it, angling his large frame in front of the person on the other side, effectively blocking their view, and hers.

He turned to her, smiling. "Ready for your bath?"

* * * *

Lilly ran her hands along the edge of the tub. Now, this was a first. A bath in a wooden bathtub. She had seen pictures online and in textbooks of medieval baths—they had looked like a large wine barrel that could fit a single person. But there had clearly been more than one style, because even though this bath was shorter, it was wide enough for her to stretch out her legs and large enough to fit at least two people.

Two people.

Gabe's face and wide shoulders appeared at the other end of the tub. She had never shared a bath with another person before and she found herself wondering what it would be like to share something as intimate as a bath with Gabe? She closed her eyes and thought about him running his hands up her legs. Pulling her body close to his, her breasts pressed against his chest, his mouth hot and moist teasing hers. His body moving in and out... Her eyes snapped open as her body and face heated at the idea. What was happening? She had other things to think about right now, like whether or not she was in the middle of a hoax, not day dream about Gabe in a hot and steamy bath.

As she pulled herself up, she noticed leaves floating in the water. Shaking her head, she reached for the fabric Edna had left for her to dry off with. Holding up the thin material, she sighed. The rough piece of linen might just be long enough to wrap around her.

Stepping from the water, she wrapped the sheet around her body and sighed again when the material became transparent. Her hard nipples pressed against the fabric, showing evidence of how arousing the simple daydream was to her. She shook her head again but this time at her foolish body. She was in the year 1503. No soft, terrycloth towels here. Or they just hadn't given her one, and were using every detail they could come up with to convince her.

Crossing to the bed, she unzipped the largest pocket of her backpack and pulled out the extra pair of workout shorts and the T-shirt she always carried with her. Her foresight at the time was paying off more than she could ever have thought it would. She quickly threw on the clothes and began to dry her hair as best she could with the wet linen. She didn't have a hairbrush, so she snapped apart the hairclip she used at work and raked the claws through her tangled hair. It didn't take long and, thanks to Edna adding some herbal oils to her bath water, she now felt clean and soft.

She sat in the centre of the large bed and scanned the room. Gabe's last words to her floated around in her head. *I will hear you, no matter where I am.*

Climbing off the feather mattress, Lilly began a slow walk around the room, examining everything. Nothing stood out, but the technology of hidden mics and cameras was incredible — they could be anywhere, could be made of anything, could look like ordinary, everyday objects.

She padded over to the small window and ran her hand along the wooden frame, replaying the conversations she'd had with the four men and then with Gabe. She played them over in her mind hour by hour, minute by minute, hoping to find some proof. She sighed, confused. Proof of what? That Gabe and the others were lying to her, that she wasn't back in the sixteenth century? That she was in some weird nightmare? Or worse, that this wasn't a nightmare, that she was still in 2012 and these men were leading her to believe she was in the past. Why would someone do that? What would they have to gain? She struggled to look through the cloudy glass pane. What was out there?

The one question that she had yet to ask was who was responsible for bringing her here. She remembered Harry referring to a professor. Professor who? How could he just take people from their lives and send them to a different world? For what purpose? And if a professor was responsible for this, did it mean she was in a controlled study or experiment of some sort? Now *that* made a bit more sense. But she would have had to give some sort of consent. It was still illegal to kidnap a person and hold her against her will. And she certainly hadn't consented to be here.

The soft knock on the door made her jump and she turned just as Gabe entered. He quickly locked on to her face, his masculine features impassive as he studied her. Her heart stopped as she noticed his gaze drifting down the length of her body to her bare legs. Heat spread over her face when she recalled her daydream. How the idea of Gabe running his hands up her legs turned her on. For a second time, she felt he could see more than what was on the surface, that he could see deep inside her mind, and she suddenly regretted not putting her yoga pants in her bag instead of the little shorts.

* * * *

Gabe focused on the bright pink flush on Lilly's cheeks. When he had stopped and listened at the door, the room had been so quite he'd panicked, thinking she was gone, and he'd entered quickly to make certain she was still there. He'd been strangely relieved to find her standing by the window.

Now that the dirt and dried blood were gone, he could get a better look at her. Her cuts and scrapes weren't as bad as he'd initially thought. Her damp hair was curling as it dried, resting on the tops of her shoulders, and the flush on her face gave her a fresh, innocent appearance. He knew she was embarrassed and he even thought about saying something to calm her, but he still couldn't stop himself from taking in the way her top clung to her breasts and how narrow her waist was, or how her shorts made her legs look long and smooth.

The image of her wrapping those legs around him flashed unexpectedly before his eyes, causing him to blink and the image to vanish. He stepped closer to her, forcing himself to focus on her face and not her long legs. Watching her, he inhaled slowly.

Fear. Confusion. There was another scent, something sweet, delicate he couldn't put his finger on and… Roses?

He inhaled again. The room smelt like roses—*she* smelt like roses. His lips pulled into a slight, involuntary smile. He liked it. He also like the other scent, too. *What was that?*

She remained still, staring at him, her face pink and her neck flushed. Holding out his hand to her, he suggested, "Why don't you get into bed? Or sit and I'll get you a blanket."

"Why?"

He exhaled slowly, telling her the truth. "Because Harry and the others are waiting outside the door. And I thought you might want to cover up before they come in." He didn't tell her that, for some reason, he couldn't allow the others to see her wearing those shorts and that shirt. That just the thought of them looking at her the way he was made him very…unhappy. "I'll have the trunk of dresses brought in as soon as our meeting is over."

Her eyes widened. "What meeting? In here?"

He nodded, reaching for her hand, and began pulling her towards the bed. "The person responsible for sending you here arrived a few hours ago. There are a few things I need cleared up and I'm sure you still have a number of questions as well. Your room is the most logical place to hold the meeting, since George wants you to rest." He paused, narrowing his eyes. "You look much better. How do you feel?"

She slipped her long, smooth legs under the blankets and, sitting upright, she crossed her legs. His gut tightened when he looked into her dark eyes. The exotic sweep of the lids combined with her dark lashes was striking.

"I feel much better. The bath helped. Thank you."

"You're welcome." He nodded. She was fine now, but how would she feel when she saw McGill? How would she react? He didn't like not knowing the answer. She was obviously still confused and nervous of the whole situation—not that he could blame her.

"Are you ready?" Harry asked, peeking around the door.

She nodded, her brows pushing together in a curious frown.

Harry caught Gabe's nod and opened the door. The three men entered and Gabe watched as Lilly smiled at each of them. She stared back at the door, watching, and Gabe knew the exact moment she recognised McGill. Her smile dropped away and she blinked hard. The pink on her cheeks changed, becoming stark white.

"Hello, Lilly," said McGill.

Nancy Adams

Chapter Seven

Lilly could not, *would* not believe her eyes. She blinked hard a second time. He was still there when she opened her eyes, standing at the end of the bed, staring at her. He pushed his square-framed glasses up his nose and twitched nervously. She knew he needed to move—he never stood still for very long. Her medieval professor, her teacher, Dr Terrence McGill, stood a few feet away from her.

Her head began to ache and her stomach rolled. She turned away from him, looking off to the side of the room, her brain still trying to register the new information. Her teacher was here, in the past. In the sixteenth century. Gabe had said the person responsible for sending her to this time had arrived, and now Professor McGill was standing in front of her. Her stomach rolled again. How was it possible? How had he been able to send her here, to this time?

She blinked, and her thought process jumped. Her stomach rolled for a third time and a nervous flutter followed it. That same uneasy feeling that things just weren't right had her looking around at the men. Where had Professor McGill brought her? If he was here, in front of her, how was it he'd been able to steal her from the future? He lived in her time.

No, her voice snapped in her head.

This place, these people...none of it's real. Time travel, or time shifting, or whatever it was called, wasn't real. She had almost believed him—believed all of them. Lilly had never thought of herself as gullible, but it was apparent she was.

Time shifting. It was wishful thinking by those who wanted to change past mistakes, or used by film-makers and storytellers to create a blockbuster. It was not real.

This was all an elaborate hoax. It had to be—which meant everything that had happened to her, everything that had been said to her...it was all a lie. These men, who had seemed so believable, had lied to her. Gabe... Her heart dipped low into her stomach. Gabe had lied to her.

She looked down at the blanket covering her legs. She had never before trusted a person she had just met. She barely trusted the people she did know. Why she had trusted Gabe and believed the story he had told her was beyond anything she could understand. It had just felt like the right thing to do.

And McGill. He was behind this lie.

The feeling of betrayal was quickly replaced by anger. How could he do this? A person she had felt a real kinship with, someone who was different, like she was—*he* was responsible for her current situation.

He had used their teacher-student relationship to trick her.

Lilly closed her eyes when her head throbbed painfully.

"I can imagine how confused you must feel, Lilly. I'm here to answer any questions you may have. That goes for all of you," McGill said.

Lilly caught and held his hazel gaze, disgust flowing through her. Once upon a time, she would not have thought twice about defending herself. But since her mother died and she had changed, Lilly had gone out of her way to avoid conflict of any sort. She didn't want the attention it would bring and she couldn't take the chance that someone might notice her unique ability. However, right at that moment, she didn't care. She felt her younger self rise to the surface and demand she strike back. "Really? You know how I feel? Then tell me, how *do* I feel, Professor McGill?"

The professor swallowed nervously as he looked at her. She could see beads of sweat on his forehead and the guilt on his face. He deserved it, too—how dare he do this to her? How dare he deceive her? He had forced her to face her own death. She had been put in an earth-shattering position and she had accepted her fate quickly, without question. She had always believed that she should have died when her mom had been killed, so she had been ready. Then he had taken it from her. How *dare* he take the only thing in her life that had been a certainty, the one thing no one could control?

Gabe touched her shoulder, his hand warm, meant to comfort her. She didn't want his comfort and shifted to the side to avoid it. She didn't want

81

anything from these men, even if they were nice, or sweet or considerate. She wanted nothing from them but the directions out.

* * * *

Gabe pulled his hand away. Lilly had gone from shocked to angry. He didn't have to inhale her scent to confirm it—he could see it on her face, feel it in her tense muscles. She was very angry, yet there was something else too.

He began to feel edgy. He knew Lilly was the cause. Maybe it was the glare she was giving McGill, or maybe it was how she kept her body stiff, or maybe he just didn't like the way she'd pulled away from him. It was the first time—from the moment he'd grabbed her wrist and pulled her to safety, until now—that she had flinched from his touch. He squeezed his hands into tight fists. He didn't like her this way—it didn't seem natural for her—and he didn't like the cause of her pain.

Harry cleared his throat and Gabe looked in his direction. Harry raised one dark eyebrow at him and Gabe instantly understood his meaning and crossed his arms, hiding his fists. He slid his gaze to McGill and grinned, gaining a small sense of satisfaction. McGill was always nervous of him, but right now, he was sweating buckets under Lilly's lethal stare.

Gabe took control of the situation. "It's time to answer our questions." He intentionally kept his voice hard. "Why did you bring us here? What is the reason behind all this?"

McGill's eyes flew to Gabe's as he pulled at his shirt collar, then began a nervous pace around the room.

"I'd like to fill you in on a little background first. You've heard this already, Gabe, but I'd like to go over it again for Lilly and the others?"

Gabe gave him a curt nod, his eyes following the man as he retraced his path on the floor.

"Thank you. First, my full name is Robert Stewart McGill. I was born in Inverness, in the United Kingdom, in 2069. I—"

George cut him off. "Scotland. Don't you mean Inverness, Scotland?"

"No, in my time Scotland no longer exists. England, Scotland, Ireland and Wales are now one country, under one government. The countries that make up the Kingdom are now territories. And the other countries in the Commonwealth, those who decided not to join, became enemies of the new Kingdom."

"Kingdom?" Marc asked. "It sounds like you live in a totalitarian society."

The professor paused. "Some aspects are—like the health care system, and distribution of food is controlled and regulated."

"People are told what to eat?" George asked, clearly shocked.

"No, of course not. The government controls what food makes it to the stores. The public is free to eat whatever they desire, as long as they buy it from an approved store. Which is all of them."

"Approved store!" George almost shouted. "I went to war twice so that mindset wouldn't find its way into England."

Gabe walked over to George and placed his hand on his shoulder, hoping to provide comfort. "Easy, George."

Gabe could clearly see the pain in the man's light blue eyes. He had lost most of his family in the First and Second World Wars, including his wife.

McGill quickly spoke up. "Really, it's not what you think."

"Then why don't you explain it...clearly," Gabe snapped. He pinned McGill to the spot with his gaze. "Well?"

Nervously, McGill continued, "It began with the Genetic Purification Act of 2040. The government had already realised the food the population consumed was directly related to the inability of their bodies to protect themselves. Even after the widespread genetic cleansing of embryos, the population still contracted diseases easily. Only the Armed Forces programmes had strict diets, aimed at keeping their bodies and minds pure. Their diets" — McGill looked at Gabe — "were implemented across the country. Any food that had been linked to any health risk was banned. It caused quite a commotion at first but then the population became accustomed to it and health-related issues dropped to an almost non-existent level. Which in turn took stress off the National Health Service and meant more money could be spent on education and other programmes. So you see" — McGill turned to George — "it is really not as bad as it sounds."

"Genetic Purification Act?" George shook his head, his eyes still full of sorrow. "Everything those people fought and died for...and it still happened." Gabe helped George to sit on the edge of Lilly's bed.

Gabe chanced a quick glance at Lilly. She was watching George and, though she had a detached look on her face, he could see tears shimmering in her eyes. But there was also doubt there. She lifted her face to his and he felt his gut tighten. She couldn't hide her feelings and that was one thing Gabe liked — that she had feelings.

* * * *

It didn't matter. It didn't matter how Gabe looked at her, or that he made her heart jump — she was still getting the hell out of here. She blinked and slid her gaze back to George. She felt bad for him, she really did — his sadness seemed so realistic — but she just couldn't find it in her to believe it was true. It was most likely another lie to convince her this bizarre nightmare was real. She was only staying in the hopes of finding out a little about what was on the other side of the door, and maybe a little more about each of the men — especially Gabe. He wasn't your normal guy-next-door, who worked at a bank, or ran a restaurant. There was something more to him — and McGill had said as much.

Only the Armed Forces programmes had strict diets, aimed at keeping their bodies and minds pure. McGill had looked directly at Gabe when he'd said that. Gabe was a soldier too, just like Harry, and if she was guessing right, he was probably very good at his job and his instincts were good. He had taken hold of her hands both times she'd had the urge to run. He had known she wanted to bolt before she did. That meant she would need blind luck to get away from him and get out of this room.

From the corner of her eye, she saw him straighten and cross his thick arms, and though she couldn't clearly see, she felt him studying her before he turned to face McGill.

"You still need to answer my first question." His voice was low, with a deadly edge to it.

Lilly swung her eyes back to McGill. She watched as the old urge overtook him and he began to move again. When she had first noticed McGill's habit in class, she'd thought he might have some form of attention disorder, but as she'd attended more and more of his classes she had come to realise his movement coincided with his thought processes — one couldn't work without the other.

As McGill marched back and forth, he continued with his answer. "In 2103, time shifting became a possibility when Dr Ian Wells was able to send his dog three hours into the future, to the loo down the hall from his lab."

There was an unnatural silence in the room.

"So..." Harry frowned breaking the silence. "Where was the dog for those three hours?" He rubbed his jaw.

"He wasn't hanging around in space or anything, Harry," Marc answered. "He would have gone straight to the destination point, where Wells was probably waiting for him. Right, Professor?"

"That's correct," McGill agreed. "The subject — the dog — travelled instantly to the landing time three hours into the future. Whereas Dr Wells had to wait through the three hours for his dog to arrive in the bathroom."

"Okay, I think I've got it. Though am I the only one who thinks sending a dog to the loo is a bit weird?" Harry said with a smirk.

"So, what does this have to do with us?" Gabe asked.

"The process that Wells discovered is the same process I used to shift you all here."

Lilly focused on McGill. He was doing that thing he did. She could hear the beginnings of it in his voice. They were talking about something McGill was interested in, something he was passionate about like medieval history, and it was beginning to pull her in. It was the main reason she'd loved his classes—his passion for the subject rivalled her own. She closed her eyes and tried to block out his excitement and just hear his words. He was the one responsible for her being in this weird...nightmare.

"And why are we here?" Gabe asked quietly, for a third time.

"I had the unfortunate luck to discover a plan to kill both sisters of King Henry the Eighth, thereby breaking the current line of succession and altering the future of England."

Chapter Eight

Lilly remained silent as names and dates of royalty directly related to the House of Tudor flew in front of her eyes. The daughters of Henry the Seventh. Margaret, the older of the two sisters and second-born to Henry the Seventh and his wife Elizabeth. Mary, the youngest of the Tudor children and very close to her older brother and future king, Henry the Eighth.

The information was so easily retrieved from her mind it sometimes took only a single word to spark an onslaught of data. It hadn't always been that easy—at the beginning, when she had first realised her memory had changed, it had taken a few minutes to gather the information and put it in the correct order. The effort of sorting through the jumble of facts and figures had caused her excruciating headaches, but she had learnt to develop a filing system where she could store the excessive amounts of information in her head and retrieve it at will. Now she was so fast she could give any search engine a run for its money.

Lowering her head she stared at the blanket as if the information compiled in her head was written there. Margaret and Mary Tudor. *If* this was really real, and she was in 1503, and the sisters were indeed to be killed, then both sisters would have to be killed before either had children. *If* she was back in 1503, it meant Mary, the youngest, was still unwed...but Margaret was married. And depending what month they were in, Margaret could still be married via proxy to King James and yet to travel the distance to her new home in Scotland to consummate the marriage. *If* what McGill was saying was true, and she was in 1503.

Her heart began to race as the doubt rose again. Were they trying to suck her in by using her interests to trap her? To make her believe? Why? What purpose would it serve?

Lilly inhaled deeply. No. None of this was real—she would not allow herself to be caught in this nightmare. Her goal was to get out of here and find help. But how far would she have to go? Would she be able to bring the police back here? What if they thought she was crazy? Maybe she was. She swallowed hard. God help her she *felt* crazy.

"What's the big deal? Who are they?" Marc said, casually interrupting her confusion.

"They are the current King's daughters, and sisters to King Henry the Eighth," McGill said.

"And?" Marc said sarcastically.

"Lilly? Would you like to answer Marc's question?" McGill suggested quietly.

She shook her head as all eyes in the room turned to her. "We are not in class and you are not my teacher," she bit out. Anger was getting the better of her but she didn't care anymore—she was tired of playing games with these men.

Throwing the blanket off, she swung her legs off the bed. Gabe was there before she decided to move, holding her by the elbow. She stared into his dark scowl and pulled her arm free. She stepped past him and walked to the large hearth.

Clenching the muscles in her jaw, she stared into the fire. Her younger self was so pissed off, she wanted to strike out and hit something. This was the main reason she stayed away from people—it was safer that way. This very situation proved her right. She had never felt so misled or trapped in her life.

"I realise you are angry with me, Lilly, but I would do it again if I had to. I couldn't let you die. You are such a talented young woman."

She swung around to face McGill and crossed the room, stopping close to him. "You don't know anything about me except I'm your student and we both enjoy studying medieval history—that's it."

"You are a good person who would have died. It wasn't fair to you. I couldn't let it happen."

"That wasn't for you to decide." She walked past him and quickly turned back to face him. "You had no right. It was *my* death, *my* fate. You had no right to take that away from me. God help me, this probably isn't real"—she clenched her hands into fists, her body trembling—"but I was ready. I'd accepted it. And you took it from me—the one thing in my life that was mine."

* * * *

Gabe felt his stomach sink as he listened to her. Lilly had been ready to die. He stared at her, shocked and troubled by her words. Twenty-six and ready to die. What could have happen to her to make her accept death so easily and not want to fight for her life?

He took note of her slight step back, closer to the door, and briefly thought her outburst might be a distraction so she could get to the door and bolt. Yet from where he stood he could see her body vibrating with anger and fear, could see the tears in her dark eyes.

She searched McGill's face, then she ran her hands through her hair, pulling it hard. "What is this place? Where am I?" She stepped towards him. "Tell me," she pleaded. "I deserve that much, don't I?"

McGill stepped back, wary of her.

Gabe moved slowly towards her. That was enough. He couldn't take any more, and neither could she. Her anxiety was becoming dangerous.

He didn't give a shit about McGill—the bastard deserved her hatred. Gabe's concern was focused solely on Lilly. Her eyes were wild as she stared at McGill. She looked hurt and confused, and even though he had an exceptional sense of smell, he didn't need it to know she was scared. She needed help. Help to make sense of her surroundings and her new life. She needed to face the truth and accept it— or he would have to force her. And he didn't want to do that. He didn't want to hurt her.

Lilly took another step backwards and Gabe stopped, pausing intentionally as she swung around and reached for the heavy, wooden door. Only when she began running down the hallway did he follow.

* * * *

Lilly didn't hesitate as she ran full speed down the hall to a set of stairs spiralling both up and down. With her mind in turmoil, she went up without a thought. The image of her mother was strong in her mind's eye. She'd had a chance to see her again, the only person who had ever loved her, and McGill had taken it away from her.

The stairs, all different widths and heights, made her trip several times but she pushed forward, curving around and around until she came to a small, thick door. She pulled it open and burst out into a damp, grey day. The sudden light was bright enough to cause her to slow and cover her eyes. She continued, half-blind, along a stone walkway, not caring where she stepped.

As her eyes finally adjusted to the light, she stopped. Looking around, she saw two stone walls, one on either side of her. One wall had square sections cut out along the top. She paused and the word and definition appeared in her mind as if she was reading a dictionary. *Crenels. The open spaces between the merlons on the battlements of a keep or castle.*

They were a means of defence for a castle or fortress, from which archers could shoot their arrows or boiling oil could be poured onto the enemy below.

"Not real," she mumbled in disbelief.

A yell caught her attention and she turned following the sound. She stepped over to the other wall, which reached her waist. Lilly placed her hands on the flat stone and gasped as she looked down. The sight before her stole her breath. She was staring at the inner courtyard, a bailey, belonging to a sixteenth century castle. She squeezed her eyes shut and opened them again. The scene remained unchanged before her.

"Oh, my God," she whispered in defeat and wiped the tears from her cheeks. Looking down, she instantly realised the battlements where she stood were easily thirty feet above the people moving around the enclosed area. She scanned the area, noticing a group of large horses being led out through a gated drawbridge by men dressed in battle gear. A couple of women carrying baskets with some type of fruit or vegetable were talking and giggling with each other as the men passed by. A loud clanging overpowered the women's conversation and echoed up the high walls. It was the distinctive sound of a hammer pounding and shaping metal.

Stepping back, she turned back to the wall behind her and looked through one of the crenels. A row of wooden huts caught her attention, interspersed with larger buildings and with paths and muddy roads weaving between them. Fenced-in areas with what she guessed were chickens and other livestock were scattered around the outer edge of the village. People were moving around, going about their business. Horse-pulled carts were transporting food, wood and other merchandise. A little village.

"It can't be." She shook her head even as her mind absorbed every detail.

The surrounding area was lush with vegetation — a forest in the distance, and fields with freshly ploughed soil on either side of the village. A wide, dark river flowed by—a ready supply of fresh water for the villagers. In the distance, as she struggled to see though the grey mist, she could just make out the outlines of large, rolling hills. Leaning further through the crenel, she caught a brief glimpse of a moat.

Her heart pounded wildly in her chest, her eyes burnt and her head throbbed. Normally, she could take in any type of information and absorb it without any problem. But this...it was too much. All the clues—the clothes, the food, the herbs—she had seen them, had touched them with her own hands, yet she hadn't truly believed until this moment. When McGill had walked into her room, she had convinced herself that the clues had been fake, planted to give the impression of being in the past.

She inhaled deeply, feeling her eyes burn again. It wasn't fake. It was real—everything Gabe had told her was real. He had told her the truth, and she felt an odd sense of relief about that. But what was she going to do? She was trapped in the sixteenth century.

Tears welled up and slipped over her lids as she covered her face with her hands. A low sob escaped before she could stop it, then thick arms wrapped around her, holding her securely.

Gabe. He had followed her. Again he had known she was going to bolt. He probably could have stopped her, like the other times, but he hadn't. When he had stopped her before, had he been protecting her from the truth?

Grateful he'd followed her, even though she wasn't used to having someone to lean on, she relaxed against him. "You let me go," she mumbled into her hands. "You knew I was going to run, but this time you let me go."

"Yes." His deep voice was smooth and comforting. "I had to let you run this time. You needed to see with your own eyes that what we said was the truth."

"You didn't lie," she said quietly.

"No, I didn't lie. There would be no point. The sooner you accept the truth, the sooner you can move on."

"Gabe?" she whispered as a sob shook her body. "I don't know if I can...move on."

He tightened his arms around her and brushed a kiss on the top of her head.

"Yes, angel, you can. It will take some time, but you won't be alone. We'll help you." He paused, resting his chin on top of her head. "*I'll* help you."

Chapter Nine

Gabe held Lilly in silence for some time. Her trembling had subsided and her breathing had slowed. He didn't care how long it took Lilly to regain her composure—he was more than willing to stand with her. In truth, he was enjoying holding her, probably more than he should, considering the situation—he just couldn't help it. Her body was so soft pressed up against his and she smelt so damn good. Yet he knew they had to go back. Questions needed to be answered and they both had to be there.

"Lilly?" He kept his voice low. "I can stay here with you as long as you need but you will still have to face McGill and the others. Questions still need to be answered."

His muscles clenched as she placed her hands on his chest and pushed back, looking up at him. Her brown eyes swollen and her freckled nose red, she sniffed. "What questions?" she asked. "I only want to know if I can get back home."

He sighed, and looked at the wavy hair on the top of her head. There was no way for any of them to return to their own time. McGill had already answered that question four times and each time he had given the same answer.

"I can't go back, can I?"

"None of us can."

She bit her lip, her dark lashes lowered, covering the sadness he saw in her eyes.

Damn it, he hated seeing her like this. But he would not lie to her, even if the truth caused her pain. "I'm sorry, Lilly. If I could change what happened, I would."

He meant it, too, for reasons he didn't quite understand. If he could undo what McGill had done and have Lilly safe in her own time, he would.

His chest tightened, his heart rebelling against the thought of Lilly being in a different time from him, but he clenched his jaw against the sensation, unwavering in his decision. "I would change it for all of us."

She nodded silently. He inhaled her sorrow and put his fingers gently under her to chin to raise her head. Gabe looked her over. She was exquisite. Even though she had been crying and her face was tear-streaked and she occasionally sniffed, she was exquisite. Her skin was soft, her eyes expressive and her lips a sin.

He met her damp eyes, then watched quietly as she looked at his mouth, then slowly moved the gaze over his face while her wet tongue slid across the seam of her lips. He wanted — no, he needed to taste those lips. Had needed to since he had first held her in his arms the day before. His shoulders and arms flexed as he drew Lilly tight to his chest. Lowering his head, he stopped, inhaling deeply. There it was again, that sweet, delicate scent. He closed his eyes, taking it further into his lungs as he touched her lips with his own.

Gabe forced himself to move slowly. Lilly's nervous fear was mixing with the scent of roses. He rubbed his thumb over the scar below her lip as he brushed his lips across hers. He had never been as turned on as he was now, and by something as simple as a kiss. He could feel the muscles trailing down his chest and stomach become tight, and the demanding heat causing his cock to harden.

Running his hand into her hair, Gabe held her securely in place as he sealed their mouths together, deepening the kiss, running his tongue along the outer seam of her lips. She gasped lightly as she pulled her mouth away and stared at his chin.

Ignoring the demands of his body, Gabe slowly inhaled, trying to achieve a measure of control, but pulled in her rosy scent instead. He swore silently in his head. What had happened? He hadn't meant to scare her. The stroke had been deliberately light, meant to entice her into opening her mouth so he could taste more of her.

"I can't believe I did that," she breathed, still avoiding his eyes. The statement was said without thought and was openly innocent.

Innocent. Inhaling slowly once again, he raised her head and looked into her eyes. Not completely innocent, by the way she had returned his kiss. Lack of experience was a better guess.

"You're not the only person standing here," he said and, without a thought, brushed his thumb across the scar on her bottom lip.

"I know. I just don't..." She suddenly switched topics. "So, why can't we go home again?"

Gabe didn't understand why she felt embarrassed, but he got the hint and didn't push the subject.

"McGill can tell you the reasons why. I'll make sure he explains them to you after we've found out more about this assassination attempt on Mary and Mabel."

Her pink lips curled up slightly. "Mary and Margaret," she corrected.

"Right, Mary and Margaret." He smiled at her. "Are you ready to go back?"

"I'm not sure why I need to be there. If things are being changed…the past I studied may never happen at all."

"I need you there because you know more about this time than any of us…but also because of your other talent."

She stiffened in his arms. He had been expecting that reaction, but he needed to know if it was true. That particular skill might save their asses one day.

"Do you have a photographic memory, Lilly?"

She looked up at him with wide eyes. "Who told you that?"

"McGill. He guessed it, actually. He was right, wasn't he?"

She sighed, nodding. "I didn't realise I was that obvious. I can usually hide it, but sometimes I get so wrapped up in whatever I'm working on that I slip up."

"You weren't that obvious. McGill is just that observant. He would have to be, being a professor and all. I'm sure he's researched how to put his pants on the most efficient way."

* * * *

Lilly smiled again. That was the second time in the past few minutes Gabe had tried to lighten her mood. And both times, it had worked. Either she was a sucker for his good looks, or he was just that good at making her feel better, or maybe it was his heart-stopping kiss that had made her feel better. Feel better? That was an understatement. She was so hot and achy and a little light headed. Not that it was a pastime she had spent hours perfecting—in fact her resume was pathetic—but it had been an amazing kiss. The way he had tightened his grip on her, the heat from his body, his sweet breath, all of it caused her body to tingle and heat up. Either way, she would take it. Any kind of distraction—especially that kind—was welcome right now. The idea of going back down to face all those men after her hissy fit embarrassed her. She felt like a fool. Gabe was right, though—she wanted to know why she was here, and the others deserved to know as well. She had no right to make them wait.

"It's time to go back," Gabe said, a hint of dominance in his voice.

He focused on her face, patiently studying her reaction. Gabe was *very* patient and she had the feeling that if she wasn't ready to go he would wait with her until she was. But from the way he studied her, she had a feeling he would know if she was stalling, too. So she accepted the inevitable.

Harry was the only one left when they arrived. He was waiting in the hall, leaning his massive frame casually against the wall next to her door. He gave her a wink as they walked towards him and she felt her face heat up.

"Feel better?" Harry asked as they stopped in front of him.

"I think so. I've never done that before. I'm...embarrassed."

"Why?" Harry asked, surprise in his voice.

"You have no reason to be," Gabe said, scowling down at her.

"I..." She looked down the hall, checking to see if anyone was around who might overhear. "I wanted to punch McGill...right in the face."

Harry burst out laughing and, red-faced once again, Lilly chanced a look at Gabe. His wide smile softened his normally focused appearance, giving her a glimpse of how handsome he truly was. Her body responded without her consent, sending a slight vibration from her head straight through to her toes.

"That's to be expected. Gabe and I wanted to do the same thing." Harry paused, smiling down at her. "You scared the shit out of him ye know?" he asked, wiggling his eyebrows. "How'd it feel?"

Lilly looked at Harry and smothered a smile. "It felt great." She heard Gabe laugh this time, but fought the urge to look at him.

"I bet it did." Harry still had a wide smile on his face and Lilly caught a brief glimpse of the scar on the side of his face. She stopped laughing, remembering where they were. For a moment, the three of them had been talking like everything was normal—like they hadn't been pulled from the future.

"Thank you, Harry." She smiled sincerely. He nodded his understanding.

Gabe stepped closer to her and rested his hand on her lower back. "Where is everyone?"

"Well," Harry exhaled as he answered Gabe. "After Lilly tore out of here, George became a little overprotective and suggested that when ye brought Lilly back she should be allowed to regain her composure in private. I agreed and kicked the lot of them out." He turned his black eyes on Lilly. "How about it, Lilly? Still need time to regain your composure?"

She shook her head. "I'm fine, really. Please, have them come back. I want to apologise…"

"No, you won't," Gabe interrupted her. She looked up him, startled by the firm command. His face was devoid of any emotion, but his eyes were blazing. He shifted his stare to Harry. "Give it five minutes, then bring them back up. I want my answers."

Harry nodded, straightened to his full height and walked down the hall.

Gabe nudged Lilly into the room and closed the door behind them. She walked over to the far side of the room, putting the bed between them. Gabe made no move to follow her—he simply watched her from the door. They stared at each other for what seemed like eternity, her heart racing.

"I said... What did I say? I'm not sure I understand what's going on here," she mumbled, almost thinking out loud, trying to read his expression. He was relaxed, or at least appeared to be. What was going on? What had she said that could have caused him to react so unexpectedly?

Very slowly, he crossed the room towards her until he stood within arm's reach of her. She froze, and so did her heart.

"You do not have to apologise to anyone here. None of this is your fault and you have every right to feel the way you're feeling." His voice was low, with a firm edge.

A shudder ran though her. Lilly didn't think he was trying to intimidate her, but he was intimidating nonetheless. This Gabe was so different from the one who had just been standing with her on the battlements—his stare alone was making her squirm. But she stood her ground as he stepped even closer, staring at her neck, and raised his hand to her throat.

The touch of his fingers was light against her pulse. "You're afraid of me."

She couldn't lie—he already seemed to know the truth. "I'm nervous."

His attention was still fixed on the pulse in her neck.

"I don't want you to be." He stroked her skin, and his eyes met hers. "Everyone I have ever met has been scared of me in one way or another. In most cases it was justified, and that was always fine with me, but I don't want it to be like that with you. Do you understand what I'm saying?" He lightly ran his hand around to the back of her neck and pulled her forward, his breath warm on her face. "I don't want you to be scared or even nervous of me. You have no reason to be." Then, a soft request, "Trust in me, Lilly." He fastened his mouth over hers once again. Where his lips had been soft and gentle before, they were hard and thorough this time, covering her mouth completely. He slipped his tongue along her lips and into her mouth. His sweet taste filled her mouth as he twined his tongue with hers, tasting every part of her mouth. And as quickly as the kiss had begun, it ended, with him tracing the seam of her lips again.

With his head still bent low next to hers, he panted, "Trust me?" His voice was low, accent thick. The combination was downright sexy. And thanks to that voice and that kiss, she felt hot and achy all over again.

Her heart jumped in response to his words; her skin heated and began to tingle as he trailed his fingers down her neck.

"Okay." She breathed out.She didn't know what else to say. She believed him when he said she could trust him—his words were so strong, and his hands on her skin so feathery light. And when his intense look turned almost pleading, how could she not believe him? Yet she still wanted to know why others were afraid of him and, a better question—why was it justified?

* * * *

Once Lilly was settled back on the bed and Gabe had made sure the blanket covered her legs, the others came in. No one said a word about her earlier behaviour, and she was sure Harry had something to do with that. Gabe stood next to the side of her bed, like a guardian. When he met Harry's stare, his friend lifted a single, dark brow and looked to Lilly and back with amusement on his face—and he knew why. Lilly's lips were swollen and flushed darker than the pink of her face. He hadn't meant to kiss her again, and so soon after he'd realised she wasn't as experienced as he was, he just hadn't been able to help himself. He wouldn't change it now, anyway. He would go back for more.

He crossed his arms over his chest as he stared back at Harry, who began laughing. "Let's get on with this," he barked, directing his attention at McGill.

Lilly watched as McGill jumped at the harsh command, then began retracing his old path on the floor.

Gabe sighed and bit out, "Damn it, McGill."

Gabe's obvious frustration was making McGill nervous. They would never get anything solved this way—and besides, she felt bad for him. She tried not to, but she couldn't help it.

"What month is it?" she asked, loud enough for everyone to hear.

With all five men staring at her, it was Gabe who answered. "It's the beginning of June. Why?" His voice was puzzled.

"Well," she began, "I would guess we have roughly two months to stop whoever means to kill Margaret and Mary Tudor."

Gabe curved his mouth up at one corner as he stared at her. She turned before he could see her face flush and quickly reminded the group of McGill's previous statement. "Professor McGill said both sisters were going to be murdered, thereby breaking the current line of succession."

"Who were—I mean, who *are* Margaret and Mary? And why do we care?" Marc asked.

Lilly looked at McGill, waiting for him to answer. Instead, he nodded his head encouragingly.

So, she began. "Margaret Tudor is the elder sister to the future King of England, Henry the Eighth, and Mary is the youngest." She caught Harry's frown. "He's the one with the six wives."

"Got it." Harry winked.

"As it stands right now, Margaret is married to the King of Scotland by proxy. That means she still has to travel to Scotland and consummate their marriage. It also means no children. Mary, on the other hand, is not married. She doesn't marry King Louis of France until 1514. That means no children for her, either." She looked at McGill, who was still pacing along an imaginary line on the floor. He carried on as if he was inside her head, reading her train of thought.

"Both sisters have children and it is their descendants who contribute to the current line of succession. Mary's descendants contribute first. After the death of Henry the Eighth, his only son, Edward, ascends the throne but lives for a very short time. By the end of his reign, he has declared both his sisters illegitimate and named Lady Jane Grey as his successor. Lady Jane Grey," Lilly explained, looking around the room at the men, "was...I mean, *will be* the granddaughter of Mary Tudor. She is Mary's contribution to the throne. But she only rules for nine days and is beheaded by supporters of Mary, Henry the Eighth's first child and heir to the throne."

McGill took over the explanation. "Mary becomes sick and names her younger sister, Elizabeth, as her successor. The throne passes to her on Mary's death. Even though Elizabeth the First is queen for forty-five years, she never marries and has no children. This is where Margaret's descendants come into the picture. At the time of Elizabeth's death, the next in line for the English throne is King James the Sixth of Scotland."

"How is he related to Queen Elizabeth?" Gabe asked.

"King James's mother is Mary Queen of Scots, cousin to Queen Elizabeth the First. He is also Margaret Tudor's great-grandson."

Gabe nodded his understanding, and McGill went on. "Upon Elizabeth's death, King James the Sixth of Scotland becomes King James the First of England. He becomes the first king to rule England, Ireland and Scotland."

"And if Margaret or Mary or both are killed before they have children" — Lilly paused and looked up at Gabe — "the current line of succession stops at Elizabeth the First."

"Wow," Marc said from his position at the end of Lilly's bed. "That was a lot of information I will never use." He muttered, rubbing his forehead. "Why couldn't this be a number problem? I could solve it and we could be on our merry way."

Gabe sighed and rubbed his chin thoughtfully. "If both sisters are killed before they have any children, then who ascends to the throne? Who would Elizabeth choose?"

Chapter Ten

Gabe watched as Lilly's brown eyes dropped to his chest, becoming unfocused. Then a strange thing happened—her eyes began to shift slightly, back and forth, as though she was about to black out.

Stepping towards her, he knelt down as he studied her face. Her pink lips, still swollen, were slightly open and her cheeks had a rosy glow to them. Her lashes fluttered, lowering over her dark eyes as they continued to dart back and forth. He didn't touch her or speak to her, just quietly watched. It was incredible. She was searching through the information she had retained during her classes, flipping page after page of information stored in her head until she found the answer she was looking for.

Her eyes began to water and she blinked rapidly, sending a single tear down her cheek, but continued to scan invisible text, almost like there was a book in front of her eyes.

After a few minutes, Gabe began to feel uneasy. The process was taking longer than he'd thought it would. He turned to look at McGill. "Does it usually take this long?" He ducked his head so he could watch her face closely.

"I don't know. This is the first time I've seen her use it."

George, who had been quiet up to this point, quickly walked to Lilly's side. "Seen what?" He bent to look into her eyes, alarmed by the rapid movement. "What's going on, Gabe?" The doctor in George became dominant and he reached for her hand.

Gabe shot out his hand, stopping George before he could touch her. "Don't," he commanded softly.

Lilly's eyes fluttered again and she blinked hard before focusing on Gabe's face. She stared at him briefly, then flushed as she took in the other men watching her.

"Does it usually take that long?" Gabe asked, smoothing away the tear stain.

Her thin brows pressed together. "I looked everywhere," she twisted her fingers together.

Gabe frowned. "Looked for what?" he asked softly, trapping her hands in his.

"There are people that she *could* choose," Lilly said, "But I don't know who she *would* choose. I never... I didn't think... I don't *know*."

"Easy." Gabe lightly squeezed her hands.

"I'm sorry," she said, regret in her voice. "I only studied the monarchs related to the current line of succession. I was never given an assignment where I had to guess who a monarch might choose as their successor, and I could never have imagined the reason would be a situation like the one we're in."

Gabe squeezed her hands a little harder and answered her patiently. "I know. We all know."

McGill's voice interrupted them. "Then let's brainstorm." He stopped pacing for all of five seconds, then started up again. "If all children of Henry the Seventh are gone and there are no grandchildren, who is most likely to ascend? Any ideas?" He looked around the room.

Gabe stroked the back of Lilly's hand with his thumb as he stood — her skin was so soft. He had never noticed a woman's skin before now. "Did Elizabeth have any other siblings, maybe illegitimate?"

"There were rumours that Henry the Eighth had a son with Mary Boleyn, but it was never confirmed."

"What about Elizabeth's granddad, Henry the Seventh?" Harry asked. "Did he have any brothers or sisters?"

"I don't remember any," Lilly said thoughtfully, "but I can look. Besides James, there would have to be a second or third cousin somewhere that would be next in line. I just don't know who it would be. The relationship would have to go back quite far, and if Elizabeth was as thorough as I imagine, she would have settled it long before her death. She probably would have kept her successor close to her and she would have made certain they shared her beliefs. I can't see her leaving England to an uncertain fate. It would be too open to both domestic and foreign threats."

"How so?" Gabe studied Lilly's thoughtful expression. She clearly hadn't liked not knowing the answer to his question. With her photographic memory, she would be used to knowing the answer to any question on a subject she had studied. Not knowing the answer to a question, especially a question about medieval history, was new territory for her. Yet she had bounced back relatively unscathed and he felt strangely proud of her for that, because he knew how disturbing it could be when your skill — the skill that gave you the edge and set you apart — didn't help a damn bit.

He knew firsthand. He was the best the UBF had to offer. He had topped every single test they had thrown at him. Mental, physical, psychological. But it was a lucky hit from an RPG that would have killed him if McGill had not intervened. It wasn't what he'd pictured in his mind when he'd thought about his death. He had always thought a younger, naturally skilled soldier would kill him in hand-to-hand combat. That he would go down fighting honourably. Not have his ass blown to bits by something so sloppy. It had been a hard kick to his ego.

"What does almost everything come down to in this time period?" She shrugged, looking up at him. The slight curve to the corner of her eyes gave her a sultry look, urging him silently to bend down and kiss her again. The idea caused his stomach to tighten in response. "Religion. She didn't bow down to the Church. They didn't like a female telling them... where to go and how to get there. Neither did Spain, and neither did her large population of Catholic followers. There were many plots against her, supported by different countries — all of them looking to get their claws into England."

"This is a great history lesson, but how do we stop this murder from taking place?" Harry asked, crossing his arms. "That was the point of this group discussion, wasn't it?"

"Yeah!" Marc added. "How do we figure out when it will happen, and who is trying to kill them? Will they kill one sister, or both of them?"

All eyes in the room shifted to McGill. "I can't help you with that, because I don't know." He faced Lilly. "Your knowledge will be an asset, but it will most likely be strictly guess work at this point. I'm going to try to figure out who in my time is organising this, and why. With some luck, I'll be able to find out when the murder will take place."

"But I don't know how to stop a murder," Lilly said, bewilderment in her voice.

"Of course you don't," McGill agreed. "That's where Gabe and Harry come in—but you can lead them in the right direction. You already know the time frame, you just have to figure out where it will happen, and Gabe will correct the situation." McGill looked at Gabe. "Right, Captain?"

* * * *

Lilly slowly shifted her gaze to Gabe. Captain? She'd known he was a soldier, of course—the air of quiet confidence radiated from him. And now she knew, it seemed obvious he was also an officer—the one in control, and not just of himself but of others as well. He was used to leading others and having them follow. That was why the other men hadn't questioned anything he'd done or said since she'd arrived. Neither had she, she realised. She had done everything he had asked of her, responding automatically to his air of quiet authority.

Gabe was still next to her bed, with his feet apart and arms crossed. The muscles in his arms flexed, stretching the material of his white cotton shirt, defining every hard ripple and bulge. He directed his annoyed stare at McGill. "Right." His answer was liberally laced with sarcasm.

Gabe hid his hands under his large arms, but Lilly caught his slow movement as the hand closest to her curled into a fist. He wasn't just annoyed with McGill, he was fuming. She looked up at his face. His expression didn't give away a single hint of his true feelings. Her heart jumped. He had such control over his emotions, turning them on and off, displaying them or hiding them at will. It was becoming very clear that there was more to Gabe than his ability to 'correct the situation'.

Gabe will correct the situation. McGill had said it casually, not giving away any details as to how the situation would be corrected. Now, looking at him, Lilly had a scary feeling she knew *exactly* how Gabe would correct the situation. She looked away, pressing her hand to her forehead. What in heaven had she been dragged into? Shifting through time, castles, soldiers from the future, a doctor from World War Two, a murder conspiracy against not one but two of King Henry the Seventh's daughters and, to top it all off, her medieval history professor, whom she had met in 2012, was born in the year 2069. She drew her covered knees up and rested her forehead against them as her head began to throb.

She knew she had to deal with this. It was all real — she had stood on the battlements of a fully functioning sixteenth century castle and looked out at a lush, green landscape. It was startling, but real. With her mind constantly active, always absorbing the world around her, she could summon any image she had ever seen, but she didn't have the creativity to produce something as breathtakingly natural as the area surrounding the castle.

It was still hard to digest, though. Not in her wildest dreams would she have believed this could ever happen to her. She wasn't one to dream up strange realities or fantasies—she couldn't, that wasn't her. So instead, she read. She loved to read. She read everything, and not just for school or to gain knowledge. She read because it kept her mind active, which she needed, but also because it helped her escape her life for a brief while. And she could honestly say what she was going through was nothing like any novel she had ever read.

She stopped in mid-thought. *Novel.* The word popped out and the image of her sliding a paperback into the outside pocket of her knapsack came to mind. She kept playing the scene, and saw her own hand begin to zip the pocket closed. She paused the scene and gasped. Her head came up quickly. She looked around and found only Gabe and McGill left in the room, both staring at her.

Gabe's accented voice found her. "Lilly?"

She smiled like a fool up at him. She remembered every detail she had seen, every sensation she had felt while he kissed her. He was so perfectly robust, so unbelievably sexy it amazed her. Gabe stepped towards her, staring intently, and she suddenly felt lightheaded and nervous, and her face felt like it was on fire.

"What is it?"

Had he noticed her blush? She watched in horror as his eyes dropped to her mouth and a slight smile came to his perfect lips.

"My bag," she blurted, feeling like a teeny-bobber drooling over her favourite heartthrob. "I just remembered I put my notebook in my bag."

He nodded, eyeing her suspiciously, and reached across the end of the bed for her knapsack.

"What's so special about your notebook?" he asked as she unzipped the main compartment and pulled the notebook free.

"It's my notebook." She shrugged. "I put notes in it."

With a smirk he held out his hand to her. "May I?"

* * * *

Lilly passed him her notebook and he casually flipped through the worn pages, stopping here and there. "This doesn't make any sense. There are just single words with..." He pointed to a page. "Are those dates?"

"Yes. I put dates next to all my notes. Let's see." She rose on her knees and moved to his side. Her body was so close to his he could feel her heat and smell her softly scented skin. Roses. She raised her hand and pointed to the page he was looking at. "See this?"

She was pointing to a single number.

"Ninety-eight?" he asked.

She nodded and looked up at him. "That number helps me track all the information I retained in school that year. The word helps with the subject and next to it is the month and day I learnt it."

"So, when you look at this word, everything you learnt just pops back into your head?"

She nodded. "Kind of...but for that year and for school only. Nothing else. I..." She stopped and looked at McGill warily, then continued. "The first few years after I got my new memory, I had a hard time sorting through the information I absorbed. Like, one time, I had an exam and needed to retrieve info on Canadian geography. It took a long time for me to sort through the trash to find the answers I needed."

Gabe glanced at her. "Trash?"

"It's what I call all the other info I absorbed at the same time." She raised her shoulders, giving him a smile. "People talking, movement around the room, the teacher writing on the board — it all gets sucked in along with the actual information I want. I needed to find a way to sort through and store pertinent information and stash all the rest."

"You created a filing system in your head." McGill stepped forward, gaining her attention. "And that notebook is your index card." The professor shook his head. "Extraordinary."

Lilly looked from McGill to Gabe and shrugged. "I needed it then. It was a way of dealing."

"So you don't need it anymore?" McGill asked.

Gabe could smell the man's excitement from across the room. His interest was purely scientific, but Gabe didn't like it any more than if his interest had been sexual. McGill was studying Lilly as if she was an experiment, and that was something Gabe would not allow. He passed Lilly her notebook and, crossing his arms, turned his attention back to McGill, watching him.

"Not all the time, but it comes in handy. I'll go through it and see what I can find."

"Good girl. I knew you'd come through."

Gabe felt his blood start to boil and was about to tell McGill to shut it when Lilly asked, "What does that mean?"

McGill shifted his eyes to Gabe only to shift them nervously back to Lilly. "You've had a tough life. First your mother's death, then your new gift, and a few years later your father leaving you alone to fend for yourself. Even in my time, I don't think many people could have gone through what you did and come out of it as well as you."

Lilly's gasp was very low and if Gabe's hearing hadn't been so acute he would have missed it, but he didn't miss it. He kept his gaze on McGill, his body tensing.

"Enough. Out, McGill. Right now."

The professor stepped back, "I thought you told her how I knew. I hope I didn't upset—"

"Get out." The words rumbled low in his chest as he stepped towards the professor.

A feathery touch on his arm made Gabe stop.

"How did you know all that?" Lilly asked. "I've never told anyone about my parents."

Gabe shook his head at McGill. She'd dealt with enough today—if she found out McGill had researched her, it might push her too far.

But her fingers tightened on his forearm. "Gabe." Her voice pulled at him and he turned and looked down into her imploring expression. He almost groaned. He didn't want her to know—it would just cause her more pain. He could tell her the truth once she'd had time to adjust to her new life here. "Please."

Her voice was soft. "I want to know." Then her tone changed, becoming firmer, and she added, "And if I don't like it, *then* you can kick him out."

* * * *

Gabe's green eyes blazed down at her. His smile was purely evil, with an ounce of seduction thrown in. He raised an eyebrow at her and nodded slightly.

"What if *I* don't like what he has to say?" Her heart jumped. Her skin began to tingle and she pulled her hand from his arm. She swallowed and smiled.

"Then *I'll* kick him out."

Gabe laughed. A deep, seductive laugh. The evil glint was gone, his smile pure seduction now. "Deal," he said and turned back to McGill, the smile dropping from his face. "Explain, but choose your words carefully."

She watched McGill's reaction to Gabe's threat. Actually, it wasn't just a threat. Gabe would throw McGill out of the door without a second thought, she was certain of it. And all because of her. Or was it? She wasn't sure. She'd never been in a situation like this before, with someone concerned about her. It felt foreign, and at the same time really, really nice.

McGill squirmed under their gazes. Finally he huffed and said, "I don't know how to be tactful. So here it is. When I figured out you had a photographic memory, I went further back into your past. And when I saw what you'd been through, I decided to go into your future to see how you'd make out. I shifted to 2013 and found out the CN Tower had been destroyed in a terrorist attack in June 2012."

"Terrorists did that?" She shook her head. "How many people were killed?" She swallowed hard, dreading—and expecting—a very large number.

"Ten—and one missing, presumed dead." He clasped his hands together. "That was you, Lilly."

She shook her head silently. "But I'm not dead."

"Of course not. But in your time, in 2012, you are. After the damage was cleaned up, a large piece of the tower was turned into a memorial for those who were killed. Your picture, along with ten others, resides on that memorial, along with your date of birth and a small memorandum about your life."

"Oh, my God." She took a shaky breath. This was scary. "So I really can't go back."

McGill shook his head sadly. "No, you can't. I checked the footage when I was there, to make sure…" He frowned.

"To make sure it was me."

"Yes. You and the others were news for a long time. All of your lives were made public—the company that owned the tower created a scholarship in your name at your university."

She rubbed her forehead. This was so weird, to hear about what happened after she had died. It was information she could have done without.

"I'm very sorry, Lilly." McGill sounded so genuine.

"So," she took a shaky breath, "that was when you decided to bring me here?"

"I didn't decide right away. I knew there was a chance—that shifting might explain why your body was never found—that's when I checked the footage and, after I found out about the plot to kill Margaret and Mary, I did just that."

Lilly sat on the bed, squeezing her hands together as she ran through McGill's confession. He had decided years later, years after her apparent death, to bring her here. She shook her head. "This is really confusing and depressing and interesting, all at the same time. So why me, again?"

McGill stopped pacing and moved towards the end of the bed, and sat tentatively on the edge. "Lilly, when I found out what had happened to you, I was...upset. I grieved for you, for the loss of a friend. And that was what you were...are. My friend. I don't have many, so..." He shrugged. "I couldn't let it happen. I had the ability to save you, so I did. I shifted you here, to this time. I had already planned to save the others, and I sent them here before you, to establish a place for you and them to live. Gabe and the others will protect you and in turn you can help them by teaching them what you know about living in this era."

Lilly stared at her professor, feeling humbled that she had touched his life in such a way. "What can I teach them? They've been here longer than I have, and I've only read about it in books. They've been living it for...I don't know how long."

"Eight months." Gabe's voice was steady.

"I don't know what I could teach you that you don't already know. I'm the one who will have to rely on you."

One golden brow lifted, giving him a mischievous and inviting appearance. "That doesn't sound too bad to me. Besides, I have a feeling there will be a lot I can learn from you." The corners of his mouth curled up, drawing attention to his lips. The thought of those lips pressing against hers was too much. She had to look away from him then; her heart was pounding.

The thought of staying here and teaching them what she knew sounded daunting, especially since she didn't want to be here in the first place. She knew she wasn't the only one to who wanted to go home, back to her own time. Harry had already referred to his old life and Gabe had said he would change this for all of them if he could. Yet they were still trying to move on. Maybe she could try moving on, too, just as the men were.

She looked over at McGill. "Why did you take all of us? Why *us*? And why take people who were about to die? Why not someone from your time who could help you?"

McGill smiled. "I chose each of you very carefully. You, because of the reasons I've already mentioned. I chose Gabe because of his extraordinary abilities as a soldier and a leader. In my time, he was a legend among the military and scientific communities. And, as was yours, his death was a waste of a great life." She chanced a look at Gabe. His expression was unreadable as he stared at McGill, listening to the legend his life had become after his supposed death.

"I chose Harry for much the same reason, and because he and Gabe had worked well together in the past. He is also the epitome of a rough-looking Scotchman — his size, accent and personality will help in dealing with the clans over the border."

She nodded in agreement "Now *that*, I can see. What about George? He's from the 1940s?"

"Yes. George is a wonderful doctor," McGill acknowledged. "I read about him at university. His skills as a medic and then as a doctor were renowned.

He applied his own method of triage during the bombing of London. It was fast and effective and his techniques were integrated into methods used in almost every hospital in England."

"And Marc?" Lilly asked. "He can't be any older than twenty-one or twenty-two. Why is he here?"

"He's twenty-three, I believe. He's what you might call a boy genius — a mathematical prodigy. He excels with numbers. He can figure out any sum in his head in a matter of seconds, and at the time I shifted him here he had just been hired by the Defence Department as a structural engineer."

"A structural engineer at twenty-three. That's incredible. So he can help by building houses, and bridges?"

"Yes, but I think Gabe has other things for him to do first."

Lilly saw Gabe's slow nod. She wanted to know what Gabe had Marc doing, but kept the question to herself. She also wanted to know about the men's deaths, or what would have been their deaths, but what Harry had said that morning helped to keep her mouth shut about that, too. If they wanted to share it with her, then they would. It was really none of her business. Besides, if she asked them, they might want the same in return, and she honestly wasn't ready to talk about it.

"So, why didn't you ask for help from people from your own time?" Lilly didn't intend to let McGill leave any of her questions unanswered, whether absent-mindedly or deliberately.

McGill gave a long sigh and shook his head sadly. "I didn't know who I could trust."

Lilly studied McGill. That sounded a bit too dramatic. "Some of the people I work with are quite fanatical—I think one of them might be behind this," he confessed.

"Don't you have a superior to report to? A department head or director?" Gabe asked.

"Yes, of course. Dr Penner. But I'm not even sure I can trust her."

Weird. Lilly looked at McGill. He was a man who made a habit of working through problems and performing experiments to prove—or disprove—his theories. Wouldn't he know whether or not his boss was trustworthy?

"She's driven by money and power, not by science," McGill continued. "If it was in her best interest to side with the person or people behind this, that's where she would be. When I go back, I'll start with her and see what I can find out."

That caught Lilly's attention and suddenly the misgivings she'd been feeling about him vanished. "You're leaving?" McGill was a part of the life she'd known, a hook holding her to her past. With him gone, what would she have left? Her heart sank.

"Yes. I have to get back. I have work to do."

She couldn't think of a reply. She knew there was nothing she could say to stop him.

"When I have some information about this murder, I'll bring it to you." He smiled at her and nodded to Gabe. "I'll wait in the alcove."

Lilly watched helplessly as her professor from 2012 turned and left the room, her past—lived in the future—leaving with him.

Chapter Eleven

Gabe's eyes snapped open at the sound of Lilly's door opening. No loud, dramatic bang or thud had accompanied it, just a slight whisper of air as wood glided over stone.

He had got used to the sounds of the castle very quickly, and the sounds of the keep in particular. He slowly sat up, his eyes adjusting instantly to the dark, and he listened as Lilly walked slowly down the hall. She wasn't running and she wasn't nervous in any way — the fall of her steps would have told him if she was. She was just walking, and heading for the stairs by the sound of it.

He slipped out of bed and reached the door a second later. He opened it without a sound and followed her down the hall. With such acute hearing, he could clearly hear her bare feet landing carefully on each step, and the drag of her palm against the wall as she climbed the dark stairwell. He sped up as he reached the stairs, not wanting her to get too far ahead of him, and easily cleared three steps at a time. He did not think she would try to harm herself, but there was no point in taking a chance. He reached the alcove that led to the battlements and stood in the dark, watching her.

She was standing in the moonlight, her hands spread open on the flat wall that faced the inner bailey. She leant forwards and peered over the wall. His body tensed in reaction to her movement. He narrowed his gaze, willing her to step back. As she did, he found he had to force the cool air into his lungs. She took a deep breath at the same time and looked up into the sky. Her back arched slightly as she bent one long, smooth leg. Gabe focused on her standing in the dark. She was wearing the running shorts and top she'd had on earlier, her feet were bare and her dark hair was hanging down her back as she looked up into the night sky. He thought about how soft her mouth was and how her nipples poked his chest as he kissed her. Lilly was a temptation he wasn't allowed in his time — then again, he wasn't in his own time.

Gabe felt his pulse rate increase, and the muscles in his chest and his cock swell as he watched over her. She looked pure, otherworldly. She looked like an angel.

He wasn't a religious man, by any means. Who was he kidding? He was so far on the opposite end of the spectrum from good it wasn't funny, but he found himself thanking God that Lilly had been sent to them.

Gaining control of his body, he stepped out of the alcove and walked towards her, deliberately scuffling his feet as he went. Her dark head swung around to face him, her hand flying to her chest, drawing attention to her firm breasts and hard nipples.

"Sorry." He raised his hands. "I didn't mean to scare you." He continued towards her until he reached her side. He looked down into the inner courtyard, a safer substitute than looking at her. "Couldn't sleep?"

He saw her staring at his bare chest, then felt her gaze on his face. He turned to meet it, despite knowing he shouldn't. "No, I couldn't. I'm sorry I woke you." She blinked up at him. The exotic curve to her dark eyes was so sensual he actually found himself starting to tense up again.

He looked away, back out into the safety of the dark bailey, and shrugged. "I'm a light sleeper." Then he asked, "Thinking about today?"

"Yeah!" She sighed. "I think that's why I came up here again. To make sure I'm not going crazy."

He shook his head. "You're not crazy." Without thinking, he reached for her hand. She stiffened briefly, her look somewhere between surprise and questioning, and even tried to pull her hand away. She finally relaxed when she realised he wasn't letting go, and stood silently beside him in the cool night air.

"Gabe," she began cautiously, her hand still in his, "do you believe McGill?" She shivered.

Now, that was an interesting question, and one he had asked himself many times. "I want to. But, it's not in my nature to trust easily." Then he pointed out, "You've spent more time with him than any of us. What do you think?"

She looked away, avoiding his gaze. "I'm not sure."

He tugged on her hand to gain her attention. "McGill isn't my friend. You can tell me the truth." She turned her head and Gabe stilled. In spite of the moon turning the area surrounding them into shades of grey, he could still see every detail of her pretty face. He forced himself to concentrate solely on her eye colour, the dark velvet brown, not the freckles on her nose or the curve of her light pink lips. "What is your gut feeling?"

The doubt on her face, in her eyes, was clear as she shook her head. "I'm not sure..."

He tightened his grip, keeping her in place. "Lilly." He kept his voice low, but purposefully used a commanding tone so she would look at him."It's okay. If McGill isn't being honest with us, we'll deal with it when the time comes."

She shivered again. "I hope I'm wrong."

Gabe remained silent. He hoped she was, too. He didn't want to hurt McGill—he didn't like the idea of killing a man who couldn't defend himself. But if that was what it came down to, then so be it.

Lilly shivered again and Gabe gently pulled her back inside the keep and led her down to her room. Once she was safely inside, she turned, staring up at him, those eyes tempting him. She wet her pink lips.

"Thank you, Gabe," she said, then focused on his chest when her cheeks flushed.

Gabe felt the muscles in his jaw clench. God, she smelt good. He lifted her face, with the intention of telling her she had no reason to be embarrassed, but she swayed towards him, her lips parting, and he found himself meeting her midway and gently pressing his mouth against hers.

Her lips were the softest thing he had ever touched, and they tasted like heaven. He watched as her eyelids became heavy and slowly closed. Except for his hand under her chin and his mouth on hers, they weren't touching, but he was acutely aware of the heat coming from her body. It was strong and alluring and he could feel it start to burn his chest. He cupped the side of her face and deepened the kiss, pressing his mouth firmly against hers, just savouring the feel of her mouth. He slipped his other hand under the back of her shirt and up the smooth skin of her back. Was she this soft everywhere?

She tentatively placed her hands on his chest as he pulled her closer. Her nervous fear once again mixed with that delicate scent. The same sweet fragrance entered his lungs every time he kissed her. Was it arousal? How could it be? Lilly was scared of him — yet here she was in his arms again. There was no way she could be experiencing two such different emotions at the same time. It didn't make any sense.

He pulled back, waiting for her to open her eyes. He wanted to see if he was right, but when she slowly opened her eyes, those sultry brown beauties were all he could focus on. His cock swelled as he bit out, "Open your mouth for me, Lilly." He brushed her bottom lip and chin with his thumb and plunged his tongue into her mouth as he kissed her a second time.

Holding her tight against him, Gabe stepped back, pinning her against the wall next to the open door. Releasing her, he braced himself in place with his forearms on the wall next to her head. Lilly's arms were trapped between their bodies, her palms lying flat on his chest. The touch was light, feminine, and he was enjoying it until her fingers curled and her nails lightly scraped his chest. His cock jerked. It was all he could to keep his hips from thrusting forward. He probed the inside of her velvet mouth with his tongue, fighting to keep his groan trapped in his chest. Lilly needed him to go slowly. He wanted to give her that but damn, he was struggling, because he needed more than just her kiss.

Running his hand up her side, he teased the rounded side of her breast with the backs of his fingers. She trembled in his arms. He inhaled as his lips covered hers. The nervous fear was stronger. He wanted to continue, hoping he was wrong, that she was trembling from desire. He stroked her mouth again, tongue slowly circling hers, and lightly teased the side of her breast again, waiting for the reaction he knew would come.

Sucking in air, Lilly turned her head away, her body shivering. Gabe bent his head, watching as his hand hovered above her breast. Closing his eyes, he fought the urge to keep touching her. Then, clenching his hand into a fist, he dropped it to his side. He wanted more, so much more, but her fear of him was something he didn't want between them. It was an unusual situation for him to deal with. In his time, the women he slept with had been there for a single purpose. Gabe had never had to be gentle or coaxing — the women were ready and most were eager. Lilly was not like those women. She was a different person, from a different time.

Gabe sighed. He would have to allow her time to get over her fear of him. Another shiver made its way through Lilly. He inhaled, her fear filling his chest. They stood together silently and Gabe was grateful she didn't pull away. He needed the time to get his body under control.

He stood to his full height and stepped back, pulling her with him by the shoulders. Her lashes were half-covering her eyes as she stared at his chest.

"Too much?"

"No." She was lying.

He lifted her face to meet his. "Yes, it was."

Her mouth opened and he waited for her to speak but nothing came out and she closed her mouth, a flush tinting her cheeks.

He rubbed his hands down her arms, feeling the sudden goose bumps that covered her skin. "You're cold—get into bed. You need to sleep." He nudged her towards the bed and waited next to the door while she slipped beneath the blankets. Satisfied, he gave her a nod. "Goodnight, Lilly." A smile grew wide on his face as he closed the door behind him.

* * * *

How was she going to face Gabe after last night? After that kiss? She slowed her nervous pacing and placed her hand to her chest. She still couldn't believe she had done that. She had never intentionally enticed a man into kissing her. Never. And she had done it without any thought, as if it was the most natural thing in the world.

Closing her eyes, she could still feel Gabe's mouth on hers, the way his tongue had stroked every inch of her mouth and the feel of his hard shaft pressing into her belly. Her eyes snapped open. Covering her warm face, she mumbled into her hands. "What's the matter with me?" She didn't do this. She barely associated with her own sex, let alone the opposite sex. Where had this come from?

In high school, the few dates she'd forced herself to go on had never worked out—she'd only agreed in the first place because she'd known she needed to have some kind of normal life. But it had already been too late for that—the boys she'd gone out with had been young and immature, and she'd been unable to relate to them. While she was struggling to survive alone after her father had left, they had been concerned about getting scratches on their newly installed rims.

Once she was in university, she'd thought she might find someone mature enough to understand what her life was like. Not much luck there, either. She'd met a few nice guys, but mostly they'd just been larger versions of the boys she had known in high school.

Gabe was different. He was nothing like the boys she had known and he was anything but immature, but she still didn't understand why she'd behaved that way with him. He was the epitome of a perfect-looking man. Perfect men did not waste their time looking at her, and she never looked at them.

Lilly stopped her pacing and stared into space, Gabe's green eyes hovering in her mind. Gabe *had* looked at her, although sometimes it seemed he was studying her rather than looking at her. But he had looked. And she had looked right back. She had taken in every detail of his perfectly sculpted face and he had allowed her to do it. Did that mean Gabe wasn't as perfect as he appeared to be? How could he be if he was interested in a person like her, with her freakish memory?

"Not perfect?" She snorted out loud. "Yeah, right!" She began to chuckle. "Maybe if he had small feet." She chuckled again, wondering where *that* thought had come from, but knew first hand that Gabe did not have small feet!

A loud knock echoed through the room and she jumped when Harry stuck his head in and looked around, frowning. He stepped into the room. "What the hell are you laughing at?"

"Nothing important." She giggled, feeling her face heat up. "Good morning, Harry."

"Good morning. I was just coming to see if you were going to leave your room today?"

Out of habit, she looked at her wrist. Her watch was gone. Stacey had given her the watch for her last birthday. She had been touched and surprised by the gesture. The last time she remembered seeing it was when she'd put it on before she left her apartment for work. Did Gabe have it?

From the light filtering through the small window, it was clear it was daytime, and she presumed it was morning — though she had no clue what the actual time was. Regardless of the time, she had no clothes to wear, so leaving her room wasn't really an option. Showing full legs was normal in 2012, but not in 1503.

"I thought... I can't go out like this." She frowned, wondering if Gabe had forgotten about the clothes he'd said he'd send her.

"Well, there's a trunk full of dresses and other things sitting outside your door. Gabe put them there earlier so he wouldnae wake you."

"Oh!" She smiled. He had remembered.

"You want me to bring it in?"

"Yes. Please. Do you want me to help?"

Harry chuckled and shook his head as he opened the door. He was back two seconds later, kicking the door open, gripping the handles of a huge, wooden trunk. She felt her eyes grow wide as he marched into her room. He was carrying it as if it weighed nothing and casually asked where she would like it.

"Uh... By the side of the bed?" Lilly pointed to the side of the bed next to the headboard. She had picked the spot so she could watch him carry the trunk across the room. Amazing! He wasn't straining his body in the slightest, and his breathing was normal.

"Guess those diets the British government had you on really worked."

Harry winked at her. "Yup, they really do."

She stared at the large trunk.

"Well, open it." He elbowed her lightly, but the playful touch was enough to make her step forward.

She knelt down and lifted the heavy lid. The entire trunk was full of women's clothes, all neatly folded and organised into different styles of dress. The owner of these clothes was wealthy, with a high status in society. The materials ranged from silk to satin to taffeta, to a cloak made entirely of velvet with a soft, fur trim. Even the colours of the rich materials screamed wealth, yet the former owner must have spent time in the country as well. The stack of delicate, more plain-looking dresses, made of fine linen and wool in softer, muted tones of green, grey and blue, seemed more practical for life away from court.

Lilly slowly ran her hand over a green linen dress.

"What's wrong?" Harry asked.

"Nothing, they're all beautiful. How did Gabe... Where did he find them?" she stammered.

"I believe they belonged to the old lord's wife. I think she died in childbirth."

"Oh! How sad." She touched the soft fabric of the dress again. The idea of wearing someone else's clothes was strange, and it gave her the creeps that the woman who'd owned them had died. Unfortunately, she didn't have a choice. She couldn't spend the whole day in her room—she wanted to check out the rest of the keep and the surrounding area and she couldn't do it in her shirt and running shorts.

"Well," she sighed, "I guess I'll get dressed."

"Good. Hurry up. I'll be waiting outside."

Waiting outside? "Why?"

He smiled at her. "Gabe thought ye might want a wee tour after you've had something to eat."

"He did?"

Harry nodded.

A light fluttering brushed the inside of her stomach. Gabe wasn't even in the room and he was putting her wants before anything else. Why would he do it? He must have more important things to do than worrying about whether she got a tour of the keep. It was the fact that he'd thought that she might like a tour and then taken the time to ask Harry to show her around that made her strangely...optimistic. An emotion she hadn't experienced much.

"Weird," she whispered.

"Pardon?" Harry turned as he was closing the door.

"Nothing. I shouldn't be long."

* * * *

As it turned out, Lilly was longer than she'd thought, and if Harry hadn't called Edna up to help, she would have still been standing half-naked in her room trying to figure out how to put on the green linen dress she had chosen. She wasn't helpless—she could dress herself. She just had a difficult time trying to lace the material closed. And the layers! She had forgotten how many layers of clothing women had to endure.

First, a chemise that was thinner than paper and was underwear of a sort. The neckline swooped low, exposing the top part of her breasts, and it stopped at the top of her thighs. When Edna handed it to her, she thought it was a nightgown and it would most likely end up being used that way. Besides, it was riding up under the other layers. Next was a longer, slightly denser chemise made of an off-white satin that went from the top of her breasts down to her feet. And last was the green linen dress. It was so soft Lilly found herself stroking the material as Edna laced it up from behind.

Next, Edna pulled a white linen cap from the trunk and held it out for Lilly. She knew immediately what it was used for, but there was no way she was wearing that coif.

"But your hair, my lady, it's not proper!" Edna gasped.

Lilly shook her head. *Nope*, she thought to herself. She was not wearing that, but she did know of an acceptable substitute.

Once fitted with a pair of slippers, which would probably fit her better once she put on her anklet running socks, Lilly stood and waited for Edna's reaction.

The older woman looked her over and shook her head. Lilly froze on the spot. Was it that bad? Would she be able to pull this off?

Smoothing the plaits Edna had woven, she said, "Maybe I should wear something else?"

"Oh no! Please, my lady—if I may say so, the green looks wonderful on you, with your dark eyes and hair pulled back. I was remembering the last Lady Sutherland—this was her favourite colour, the poor dear."

Lilly looked down at the dress she was wearing and asked, "Is it proper for me to be wearing this? I feel like I'm stepping where I don't belong."

"What else is there, my lady? All your belongings were stolen when you and your entourage were attacked. You are lucky to be alive." The concern in her voice was obviously genuine.

Lilly slowly raised her head, going over the words in her mind as Edna continued. "The old lady Sutherland has no need for them now, and they are such beautiful gowns, it's a shame for them to sit in a trunk. And the way they fit... It was meant to be, my lady."

The old Lady Sutherland? Who was the new Lady Sutherland?

Lilly gave the woman a half smile. "Meant to be."

Chapter Twelve

Lilly absorbed everything around her as Edna led her to the kitchen. Harry, who was close behind her, had to nudge her a few times to keep her moving.

The stone floors were a light grey and the large areas had fresh rushes thrown down. She noted the different sized steps on the spiralling staircase, used to trip up any enemy that might have gained entrance to the keep. The great hall wasn't really that great, and was more like a very large room. Except for candles and the odd tapestry hanging on the walls, the room was rather plain-looking, although it did have a large, stone fireplace that made the room cosy and was probably also used for cooking.

Lilly smiled like an idiot. She felt as though she was on a paid tour — all that was missing was the loud, obnoxious tour guide, ice cream and the token screaming kid. It was scary, because this was her life now, and exciting, because she was finally seeing, firsthand, all the stuff she had studied over the past few years.

There were only two pieces of furniture in the room. The first was a long, rectangular table with benches running the length of each side and a large, traditional, high-backed chair at the head of the table. The other, on the far side of the large room, was a smaller, round table with stools circling it. A very large man occupied each stool, and each of those men was listening intently to one person—Gabe.

She stopped in her tracks as her pulse quickened. She saw him before he noticed her and for that brief second she was able to take him in without feeling his intense stare. His light brown hair was darker in the shadowed corner, but she could still make out the traces of gold running through it. The sleeves of his cream-coloured shirt were rolled up and she knew there were scars tracing over his tanned skin. He was leaning on the round, wooden table, talking and pointing to different spots on its surface, perhaps to a map. Outwardly, he gave the appearance of being relaxed, but that strong, observant air still clung to him.

She studied his face carefully. He was calm—tranquil, even. Yet he was still very much in control and very much in charge—there was no mistaking that. Just like he had been last night. Sure, she might have started it by leaning in to him, but he had been quick to take control of their kiss and had led her to new feelings, erotic feelings. Control was a must for Gabe. Of course, it would have to be. He didn't have a choice. He was the lord in this weird, medieval world, and as lord he had no room for fear or doubt. No man would follow a leader who had no confidence in himself, especially in this time. Well, Gabe certainly didn't have that problem. He was the embodiment of skill and confidence. These men, his men, would follow wherever he led.

Harry gave her a nudge and she snapped out of her haze. Blinking, she realised she was staring into Gabe's curious gaze. His brows slowly rose as he watched her. Despite her natural instinct to avoid attention, she stared back — but she was grateful when Harry pushed her in the direction of the kitchens and out from under Gabe's all-knowing stare.

* * * *

The kitchens weren't at all like she'd thought they would be. From the number of books she had studied over the past few years Lilly had pictured a dark, very hot, confined working area with a large hearth, situated away from the rest of the keep. The authors of her study material had apparently been misinformed. Edna's kitchen was situated off to the side of the great hall, with only a short walk separating the two rooms. Held within its stone walls and high, wood-beamed ceilings, stood a large wooden island where one woman rolled dough and another chopped vegetables. Herbs hung from the doorway, baskets of fruits and breads sat in large baskets on another long wooden table close to a fair-sized window, and a large hearth with iron racks and pots took up most of the outer wall on the opposite side of the room.

Despite the fact that the room was hot and stuffy, this was a very nice kitchen. And the smells...her stomach rumbled. Lilly looked up at Harry's wide smile.

"You shouldnae've hid upstairs for so long," he teased.

"I wasn't..." She shook her head.

"Mmm. Of course you weren't."

"No need to worry, my lady," Edna piped up. "We'll make you up a small plate to tide you over. Audrey!" Edna snapped out the name, and the young woman cutting the vegetables responded at once.

"Yes, miss?"

"A plate and some bread for the lady." The young woman turned her narrowed eyes on Lilly, and she was surprised the look didn't cut her in two. With a loud, deliberate sigh she walked away, swinging her long, chestnut braid over her shoulder. "Clair," Edna ordered. "Go to the buttery and fetch some cheese." The second woman hurried away as Audrey returned, her full, curvy figure swaying back and forth.

She placed the plate with the bread down on the wooden table. "Is that all, miss?"

"Yes, go on—get back to your chopping. There's lots to be done before the evening feast."

With the large pile of food still to be chopped, it was obvious the three women had a fair amount of work still ahead of them. Guilt swept over Lilly as she watched Clair hurry in with small chunks of cheese in a cloth. "I'm sorry if I've interrupted you. I can wait until later to get something."

Edna turned to face her. "Are you not hungry, my lady?"

"Yes. But I don't want to get in the way. In fact, if you need some extra hands I'm pretty good at chopping myself."

Except for the crackle of the fire, the kitchen was dead quiet as the three women stared at her.

"Do you wish to change the meal my lord has ordered?" Edna asked, puzzled.

"No, not at all. I just thought you could use some help," she offered.

"My lady, it would not be proper," Edna explained softly, as though speaking to a child. "You give directions to your servants, and we do as you have ordered."

Servants. Lilly frowned. She had servants? She shook her head, not understanding what the woman was saying.

Edna stepped closer. "That is the way it is done. You are the lady of this keep. We follow your instructions."

"Lady of this keep?" she whispered, shaking her head again. "I'm not..." She felt Harry rest his large hand on her shoulder as she stared at Edna. Lady of the keep. But she *wasn't*. One would have to be married to the lord of the keep to be considered its lady. And the lord was... Gabe?

Lilly quickly scanned her earlier conversation with Edna.

The older woman had referred to the former lord's wife as 'the old Lady Sutherland'.

All your belongings were stolen when you and your entourage were attacked. You are lucky to be alive. Did they think...? *Was* she the...?

Oh! She placed a hand on her stomach when she felt it turn. She could be wrong — maybe that wasn't what had happened. But what if it was? The higher class *certainly* did not offer to do their servants' work for them, and she had just said... Oh, boy.

She needed to fix this right now. How stupid. She cursed herself. How long had she studied this era? Months? Years? Apparently, it didn't matter that she was dressed as though she belonged in 1503, because her mind was still stuck in 2012. This was so weird. Was she even capable of bossing servants around? She hadn't even been comfortable when she'd had to delegate jobs at work, and had usually opted to do the task herself. How could she do it here?

But there was no choice in the matter. This was the sixteenth century, and if she was the lady of the keep—which would most likely be temporary at best—she would have to act as though she belonged until the time came when she *didn't* belong anymore.

Edna's gaze was patient, but puzzled. Lilly smiled. *Remember, sixteenth century.* With that mental note firmly implanted, she pulled together the relevant information and began explaining her actions.

"In my father's home, he and my mother...thought it best to have each servant show me what their...duties were, so I would have a better understanding when the time came to run my own household. My mother also believed that idle hands were useless hands." She smiled. Her mom had said that to her many times. "And when a chore needed completing, many hands would pitch in to complete the task." She folded her hands together and did her best to act like a gentle, well-bred lady. "I realise my parents' teachings are most...unconventional, and not accepted in traditional households. With that said, I am willing to adapt to how this household is run," she finished politely.

"As you wish, my lady." Edna returned her smile, then bowed her head respectfully. "My lord."

Lilly quickly turned and saw Gabe directly behind her. How long had he been standing there? She had concentrated on making her explanation sound genuine, but not so much that she couldn't hear what was going on around her. She hadn't heard him even enter the room, let alone stop so close behind her. How did he do that? He was very close, too—close enough that she felt the heat from his body.

"Edna was kind enough" — Why was her mouth dry all of a sudden? — "to explain how your household was run." He moved forward and wrapped his arm around her waist, pulling her in to his side.

He nodded at Edna. "Yes, I heard. And now that Edna has listened to your explanation, I'm sure she will be happy to explain the other duties within the keep, in keeping with your family's tradition."

"Yes, my lord." Edna dropped a curtsey.

"Now we have that settled..." Gabe nodded again at Edna and turned, pulling Lilly towards the door. With a man on either side of her, she walked into the great hall.

"Once you've had something to eat," Gabe began casually, "Harry will take you around the keep so you can familiarise yourself with it." Gabe stopped her and stared down. "I have to go to the village, but I will see you later at the evening meal." He paused. "Stay close to Harry... I don't want you offering your services to anyone else." For the first time, he presented her with a breathtaking smile before he teased, "The thought of you volunteering to fit the horses with shoes scares me."

She couldn't help but smile back. "Well, then, maybe Harry should skip that part of the tour."

* * * *

"So," Lilly said. "If I'm lady of this keep, what does that make you?"

"Your humble servant." Harry bowed formally.

Harry's attempt to make her laugh fell flat. "You are not a servant, and I am definitely not a lady. Harry, why did Edna say all of that?"

Lilly thought she knew the answer, but asked all the same. She needed to hear it. "Why would they...why lead the people here to believe such a thing?" Her stomach flipped and she began to feel a little lightheaded.

Harry shrugged his large shoulders. "I could tell you why. But I'm not the right person for you to be talking to about this."

"And" — she swallowed hard — "Gabe is the right person?"

His eyes softened slightly — it was surprising in such a formidable-looking man, but it suited him. "Why are you asking, if you know the answer?"

"Just making sure."

The people here believed she was Gabe's wife. The thought unsettled her. Marriage was something she had never considered for herself. Not with her memory the way it was. It was easier to be alone. She liked being able to used her memory freely, without fear of strange looks or whispers. Her ability was part of who she was now — it had taken years for her to learn that if she tried to suppress it, she would never be at peace. But the idea of trying to explain her skill to someone she cared about, just to have him or her turn away from her... It would be like the pain she had felt when her father left, all over again. No, marriage would never work for her. She would not willingly go through that pain again.

* * * *

Harry's tour and the day passed quickly. By the time they were finished, the sun had set, and she was both disappointed their explorations were over and nervous that he was leading her back to the great hall and back to Gabe.

"There's no time to see the village?" she asked, hating the pleading sound of her words.

"I'll take you tomorrow. Assuming you don't take too long in getting dressed," he teased.

She looked up at him, smiling, and almost tripped as she tried to keep up with his longer strides. "Give me a break — it was the first time I've put on so many layers that didn't involve the need to protect myself from frostbite."

"Frostbite!" He laughed. "The temperature doesn't drop that low now... I mean, in my time."

She looked down at the ground, watching her steps. The sun had almost set, casting the inner courtyard into darkness.

"What do you mean?" She inhaled deeply, trying to catch her breath. She loved to run, but found she was becoming breathless trying to keep up with Harry. "You must be really hungry," she blurted out.

"Sorry?" He eyed her.

"Can you slow down a bit?" she panted.

"Sorry about that." He smiled sheepishly and slowed his pace just as they reached the entrance to the keep.

"Thank you. Now tell me — what did you mean?" She slipped through the heavy wooden door when he held it open for her, and they walked towards the great hall.

His voice was low as he continued. "In our time, my time, the damage caused to the ozone layer was finally stopped. But, in some areas, it was too late. North America was the worst affected. Winters are all but non-existent there now. Then. I mean, in my time."

"No winters?" She could hardly believe it, let alone imagine what it would have been like to grow up without any snow! No tobogganing, no skating on ponds or backyard rinks, no cross-country or downhill skiing... "Wow! I'm glad I wasn't there for that. I loved the snow."

"I think there's still some snow. Just not as much, and it's definitely much warmer. No layers required."

Stopping before they entered the hall, Harry asked, "Did you maybe want to change before dinner?"

She couldn't help but frown. "Isn't that where this conversation started, with me trying to dress myself?"

"Right." He chuckled.

She narrowed her eyes at him. "Are you trying to tell me something? Am I covered in dirt or something?" She looked down at her hands and dress then up at his unreadable eyes.

"No. Not at all."

"Then, do I smell bad? I don't see how I could. You didn't take me by the stables or blacksmiths."

He chuckled again. "Hey, you were the one who said I should skip that part of the tour!"

Lilly laughed. Harry's good-natured humour was in direct contrast to his dark, menacing looks, and his laugh highly contagious. She felt very comfortable with him and, strangely, at ease. She could be herself with him. She liked him even more for that.

"Go on, then." He nodded to the entryway to the great hall.

She had only taken a single step into the large room when she stopped dead in her tracks. Every pair of eyes in the hall was on her the second she entered the room, and every man stood a moment after that. The entire room was full of men. Big, hard-looking men. Soldiers. Warriors.

Harry had to push her farther into the room, because her legs refused to move on their own. She never liked being the centre of attention and she did not like it now. Her hands began to feel clammy and her face heated just as Gabe stepped up in front of her, blocking her view of the men. He grasped her hands and held them in his own. She looked at him, nervous fear beginning to consume her. "Lilly?" His grasp tightened and she realised she was leaning back, getting ready to run.

"Lilly." His low voice commanded her attention. "These are my men. And as soldiers they have been taught to stand whenever a lady enters a room." She continued to look into his fixed stare, and it seemed all the more intense thanks to his thick lashes. He squeezed her hands. Blinking rapidly, she remembered reading something about this — her lids lowered as she quickly scanned.

Her eyes snapped open.

"And? What did you find in there?" He lightly brushed her hair with his fingers.

"They'll sit and begin eating after I curtsey to them."

He nodded as his thumbs grazed the backs of her hands. "So stop panicking. They just want to eat."

Lowering her gaze, she chastised herself. Gabe must think she was a coward.

"Now, please acknowledge them so they can sit down — they're starving." His words were stern but his tone was teasing. When he released her hands, she nodded her head slightly and gave them a polite curtsey. Almost in unison, the men sat and began noisily chatting and eating.

"Weird." She sighed.

Turning, she narrowed her eyes at Harry. His smile was a little too mischievous.

Chapter Thirteen

Dinner wasn't as bad as she'd thought it was going to be. She sat along the side of the long table next to Gabe, and Harry sat on her other side, effectively blocking her from the other men. George and Marc sat across from her and kept her distracted with chatter, asking her about her day.

The food was tasty and there was plenty of it. She also found that the books she had studied had been absolutely correct in describing sixteenth century mealtimes. The food, how it was prepared and served, what utensils were used, what drinks were served to accompany the meal... Lilly studied each and every detail of the meal in awe. It was like the descriptions in her textbooks had come to life right before her, no illustration or imagination needed.

As soon as they had finished their meal, the soldiers rose in groups and scattered around the room. Some moved to the other table and began talking, and some left the hall. But every man, before he left, caught Gabe's attention and nodded. Intrigued, Lilly continued to watch. She turned to face Gabe just as the last of the men were leaving. She watched as he nodded to the group before turning his attention back to her.

"Are they…?"

He leaned closer to her. "Are they what?"

"Asking for your permission to leave?"

"They don't need my permission to leave — they are free to go whenever they like."

"Oh. It just looked that way."

"It is a sign of respect to thank the person who has fed you. They were being courteous." He inhaled and smiled. "You look very nice today. You smell nice, too. Like roses."

"Thank you."

He scanned her face. The swelling from the cut on her forehead was almost gone and the bruising was beginning to fade. He didn't like the constant reminder of her near-fatal journey. Actually, considering everything she had been through, last night's drugging kiss included, she was adjusting better than he'd thought she would. Although, there were a few more revelations that might change that…

Gabe watched as Lilly restlessly moved the food around in front of her. Something wasn't right — something was bothering her — and as long as the others surrounded them, he had a feeling he would never get it out of her. He studied her briefly, then stood, holding out his hand to her.

Without so much as question, she allowed him to lead her out of the hall and up the stairs to the battlements. He wasn't sure why he chose the battlements — it just seemed like the right place for them to be alone.

She walked out in front of him and stopped, looking through a crenel, her arms crossed defensively over her breasts.

Gabe rested against the smaller half wall. He kept his voice low. "What is it, Lilly?" Her bottom pink lip caught between her teeth and her thin, dark brows pressed together. He felt his body grow hard as he stood watching her. She was beautiful. She was also innocent, Gabe had to remind himself.

He shifted uncomfortably.

"I need something... No. That's not right."

Gabe felt the muscles in his arms and chest tense as she stepped towards him.

Probably not the best idea in his present state. The demands his body was making were strong, when he was this hard and Lilly was close enough that he could easily reach out and pull her to him, take what he wanted. Even so, he would never allow himself to break a promise — he'd meant it when he'd said she could trust him.

He took a centring breath, blocking out the memory of the taste of her soft lips.

"May I ask you a question?" she said. He scanned the distance between them. She was only two or three feet away from him — a distance he could cross before she even registered his movement. The thought had come automatically, but he resisted acting on it. Shit! This was going to be harder than he'd thought.

Taking another slow breath, he nodded. "Of course."

Lilly opened her mouth. She knew what she wanted to ask him — why Edna had referred to her as the

Lady of the keep—but didn't. The memory of him last night, holding her, kissing her, kept replaying itself in her head. She shook her head, trying to rid herself of the sensual memory. "How did you come to be here?" *Argh!* What a huge chicken she was.

"That's what this is about?" Gabe obviously wasn't fooled.

"No," she blurted, before she could stop herself. "I just need time to gather my courage."

"Okay." He grinned. "But you'd better gather it quickly, because my story isn't that long."

Lilly nodded.

"My trip here isn't as dramatic as yours, or the others'." He leaned casually against the small wall facing the courtyard. Lilly studied him, amazed he was sharing this with her, at her request, because she didn't have the guts to ask him what was really on her mind—and he knew it. Gabe was putting her first, putting her fears first.

He looked out over the courtyard as he continued. "I was ordered to take a small team into a building that was used as a rebel base."

"Rebels?" She couldn't hide her surprise. "I imagined your time to be more peaceful than mine or George's."

"My time wasn't peaceful, Lilly. No time is." She heard the weariness in his words. "The rebels that we were after were the ones who'd planned an assassination attempt on the king the previous year."

"The time when Harry was shot and brought here?"

Gabe grimaced. "That day, I watched Harry get shot, then vanish right in front of me. There was an explosion just after he vanished that would have blown him apart if he'd still been there."

She felt a bit sick. "Harry never mentioned that part. It must have been horrible to see your friend..." She didn't know how to end the sentence. *Killed* would be the most logical ending, but Harry wasn't dead — yet in his own time, before he'd been brought here, how could Gabe have known that? She shook her head — all this time stuff was confusing.

"Killed," Gabe said flatly. "I thought he'd been killed. It was the only logical answer at the time, because the alternative" — he spread his arms wide, gesturing around him — "was unthinkable."

"So you found the people responsible for Harry's 'death'?"

He smiled at her, then. An evil smile that told her he was not above revenge. "Yes, I did," he purred. Pure satisfaction.

Lilly blinked, stunned by his confession. Her heart began pounding in her ears.

"The operation was over and we were exiting the rooms for the cleaners. Standard Operating Procedure calls for the highest rank to leave the scene last. I was just leaving the main room when I first felt the vortex spinning around me. And the next thing I knew, the outer wall exploded in flames just as the vortex closed over me — then I arrived here."

She swallowed. "I don't know, that sounds pretty dramatic to me. It must have been terrifying."

The expression on his face turned unreadable. "A tower was about to fall on top of you" — he shook his head and his voice dropped low — "and you think *my* story was dramatic."

She flinched when he mentioned the day McGill had shifted her. "McGill told you?"

"Is it true?"

"Yes." She saw no reason to lie. "I was next to it. When the space deck exploded, it slid to the side and fell, I was right under it."

She heard his deep inhale and looked up just in time to see him push away from the wall.

"I'm a soldier. Soldiers die in combat. You were innocent, a civilian—that should never have happened to you. Someone should have been there to protect you." Angrily, he turned from her and walked back towards the dark alcove.

There was a dark side to Gabe. How could there not be? He had done things that frightened her just thinking about them. But he wasn't all dark. The way he had touched her and gently kissed her...there was good, too. Regardless of the good and bad in him, Lilly liked it when he was near. She felt... She wasn't sure what she felt, but it was good. She liked it. She watched him walk towards the alcove, panic rising. She didn't want him to leave, not like this, not while he was angry. More importantly, she didn't want him to leave her alone. She didn't want to be alone.

"Don't go. Please," she whispered, almost to herself.

Gabe stopped dead in his tracks and slowly turned to face her. "I wasn't leaving."

Eyes wide, she opened her mouth to ask him how he had heard her, but the words wouldn't come out. How? There was no way he could have heard her. She had barely opened her mouth. She had whispered it because she was ashamed of her weakness.

"Lilly." He stepped slowly towards her. "There are things about me you may not understand or even like. But I won't lie about them, or hide them from you." He took another step, then stopped and turned his head towards the forest beyond the keep.

* * * *

Lowering his bow, Sergeant Major Eric Graves watched as his arrow flew towards the battlements of the keep. Narrowing his eyes, he waited for Sutherland to jump to the woman.

"He hears the arrows. Why isn't he moving?" Corporal Jason Hardy asked in a whisper.

"He's trying to locate the direction the arrows were released from," Eric replied, still watching the keep.

"He can do that?" the younger man asked, amazed.

"I doubt it," Lieutenant John Patterson sneered. "It looks to me like he's trying to figure out what to do." John lowered his thermal binoculars and looked at Eric with glass-blue eyes. "The legend is more impressive than the man. You're giving him too much credit."

Eric turned back to the keep and shrugged. "Maybe."

But as he spoke, Sutherland, the legend, looked in their direction before clearing the distance to the woman in one jump. The arrows hit nothing but the wall.

Eric turned to his commanding officer. "He knows we're here. I recommend we go before he arrives."

John pressed his thin lips together and nodded.

Chapter Fourteen

In his entire life as a soldier, Gabe had never once felt the fear he felt when he heard the arrows soaring towards them. One by one, he heard the launch of the arrows, and knew it was only seconds before they hit. Instinct took over and he easily cleared the distance to Lilly, each of the six arrows hitting the wall behind him, in sequential order.

Eric.

For months, the keep had experienced sporadic attacks by an unseen force. Each time it had been at night and each time the party responsible had disappeared, with no evidence suggesting they had been there in the first place. He hadn't really been bothered by the attempts, and found them quite entertaining, that little spark to liven up the day. But that had changed the moment he'd heard the arrows flying towards Lilly.

Gabe tightened his arms protectively around Lilly. The bastard hadn't been expecting him to jump, because if he had, the arrows would have succeeded in hitting their target, or at the very least done some sort of damage.

With Lilly still pinned beneath him, Gabe took a breath and rolled to the side. Her body trembled as she struggled against him. In an effort to calm her, he finally pinned her to his chest.

"Are you hurt?" he whispered.

She kept her face buried in the hollow of his shoulder, still trembling.

He forced her away and focused on her face. "Answer me, Lilly," he commanded. He wanted to get her inside, where it was safer, but he wasn't moving her until he knew for certain she wasn't injured.

He breathed in her scent and cursed under his breath. "That fear you have of me..."

She looked up at him.

"Now's not a good time." She nodded, her face pale from shock.

"I didn't mean to hit you that hard. How are your back and shoulders? Can you crawl?"

"Crawl?" Her voice was little more than a breath.

"Yes, crawl. Look to the left—can you see the arrows?" As she turned, Gabe saw her flinch from the slight movement.

"What...?" she stammered.

"We were just attacked and they will be waiting for us to make a run for it. I don't want to give them another chance to fire at us." With his free hand, Gabe began rubbing the tenderness from her neck. "So we stay below the wall and crawl back to the alcove."

She nodded her understanding. "You're very calm."

He continued working the stiffness from her neck. "Yes. And so are you."

"I don't feel calm."

"But you are. And I need you calm, because I need you to do exactly what I say."

Gabe heard the slight increase in her breathing. He looked at the pulse pounding in her throat, then back to her face. "I want you to trust me." He focused on her eyes. "Trust me to take care of you."

He lowered his gaze to her pulse again and nodded when it skipped a beat. "Good. I'm going to roll onto my stomach. I want you to crawl onto my back and hold on to me."

"You're going to crawl with me on your back?"

He almost smiled at her shocked expression. "Yes. So hang on tight—we'll be moving fast."

Her breathing increased again.

He smoothed the hair from her face. "It'll be over before you know it."

* * * *

Sitting on the large bed, Lilly pulled her knees up under the long gown, replaying in her mind how Gabe had moved with such speed. She had never seen anyone move that fast. How was that possible? How could he do that? And Gabe had been right—he had moved so fast that she'd barely had time to register the idea of him crawling with her clinging to his back before it was all over.

There are things about me you may not understand.

His statement floated around in her head. *Things? What things?*

She had gone over the scene a dozen times. She wasn't losing her mind—she had seen him jump to her. He must have been standing ten or twelve feet away from her, and he had jumped to her with no effort, no strain. He had crossed the distance as though it was no more than a single step. That incredible feat of athleticism wasn't all—she hadn't forgotten how he had heard her whisper from that very same spot. She had uttered the words so softly, yet he had heard her.

She rested her head on her knees, allowing her mind to run through the day's events. She had been sitting there since the moment Gabe had carried her in, and through George's brief exam. Once George had assured Gabe she was unharmed, Gabe had called for Harry then, raising her chin gently, ordered her to remain in her room. He'd left after that, and she had been sitting there ever since, waiting and wondering. She knew Gabe had gone after the people responsible for attacking the keep. Why had they attacked the keep in the first place? Nervous waves rolled in her stomach. She felt so trapped.

Except for a single lit candle, the room was dark. Automatically reaching for her watch, Lilly rubbed the bare skin on her wrist. She didn't like being without her watch. Guessing it was late, she rested back on the bed and closed her eyes. The questions running through her head would have to wait until morning.

* * * *

Gabe stood in the centre of the battlements, looking into the dark void surrounding the keep's outer walls.

He knew the exact spot the arrows had come from but, like every time before, the party responsible had been long gone by the time he and Harry had arrived.

His nostrils flared and his jaw clenched. Someone had been watching them, and whoever it was knew both he and Lilly would eventfully go to the battlements. A properly trained soldier had the patience to wait for the perfect moment to make his kill.

Eric.

Gabe heard Harry before he reached the top step. "A herd of eight-year-olds would make less noise than you."

Harry's deep chuckle circled the air around them. "I didn't want to startle you. Feeling a bit edgy?"

Edgy didn't describe half of what he was feeling. He was angry someone had tried to attack his castle. Lilly could have been hurt or killed. And he was pissed off with himself

because she wouldn't have been up here if it hadn't been for him.

"So, you think it was planned?"

"There was no way it was luck. Those arrows were fired under the assumption I would run to Lilly." Gabe turned to the arrows still littering the stone walkway. "What are the odds that this was planned by Eric?"

"I'd say good," Harry confirmed, then reminded Gabe, "Ye wouldnae let me kill him, remember? And he's not alone."

"I noticed that."

"What do you want to do?" Harry's deep voice dropped, becoming downright menacing.

"I want to find him, and ask him why he attacked my keep."

"What about Lilly? Do you think she was the target?"

Gabe shook his head. "Don't know. But let's be cautious. No one else knows about this other than the five of us. And I want someone with Lilly at all times."

"Done." Harry assured him. "Anyone in particular? What about Charles? He's good in a fight, not to mention loyal, and the others look up to him."

"No," Gabe bit out. There was no way the handsome blond was going to protect Lilly. "Only one of us stays with her. When we're away, George and Marc are with her. No one else."

Harry didn't try to hide his smile. "If it makes any difference, Charles spends his time with a black haired beauty in the village. She's already given him one kid, and from the look of her another is on the way."

"No, it doesn't make a difference." Gabe growled and started towards the stairs.

"When are we leaving?" Harry called as Gabe reached the alcove.

"At first light. Tell George and Marc and mention that one of them has to be with Lilly at all times."

Then he stopped. Lilly's safety was more important than his jealous streak. To be honest, Lilly was more important than anything. The overwhelming feeling had overtaken him the moment he'd held her in his arms and she had looked up at him. He shouldn't have allowed it to happen. He actually agreed with the UBF's rule of No Emotional Attachments. No spouses, no family...*no* emotional attachment, was tolerated for any serving member of the UBF. It made sense. How could a soldier focus on his job when his mind was somewhere else? Yet every time he thought about Lilly getting hurt, all common sense became obsolete.

Damn it, he was trained to look at situations objectively, not let his emotions get in the way. He was fighting a losing battle. It didn't matter what he should do or what he had been trained to do — he was going to do what felt right. What felt natural.

"Shit." He had asked Lilly to trust him to protect her. Leaving her in the care of a doctor in his late forties and a kid whose best friends were numbers wasn't protection. He had to leave her in the hands of a man capable of killing in order to protect her — neither George nor Marc was that type of man.

He turned back to his friend. "You're right. Tell Charles, too. Have him keep an eye on Lilly — *from a distance*. If he feels anything's out of the ordinary, have him take care of it."

"Now you trust him?"

He looked Harry in the eye. "No, I don't. But you seem to think he's trustworthy, and I trust you. George and Marc aren't soldiers — they can keep her busy and out of trouble, but they can't protect her like Charles can. Have them remind her that Edna was going to explain each of the servant's duties. And ask them to show her the village — she'll enjoy that. Fill Charles in, and stress the fact that she goes no farther than the village — I don't want her near the forest. It's too dangerous with Eric and his friends in the area."

Harry grinned, then teased, "You're giving this a lot of thought."

Gabe pointed a finger at him. "Don't you bloody well start."

Harry burst out laughing, his deep voice echoing around the courtyard below.

"Damn it Harry, I'm feeling really mean right now," Gabe warned.

"Yes, sir." Harry saluted. The wicked grin remained. "How long are we going to be gone, sir?"

"You're pushing it," Gabe growled.

"Of course. It's my job as your friend to take the piss out of ye when you've fallen on your arse for a woman."

Gabe sniffed, trying to hide his amusement—and the fact that what Harry pointed out was true. "Who said we were friends, Sergeant Major?"

* * * *

Gabe knew before he opened the door that Lilly was sleeping. He moved silently across the room and stopped when he reached the side of the bed. He stared down. She was lying on top of the blankets fully clothed, her breathing slow and deep. The room was black except for a single candle, the orange glow highlighting her pretty face. She looked so peaceful. He didn't want to wake her just so he could tell her he was going after Eric. George could tell her tomorrow. Yet he still found himself sitting down beside her.

Reaching for the blanket, he tucked it around her and waited for her to stir. Nothing. He lightly stroked the side of her face, watching for a reaction. Still nothing. He decided against waking her and trailed his thumb across her bottom lip, tracing the scar. "How did you get this?" he whispered.

Then he caught sight of it. The slightest irregularity in the pulse at her throat. Watching the pulse beating steadily in her neck, he traced her lip again, and it stopped for the briefest of moments. He looked at her face, watching for a sign she was awake. Listened to her breathing, waiting to hear a difference. There wasn't any. She was still asleep. She was responding to him even though she was sound asleep. Was her brain still active, even though her body was asleep? Did it ever shut down at all? A better question was, would she remember this tomorrow, when she woke?

He would bet good money that she would. He slowly leant down and brushed his lips against her ear. "Harry and I are going to find the person who attacked us. It shouldn't take too long, no more than a day or two. While I'm gone, stay close to George and Marc and" — he stressed the next part — "*do not* go any farther than the village. It's not safe." He took a deep breath, and the scent of roses filled his head. "I'll come to you when I get back. No matter how late, I'll come to you."

Before Gabe could pull himself away from her, she stirred and turned her face so his lips rested on the corner of her mouth. His heart slammed in his chest and though he knew better he needed to feel her sweet-tasting lips pressed against his.

Her lips twitched under his and her body stirred slightly as he gently kissed her. She even responded to him physically in her sleep. His groin tightened. His normally comfortable breeches became tight as he pulled away. In his present state, the only thing he could do was leave the room.

His need for sex was very strong, thanks to genetic improvements. In his own time, the military had, of course, supplied him with everything he could need, including women who were pre-selected as a genetic match, all conveniently available to him whenever his need arose. The women he spent time with had been created to entice him, to stimulate his body. They'd had few unique characteristics, no real individual personalities, since they were all cut from the same mould. Of course he knew why the women had come—the military wanted to produce stronger, smarter soldiers, and they were using their best to achieve it. He had forced himself not to think about why the women came to him during those times, had detached himself from the women with whom he spent the night. Yet here, with Lilly, he didn't have to separate himself—there was no need.

Lilly was different from those women. There was something about her that pulled at him. He wanted more than just sex—he wanted to be close to her, to know her inside and out. He liked the freckles sprinkled on her arms and nose. He liked her curvy figure and the way her dark eyes swept up at the corners. The one trait that he liked most was the way her emotions were always at the surface. The nervous fear when she had first awoken, her anger at McGill, the interest and excitement she'd shown while walking through the keep, her interest in how the evening meal was served...

There wasn't much he *didn't* like about her.

Like? He shook his head. What he felt for Lilly was more than a grade-school crush. 'Like' didn't fully describe what he was feeling.

Fixated? He frowned, not liking what the word suggested.

Yet why did he feel this way only with Lilly? Why not with another woman from this time? Since assuming the role of Lord Sutherland, Gabe could have any woman he wanted. He could choose, not have the decisions of others forced upon him.

Leaning his head back, he took a deep breath, acknowledging two truths. One, he didn't know why he felt anything for her, he just did. The muscles in his neck and shoulders became tighter. Two, he *was* fixated on her. But it went deeper than that. He wanted to know her, what her life was like, what she enjoyed doing, why her father had left...everything. There was also this need he had for her. This physical need. It was strong, almost overpowering. He needed to feel her move beneath him, needed to feel the weight of her breasts in his hands, needed the taste of her soft lips—he needed to have her in his arms, in his bed.

He caught himself leaning towards her and closed his eyes, inhaling deeply.

Roses.

"Shit." He stood quickly and, without looking back, walked quietly from the room.

Chapter Fifteen

I'll come to you.

Those words floated around in Lilly's head the entire first day Gabe was gone. He had said them to her in her dream.

It had been a strange dream. Gabe had come to her in the middle of the night, saying he was going away and that she should stay close to George and Marc. He'd continued by telling her to go no farther than the village, that it wasn't safe. Then, he'd kissed her. A soft kiss. Her heart began to beat wildly as it had in the dream. She recalled feeling warm and lightheaded and her arms and legs had tingled when he'd touched her.

The more she thought about it, the more real it seemed. Actually, she wasn't altogether sure it had been a dream and second-guessed herself when George mentioned that Gabe and Harry had left.

"Weird," she said.

"What's weird?"

She looked over at Marc, who had decided to join her on a walk to the village. She hadn't been alone from the moment she'd found out that Gabe really was gone. That had been three days ago. Three days of constant companionship, either from George or Marc... And then there was the soldier with the blond hair and bright blue eyes, who seemed to be everywhere she turned.

"Nothing important."

"If it's weird, then it's totally important."

"Totally?" Lilly asked with a playful smile.

"Yeah. Totally." Marc looked confused.

"You really did grow up in the 80s, didn't you?" It was a statement, but Marc answered as though it was a question.

"Yeah. How can you tell?"

She could hear a slight lilt to his accent. Irish?

Lilly laughed. "Call it, like, an educated guess."

Marc stared at her. "I don't get it."

"After 2000, when someone said 'totally' or 'like', they were usually making fun of the 80s."

"Oh, that's just fantabulous!" Marc said in a huff, then put a hand on his chest and lifted his other arm into the air in a dramatic gesture. "Wouldst thou prefer I spoke like a Shakespearean actor? What is thy beef?"

They laughed together this time. Boy, she really needed that laugh. She hadn't realised how much until just now.

"So, how did Edna's orientation about the masses go?" Marc asked, a smile still on his face.

Still smiling herself, Lilly shrugged. "Good. It took no time at all." The light conversation with Marc was comforting. He was very easy to talk to, and their common knowledge and present situation had helped to create a bond faster than normal. So she didn't hesitate when she asked, "Did Gabe tell you and George to keep an eye on me?"

"No." He frowned at the sudden change in conversation. "Harry did, though."

"Oh!" Harry? She hadn't expected that, especially after her dream.

Marc must have seen her surprised reaction. "But the request came from Gabe. I think he was worried after what happened with the arrows and all."

"Yeah, right," she said, a little relieved. "That was weird. I've never been attacked before."

They reached the end of the village and turned around, retracing their steps. The late afternoon sun was warm and the stroll was a nice way to end the day. It was also a good way to give her mind a rest before she went back to her room and continued with her search for information about Margaret Tudor.

As cold as it sounded, she didn't believe the death of Mary Tudor would make too big an impact on the current line of succession, so she had focused on Margaret and her life. She had covered a large chunk of her notebook, stopping her quick scan now and again to write down important facts and dates relating to Margaret. It was a good distraction from the fact that Gabe was gone and for the first time in her life, she missed someone other than her mom. She looked forward to seeing him again. She was worried about him, too, an emotion she had not experienced for a very long time. The last person she'd worried about had been her mother, when she was in the hospital after the accident.

Mom. Gabe. Fear all of a sudden caused her throat to close.

As they reached the river, she turned to Marc. "I'm going to sit by the river. Want to come?" The request was casual, but she was desperate for his company all of a sudden.

He shrugged his narrow shoulders. "Okay."

She stepped into a bare spot surrounded by high grass. Sitting on the ground, she slid off her leather slippers and raised her beige-coloured dress to her knees, dipping her feet into the cool water.

"That's nice. Try it."

"No, thanks," he said as he settled beside her, sitting cross-legged. "There's fish in there. I don't like fish, and I don't like nature."

"Marc," Lilly laughed. "I hate to break it to you, but you're sitting in nature right now."

"Don't remind me," he mumbled with a look of disgust.

Lilly wrinkled her nose. "Didn't you play outside when you were young?"

"No. I was never good at playing sports or playing at the park or running. Sometimes walking is hazardous for me—I'm not the most coordinated person, which is probably why I never had many friends. Besides, it was safer for me if I stayed indoors. So I studied."

"Well, you didn't trip or fall on our walk," she pointed out.

"Walk's not over yet. We still have to cross the bridge to get into the keep. I'll probably trip and fall over the side. And I can't swim," he said, straight-faced.

Lilly smothered a smile. "You really are a geek, aren't you?"

"Yeah."

"Me, too." She wasn't as uncoordinated as Marc believed he was, and she enjoyed the outdoors very much, but she could relate to him. She'd never had many friends either, and books were a salvation for her as well.

She changed the subject. "Can I ask what happened when you were brought here?"

He shrugged. "I was going to a department store when a bomb exploded. I was standing next to a police car when I felt the wind, and I got a really bad feeling. I tried to move but couldn't, and just as the police car exploded I was brought here. I had a feeling it was an IRA attack and McGill said I was right."

Goosebumps formed on her arms. "That sounds scary."

"Not really — it happened so fast. I only went there because of the bonus the military gave me when I was hired." He looked at her, wiggling his eyebrows. "Went to get some cool new digs. For, you know, all the ladies that wouldn't be able to keep their hands off me." He rolled his eyes. "And I get blown up instead. Well, kind of."

"Your family must have been devastated," she said gently.

"I only had me dad." Lilly could hear a faint trace of an Irish accent mixed in with his English. "And most of the time he was too pissed to even notice me." He shrugged. "McGill said that I wasn't reported missing, and not one person noticed me standing there. They saw the coppers, but not me." He shook his head.

"I'm so sorry, Marc." What was the matter with McGill? Why would he tell Marc that, even if it was the truth?

"What about you?" he asked seriously.

She wasn't ready to talk about it yet, but she couldn't ask and not tell, it wasn't fair.

"The CN Tower would have fallen on top of me if I hadn't been brought here."

"Wow!" Marc threw his hands up. "You win."

She frowned at him, "It's not a game..." She paused when two voices caught her attention.

"Where do you think he found her?" A high voice.

"I've no idea. But let me tell you this — that woman is no lady."

Lilly looked up as the two women passed. She recognised the face the second voice belonged to. Audrey, the young woman who worked with Edna in the kitchen. Lilly had spent the better part of an hour with the young woman as Edna had explained her duties. She'd quickly realised Audrey did not like her.

The two women continued to talk as they headed towards the bridge.

"Why's that?"

"She offered to help cook the evening meal," Audrey sneered.

"She never."

"She did too. I heard it meself. And Edna said she didn't even know how to put on her gown. Now what lady doesn't know how to dress herself?"

"But her lady's maid was killed," the other woman pointed out.

"Yes, but why did she wait so long to ask for help? If she were a proper lady, she would have ordered one of us to help her. And look at that hair of hers. It's so short, and it just hangs there. Do ladies style their hair like that?"

"No. They have a lady's maid to do it."

Lilly pulled self-consciously at her shoulder-length hair.

"And why hasn't he got her another maid, I ask you?" The other woman didn't get a chance to answer before Audrey continued, "Because she never had one and he knows it, too. That's what I think. I think he found her out and about in the woods and scooped her up and brought her here. Just so's he could have a good romp."

"No, Lord Sutherland would never do that. He's a good man, just like his uncle."

"Then why do the soldiers think the same thing?"

"They don't," the other women said in disbelief. "Surely!"

"They do, I tells you. I've heard them. The poor man didn't have to go to all that trouble — all he had to do was look right here."

"Audrey." The other woman's voice was shocked, but she giggled at the suggestion.

"If that's what he's after, I would make the perfect Lady Sutherland."

"Audrey, you're awful."

"He'll soon realise the mistake he's made. He'll find her lacking, I tell you. In more ways than one. And if that's the way of it... Well, I'll just have to make myself available to him."

"Don't say such things," the other woman whispered.

The laughter of the two women faded as Lilly stared blindly into the river. The truth of Audrey's words hit her hard, and just like everything she had heard since she was twelve, she would absorb it and file it away, not having a choice. She would always remember.

"Don't listen to them, Lilly." Marc said next to her. "They don't have the ability to understand what's happening."

"It doesn't matter." She pulled her feet from the water, slid them back into her slippers and stood.

Marc stood next to her, his young face looking grave. "Those women don't know you, Lilly."

But they did. Even after her years spent studying, they knew she wasn't capable of acting the part of a lady. All that time and energy spent studying, and she couldn't pull off the one role she should know better than anything.

"We should go in before George comes looking for us." She turned and headed for the keep.

* * * *

Gabe listened outside Lilly's door for movement. When he heard none, he once again silently opened her door and entered. He expected to find her in the bed, asleep, like the last time, but the blankets were neat and untouched. He quickly scanned the dark room and found her sitting on the floor next to the large chest. Her legs were crossed and her head was resting back against the wall. Her eyes were closed. Positioned between her crossed legs, her notebook and a pen. Her backpack was sitting next to her.

He knelt down and slowly tugged at the notebook, with the thought of putting her to bed. Unexpectedly, her hands shot out and held the book possessively in place.

"I didn't mean to startle you," he whispered. "I was going to put you into bed."

"I was going through my notebook looking for..." She paused with a confused look on her face.

He sat down in front of her and crossed his legs. "Looking for...?" He prompted gently.

She rubbed the sleep from her eyes. "Looking for something that might give us clues as to when Margaret will be attacked."

He studied her. "Only Margaret?"

She nodded drowsily. "If Mary was killed, I don't think it would cause too great an impact on the current line of succession. Her only contribution to the throne was Lady Jane Grey. It's Margaret's descendants that fill the void after Elizabeth the First."

He rested his elbows on his knees and clasped his hands together. "And the decision is made by Elizabeth the First?"

"Yes."

Gabe studied her closely as she tucked a strand of dark hair behind her ear.

"She appoints her cousin, King James the Sixth of Scotland. The line continues with him." She chewed her lip. "I think we should focus on saving Margaret."

"I think you're right."

"You do?"

"Yes. I trust you and I trust the knowledge you have about this time. If you believe we should concentrate solely on Margaret, that's what we'll do."

She stared at him, unblinking, her surprise evident.

He held back a smile. "What else did you remember?"

"I've been writing down everything I can find on Margaret." She flipped through the pages of her notebook. "But I still have lots to go through." She shook her head. "I'm not sure how helpful any of it will be. Did you find the person you went looking for?"

The sudden change of topic caught him off guard, but he answered her truthfully.

"No. We didn't find him. He covered his tracks very well."

"What does that mean?"

"He covered his footprints and what we did find felt staged — it was leading away from the area. So, we came back."

She looked down, brow furrowed in concentration. He was beginning to understand how her mind worked, and right now it was in overdrive.

"Lilly," he said, purposely using a compelling tone.

"Hmm?" Her thoughts were elsewhere.

He lifted her chin with one finger, forcing her to meet his gaze. "Ask me."

She blinked. "On the battlements... How did you do that? Jump to me from so far away?"

He hesitated. "Don't be afraid to ask me questions. I told you I wouldn't hide anything from you. But I will warn you, my time is different from yours."

"I know."

Inhaling, he began. "In 2040, King Harry put into effect the Genetic Purification Act. From May of 2040 and beyond, all embryos were scanned for two different criteria. First, if the embryo showed signs of any type of defect — mental, physical or genetic disease—it was terminated. And second, if the embryo showed signs of superior intellect, hearing, sight, strength or speed, it was classified as military property. Once born, the child was placed in specific programmes that strengthened its natural abilities as a future soldier." He studied her face, looking for signs of disgust, but he saw only fascination.

He continued. "Harry was one of the first children selected. By the time I was scanned, the government had changed the Act to include genetic strengthening before the actual birth and deletion of almost every known genetic disease. After which, the termination of an embryo became rare."

She looked thoughtful. "No genetic diseases. No Huntington's disease, or cystic fibrosis or Down's syndrome..."

"Not that I'm aware of."

"That's..." She shook her head. The sadness in her eyes made something in his chest squeeze and he reached for her hand. "What's wrong?"

"It's something I never thought I'd hear. Just those three diseases alone caused so much pain for so many people. It's nice to know all that pain comes to an end."

She was so compassionate. God, he liked that about her. He turned her hand over so her palm was facing up and stroked the centre with his thumb.

She cleared her throat. "So, you were genetically strengthened before you were born?"

Still stroking her palm, he nodded.

"Because you showed signs of superior strength, and speed."

"Yes."

"And your hearing?"

"And my hearing," he agreed. "And many other things. All five of my senses are at a heightened level, as well as my speed and strength."

"That's why you heard me when I whispered." He watched as the tops of her cheeks turned pink.

"Yes, I heard you."

As much as she enjoyed Gabe's touch, Lilly wished he would stop. The light strokes increased the embarrassment she already felt, not to mention it was distracting her from their conversation.

She tried to pull her hand away. "Who else benefitted from the process?" She scowled when he wouldn't let go.

He continued to stroke her palm. "The strengthening started with military, but it soon encompassed other fields — from medical personnel to musicians to teachers. If an embryo showed an elevated aptitude, it was strengthened even further in that area, then placed into a school that would help develop the enhanced skill."

Her mind absorbed the new information. Genetic modification. Why was she surprised? They were talking about the future — it was bound to happen sooner or later. But to take the children away from their families? That wasn't right. She had experienced it firsthand. It sounded as though Gabe had grown up the same way she had, alone. "So once born, the children are taken away from their parents and placed in these schools or programmes? Didn't you have any sort of childhood, get to play, or — ?"

"No." He said flatly, cutting her off. "It wasn't like that." He gently pressed his thumb into her wrist. She looked down and saw her hand clenched into a fist. The pressure from his thumb caused her hand to open and he held it with both of his. "I had a good childhood. I didn't know my father—he died before I was born—but my mum was always there. And yes, I played. It was encouraged. I couldn't enter the training programme until I was ten, and then it was more like a school, with school hours. We even had classes, and I went home at night. I had friends and got into trouble with those friends. And once I turned eighteen, I joined full time."

Staring down at the hand Gabe held, she felt silly. She had just assumed he'd had no childhood, and been angered by the thought. Why had she done that?

"I overreacted. I shouldn't have jumped to conclusions like that."

"I don't mind. You were upset over the thought that I had been taken away from my parents and didn't have a proper childhood." He turned her hand over and studied it for a moment before saying, "You care about people, probably more than they deserve. I like that about you."

Confused by his statement, Lilly asked, "What do you mean, more than they deserve?"

Gabe met her stare. "You never felt any anger towards your father for leaving, did you?"

She shook her head.

"How old were you?"

"Seventeen."

He nodded. "You see? More than he deserves." The corners of his mouth curled up into a slow smile. "You shouldn't waste your time on me, either. But I like the idea of it."

Lilly watched as he brought her hand to his mouth and brushed a soft kiss on her knuckles. Her breath caught and her heart skipped a beat. God help her, she liked the idea of caring for him, too. Except, she had just met him — these feelings she was having couldn't be real. Love at first sight only happened in trash novels. Real life wasn't like that. But she wished with her entire being that it was…just this once.

It was at that moment, with Gabe's lips on her skin and her heart pounding fanatically, that her stupid memory had to recall the one sentence she'd overheard that afternoon that made her feel like a fool.

I think he will find her lacking in more than one way.

The truth. Audrey was right. He would find her lacking, and no matter what she did, Gabe would know — if he didn't know already. She remembered how he had skimmed the side of her breast. It was the slightest of touches but she had trembled like a coward. She had never felt so inadequate as a woman before. She changed the subject before she could think too much about it.

"Did you tell your soldiers that I was a lady and that I would become your… Your wife?"

He narrowed his green eyes. "Yes, I did." He grinned. "Do you realise you jump from one subject to another without any warning?"

Lilly babbled, caught off guard by his question. "I… Yes, I know. I try to control it, but…sometimes it's hard." He stroked her hand again, his grin turning mischievous. Instead of smiling back, she bit her bottom lip. "Why did you tell your soldiers that?"

"Harry and I left the keep alone, and we came back with you. I was carrying you in my arms, on my horse, wrapped in my cloak. I couldn't say you were some woman we found hanging on to the side of a ravine for dear life."

"A ravine… It was steep. I remember sliding."

"It was steep," he confirmed. "If you had let go, you would have fallen into the river below."

She soaked in the idea, remembered clinging so desperately to the root.

Gabe tightened his grip on her hand, bringing her attention back to him. "I told them you were my bride-to-be and we had gone to meet you and found that you and your escort had been attacked. That explained why you had no clothes or servants with you. We're living in 1503—it isn't safe for women to wander around by themselves. You know that."

Yes, she did know it. No females travelled alone, including maids and other female servants. They always had an escort of some kind. His explanation did make sense, but… "Why did you say bride? Couldn't you have just said I was your sister, or a cousin?"

He shrugged. "I suppose I could have. But you being my bride made more sense."

"It did?" She cocked her head to one side. "How?"

"Because…" He tightened his grip on her hand and pulled her towards him. "If we were related…"

Her heart nervously skipped a beat as he reached for her, Audrey's cruel words invading her thoughts. Gabe slid his hand around to the back of her neck and pulled her towards him, desire in his hooded eyes. That look and his touch became her sole focus, nothing else. His mouth was no more than an inch away from hers. She could feel his breath on her face, feel the way his hand gently cupped the back of her head. He brushed his lips against hers as he spoke.

"...I couldn't do this."

Her eyelids drifted down as he pressed his mouth to hers. She couldn't move, couldn't think—all she seemed capable of was feeling. Feeling Gabe's mouth, the strength of his hands, the heat of his body so close to hers.

He moved his hand to her cheek as he traced the old scar on her bottom lip with his tongue. She inhaled deeply at the seductive touch. He pulled away from her then, and her lips felt cool and lost without his. She slowly opened her eyes and found him staring at the pulse in her neck. It was pounding with excitement—she could feel it, just as she knew he could see it.

Giving her an evil grin, he pulled her back, his mouth sealing roughly over hers. She parted her lips automatically, and with an arrogant grunt he slid his tongue smoothly into her mouth. She had never felt anything like the way she felt when Gabe slid his tongue into her mouth. The sudden nervous flutter in her stomach was being quickly replaced by something hot and needy. It was as if her entire body was in some drug-induced state of euphoria. Every nerve, every muscle seemed to come to life, craving more of him. The sensation was new and confusing. It felt like she was losing control, but what he was doing to her felt so good, so right. She fought to keep her fears at bay and, following his lead, she gently, without hesitation, stroked his tongue with her own.

Gabe's low groan gave her the courage to continue and she leaned in to him, deepening the kiss. His hands fell away from her face to grip her waist. She felt a brief tug at her gown and he lifted her without any effort and had her straddling his crossed legs. He closed his arms around her and pinned her against his muscled chest. The heat from his chest seeped into her breasts, causing her nipples to become tight and sensitive. He ran his hands down her back to her bottom, where he gripped almost painfully, pulling her damp centre tight against his hard length, his mouth hard, demanding.

At that moment, she became acutely aware of where his hands were—that they were sliding along her bare legs, under her dress, to her bare behind. Oh, God. She gripped at his shoulders, her body rigid. She wasn't wearing any panties. Her face flushed. She had been washing them nightly so she could wear them the next day—a nightly chore she had already completed.

He squeezed naked flesh this time, grinding his swollen cock against her wet mound. The rough texture of his breeches caused her hips to jerk in response. She felt both exposed and wanton, confused whether she should stop or just let the warmth of Gabe's mouth and hands take her away. Then the decision was made for her as she felt Gabe's finger brush along her inner thigh. A nervous flutter swirled in her stomach as her skin flared with expectant heat, her breasts swelling, hot and heavy. Slowly, he stroked her, teased the achy heat pooling in her core, and when he eased a finger deep and her body clamped down, something between a sigh and a moan escaped before she could stop it.

"Jesus, you're wet," Gabe breathed against her mouth, inhaling deeply, moving his finger in slow strokes. "I need to know right now if you want this." When she failed to respond quickly enough, he removed his finger and clamped his hands around her waist, demanding, "I'm getting mixed signals, Lilly. Tell me if you want this." His voice was low, with a rough edge.

Opening her eyes, Lilly felt the sensual haze lift and she tensed, staring at Gabe's face. A sinful mask was playing with the shadows of his face. He looked dark, almost to the point of being dangerous.

"Don't do that." He closed his eyes and took a deep breath as he pulled her close. His lips brushed her ear. "Lilly, please. How many times do I have to ask you not to be afraid of me?" The warmth of his breath brushed her cheek.

"I'm sorry, it's just that you looked..." She was lost for words.

He pulled back, asking, "Hungry?"

She swallowed. Was that what it was? Hunger? Was he hungry for her?

"I want you, Lilly." His strong hand squeezed her waist, making her feel small and vulnerable. "I want to hold you, to touch you, to kiss you. I want to look at your body when you're hot and wet and ready for me. I want to lay you down and do things to you...your body...that you have never imagined." He pulled her close, buried his face in her hair. "You want me, too." His breath warmed her neck. "But I can't, not like this, not when you are scared and confused."

He knew. She bit her lip, keeping them from trembling. How did he know? She inhaled a choppy breath, her body shivering. Things she had never imagined! He was right—she couldn't imagine them. Her only real experience was with a boy she'd met at university, and their goal had been the same—to lose their virginity and become part of the adult world.

But the experience had left her with lots of questions, and no one to answer them. She took a deep, shuddering breath. She had no idea what to do, or how to do it. She was completely unprepared, and that was something she wasn't used to.

After a few minutes, he lifted his head, cupping her cheek. She looked into his face, the dark mask gone, and was amazed at the patience she saw instead.

"I'm making up your mind for you." He gripped her waist and was on his feet before she could understand what he was doing. "And you've decided to go to bed. Alone."

* * * *

Lilly felt her brows push together as he placed her on the bed. Why did she feel so dejected all of a sudden? He was doing this for her own good, right? She had been the one having doubts. Or maybe...he would simply go elsewhere and get what he seemed to need. Audrey's face flashed in front of her eyes. Her stomach turned and she suddenly felt like she was going to throw up.

Oh God! Her stomach rolled a second time, and then sank at the memory of Audrey's words. I'll just have to make myself available to him.

"Gabe?" She closed her eyes, hearing the desperate tone in her voice and hating how weak it made her sound. She wasn't sure what was going on. She wanted to be with him, to do the things he wanted, but he was right—she was scared and confused. She didn't want Audrey to be right. She didn't want Gabe to go to her. She placed her hand on her stomach. Why? Why did it bother her so much?

He sat on the bed facing her, his intense gaze not missing a thing. "Yes?"

Help me! she whispered in her head. She wanted to ask him why she was feeling this way, but the idea of him knowing her fears kept her from voicing them. Her head started to ache. She asked instead, "You came to me before you left." She licked her dry lips. "You talked to me, didn't you?"

He studied her, then nodded, his voice sounding harder than before. "I was wondering if you would remember." Holding her gaze easily, he demanded, "What was the last thing I said to you?"

"That you would come to me," she said breathlessly.

He gave her a brisk nod of satisfaction, and stood. His hand cupped her chin, and he raised her face. Gently, his thumb stroked her bottom lip, "Good night,   angel."

Chapter Sixteen

Lilly sat at the round table in the corner of the great hall, surrounded by all four men. Seated between George and Marc, she was on the opposite side of the table from Gabe, listening quietly as they discussed their options for stopping the assassination of the young queen.

Two weeks had passed since that night in her room, the night Gabe had kissed her. *Kissed her.* She scoffed in her head. He had done more than just kiss her and, in spite of her fear and confusion, his mouth and hands and words had left her desperate for more. But she had hardly seen him since then. He was either busy training his men or taking care of problems in the village. When she did see him, his only acknowledgement was a curt nod in her direction or a polite greeting. At least that was something...until one evening she saw Gabe following Audrey into the kitchen. The look she'd given him over her shoulder was nothing less than a blatant invitation. It was, however, the smile he'd returned that had Lilly deciding she would be better off spending her time alone in her room, giving the excuse that she was searching her memories for information on Margaret.

Lilly really had helped them as best she could, had spent hours every day scanning her notebook, looking for anything that might aid in saving Margaret. The information she had retrieved now sat ready on the table, neatly written down should they have any questions.

So she sat there waiting for the men to acknowledge her, listening to them debate over the best course of action. She scanned the hall as they talked, wondering if they even knew she was sitting with them, feeling suddenly very…alone.

The feeling was new. She was used to being alone, it was normal for her. She had often been alone and not had any problems with it. Except now, she didn't want to be alone. But she had realised over the past two weeks that it didn't matter what she wanted. Being alone was much easier and safer than being with someone.

It wasn't the first time she'd experienced these conflicting emotions. Her father had behaved much the same way after her mother died, keeping a casual distance from her, often ignoring her. At the time, Lilly had believed grief over her mother's death had caused his behaviour. Four years later, around the time of her sixteenth birthday, she'd made the mistake of showing him her newly acquired talent, hoping he would become interested enough to want to spend time with her. Her plan had backfired. Her father had been shocked and scared by her ability, saying it was unnatural, and within the next year he had completely removed himself from her life.

Lilly had quickly made peace with her father's decision to leave. His actions had taught her a valuable lesson—it was safer to remain alone, because when you were with another person it just left you open to rejection, and that particular abandoned feeling had a strange way of crushing the air from your lungs.

Funnily enough, she'd had that same feeling lately—she hadn't taken a full breath in two weeks. The same two weeks during which Gabe had been keeping a polite distance from her.

Of all the people she had met—and the list was very short—he had been the only one to make her feel safe, to instil a feeling of trust in her. She enjoyed his company for many reasons, but mainly because he was honest with her—he forced her to see the truth even if she didn't want to. He was the only man she had ever wanted. She missed him. Missed his stare, missed the way she felt safe around him, missed his kiss, his touch. And she really wanted him to do the things he'd said she couldn't imagine. Actually, she had caught herself daydreaming about it. But somehow, she'd made the mistake of showing her fear of the unknown and he had pulled away from her. Now she was left wanting something that she knew in the end would never happen.

Picking at the wood on the tabletop, she vaguely heard Harry ask a question and mention Professor McGill. The name sparked a memory of the day she'd been shifted and the image of the tower falling towards her. Blinking rapidly, she rewound the memory in her head until she saw the bright smile on

Stacey's face and felt the warm hug her friend had given her. She rewound further back until she was riding her bike to work for the last time and felt the memory of the warm wind tickle her face. The air had been so clean that day and the water of the lake had seemed crystal clear. Her throat closed up and her heart suddenly ached.

Reminiscing wasn't something she did on a regular basis — there was nothing in her life that was worth looking back at — but she had found over the past two weeks it was fast becoming a habit. She missed the life she'd had, even in Toronto where she'd been alone a lot of the time. She missed the few friends she did have, and her classes and work. She belonged back in her own time. Not in 1503, with a kid genius from the 80s, a doctor from the 40s and two soldiers from the future. One of whom wanted nothing to do with her now that she had shown her true colours, which were apparently the same as a cold fish. She wanted to go back to the simple life she had made for herself. She didn't want to be here, in this time. She wanted to go home.

Home. She'd been safe there.

She felt a sharp jab to her ribs. "Lilly? You awake?" Marc raised his voice.

She turned to look at him, feeling a little disoriented, a normal side-effect of scanning her memories.

"Yes. Of course." She looked around at the men and stopped, coming eye-to-eye with Gabe. Her lungs felt tight, so she looked back to Marc.

He frowned at her. "Well?" he asked sarcastically.

Surprised by his tone, she straightened, asking carefully, "Well what?"

"Didn't you hear Gabe's question?"

Question? She hadn't heard anything. How long had she been inside her own mind?

She chanced a look at Gabe. He was resting his arms on the table, hands clasped together, studying her.

"No, I didn't."

He tilted his head slightly, giving her a curious look.

She felt a hand on her arm and she turned to face George. "Are you feeling all right, Lilly?"

"Yes, just daydreaming." She forced a smile. "What was the question?"

"Gabe asked about locations or stops Margaret might have made on her journey to Scotland," George repeated politely.

She nodded. Now, *this* was why she was here—she could handle this. She opened her notebook and looked at a single word, *travels*, and the information appeared in front of her. Looking at the centre of the table she felt her eyes lose focus as she began to speak.

"There are a few places. First, she stopped in to see her grandmother, on her father's side. She lived outside London somewhere along the Thames. Then I found information saying she stopped in a small town with her entourage and had lunch under a large oak tree—but that might be hearsay, and I never studied the name of the town, so I have no idea where it was. Next stop was the town of York—her visit was supposedly commemorated with a plaque. Further along, she stopped in the town of Berwick. And her last stop was in Lampton Kirk, which is where King James was...I mean *will be* waiting for her." She toyed with the pages in front of her and blurted out, "I

wrote everything down for you, in case you need it."
With that said, she slid the pages across to Gabe.

He regarded her steadily but broke the contact
when Harry spoke. "Berwick isn't too far."

Gabe nodded, deep in thought. "No, it's not. But it's
a fair-sized town. If I was planning this, it wouldn't
be in a town, and nowhere near the border." Without
hesitation, he said, "I'd do her before she got to
Berwick."

Harry nodded in agreement.

"Lilly did say she has her entourage travelling with
her." George reminded him. "There will be people
protecting her. Surely they won't attack with so many
people around her?"

"It only takes one clear shot from a distance to get
the job done." Gabe pointed out candidly.

Lilly repressed a shudder. Gabe was so casual when
talking about killing. He seemed very comfortable
with it. The idea of him killing so easily scared her.

"Besides," Harry chimed in, "if they want her dead
badly enough, they'll have more than one plan, and
more than one person waiting to finish it. The amount
of people protecting her won't matter."

Gabe looked at Harry and shrugged his shoulders
questioningly, then turned to Lilly. "Margaret's
entourage. Who and how many?"

His cold tone caused her to flinch. "I don't know the
exact count, but I'm under the impression it was a
very large group."

"Who will be with her?" Lilly couldn't help but
notice that the others talked about Margaret in the
present tense. It seemed they had adjusted much
better than she had to the bizarre reality they shared.

"English lords and ladies accompanied her, as well as knights and servants. There were also armed soldiers escorting the entire entourage."

"And the date of their wedding?"

"August the eighth, 1503." She looked down at the table. "Maybe..."

"Maybe what?" Gabe asked.

"Maybe George is right. Margaret is Queen of Scotland now. Her marriage to James sealed the deal to end the war between England and Scotland. For political reasons, her father wouldn't allow anything to happen to her."

* * * *

Gabe sighed, doing his best to hide his frustration. He was beginning to lose his patience. Lilly couldn't avoid his gaze forever. She had been doing it for the past couple of weeks and he hated it. Damn it, what had he done? He had backed off with the intention of giving her space, and now she wouldn't look at him. He knew he had scared her when he told her how much he wanted her, but he was positive she'd wanted him as well. Her entire body had been screaming at him to take her—not only could he feel it in the way her body trembled, he could smell it. That delicate, sweet scent of hers had become heady and erotic. It had him wanting to lay her on the stone floor and take her. But that nervous fear had been present as well, and for the first time in his life Gabe had done the noble thing and let her be, so she could figure things out for herself without any pressure. But his plan had backfired.

He sighed again and placed his hands palm down on the table. "You could be right. Nothing might happen at all and I'm sure the soldiers protecting her are very capable men. Except they won't be defending her against people from their own time. If what I suspect is right, her soldiers will be trying to protect her from people like me."

Gabe watched as a frown wrinkled her thin brows, and though he heard the others begin to talk and ask questions, it was only Lilly he answered.

"The attack on the battlements?" She wet her lips and Gabe nodded as he watched, entranced by the way her tongue moved over the pink skin. That mouth had haunted his every waking hour, as well as his dreams. The way she tasted, how her body had melted into his, the soft whimpers of pleasure as he stroked her wet body. Some dreams were so vivid, so erotic, that he woke in the middle of the night painfully hard, his body demanding some kind of fulfilment. And every night he gripped his swollen cock and thought of nothing else but Lilly as he temporally sated his need.

"The one you went looking for? He's going to kill her?"

He nodded again, not bothering to tell her there was more than one man behind this. "Yes. I think he was sent here to kill Margaret."

"Are you sure he's from your time?" George asked, concerned.

"Maybe not from my time exactly, but damn close. He used a few evasive manoeuvres we're familiar with—not to mention some we weren't so familiar with, which is why we had a hard time following him."

"So, he was sent by the people McGill works for. To kill Margaret and change the line of succession?" Marc asked.

"Thanks for the recap," Harry said dryly.

Marc looked at Harry and raised his middle finger. "You know what you can do with it."

Harry laughed out loud.

With a smirk, Marc continued. "I don't fully understand why these people McGill works for would want to do that? What do they have to gain? Is it for money? A new political leader? Or maybe something else is going on that McGill hasn't told us." He looked each of them pointedly in the eye. "I don't trust him."

He turned to Lilly, shaking his head. "I'm sorry. I know he's your friend, but there's just something odd about his story and the reasons he's given for bringing us here."

Gabe felt the muscles in his jaw tighten when Lilly turned to Marc and gave him an understanding smile. "It's okay. I'm not sure about a few things myself."

Gabe cleared his throat just as Lilly reached out to touch Marc's shoulder, interrupting her. "What don't you trust, Marc?" he snapped, ignoring the slight kick Harry gave to his foot.

"I'm not sure. The idea of sending another soldier to kill Margaret seems wrong. Did the people McGill suspects are behind this send him? Is this soldier in the same boat as us — would he have died if he hadn't been brought here? And if so, how could he know to kill Margaret?"

Gabe focused on Marc, not liking his train of thought. "Keep going."

"Maybe this guy was sent by McGill's bad guys and he is under the impression he's going back. The bad guys didn't tell him it was a one way ticket, but had prepared him ahead of time for what he had to do."

"You're saying he was tasked with a mission," Gabe guessed.

"Yeah, if that's what it's called."

"So he completes his mission and they leave him here. Nasty little double-cross."

Marc leant forward. "Totally! Or...what if...he *is* going back?" Marc paused, leaning forward. "It would make more sense if he was the one to control the tracker, because he's the only one who will know when the mission has been completed."

"So he goes home once the job is done and reports his kill." Gabe rubbed at the stubble on his chin. "What happens if he doesn't make his kill?"

"Well..." The younger man looked nervous all of a sudden as his dark brows pushed together.

"Marc," Gabe said firmly. "Just give me your best guess."

"Wouldn't whoever is responsible for all of this know right away? The line of succession would change." Gabe stilled as Lilly looked up from the table. Her wavy hair hung around her face and the light sprinkling of freckles gave her a sexy-innocent appearance. His body hardened despite the fact there were three other people sitting with them. He didn't care. All he cared about was Lilly. Shit, he wasn't even sure if he would help this queen if Lilly wasn't here — it wasn't his concern, and as long as it didn't affect the people under his care, he didn't give a fuck who was killed. But it mattered to Lilly, so it mattered to him.

"So, there is a possibility that he might have a tracker on him to take him back to his own time?" Harry asked.

Gabe shifted his eyes to Marc.

"If he has, then yeah. It would take him back. Why? What are you thinking?"

Harry ran a hand over his face. "I don't know. I don't really understand this stuff. But it'd be nice to get our hands on it. Maybe sort this out at the source."

"That would be nice," Gabe agreed. "Marc, if I let you have a look at McGill's tracker, would that be possible for us?" Gabe asked.

"Totally! Or I think so, anyway. But I'd need to study it more before I'd attempt to activate it," Marc answered. "Having McGill explain how it works would be better."

Gabe nodded at the kid.

"I'll keep that in mind the next time McGill puts in an appearance."

"Hey." Marc gave him a serious look. "Then maybe we could go back home."

Gabe shook his head.

"Why not?" Marc frowned. "McGill said nobody saw me there and me dad didn't report me missing." He looked around the table. "I could go back."

Gabe took a deep breath. If what McGill said was true, which it turned out to be more times than not, then Marc *could* go back.

"What about you, Harry?" Marc asked. "Any way you can go home?"

Gabe shook his head at the same time as Harry.

"Why?" Marc pushed the issue.

Harry sat back and crossed his arms. "I almost got shot in the face." He pointed to his cheek. "And I was shifted just before a bomb exploded in front of other members of the UBF, the king and thousands of civilians. I'm not going back."

"Gabe?" Marc asked hopefully.

"No. Too many UBF."

He squeezed his hands into fists when Marc turned to face Lilly. "What about yo—"

She was already shaking her head, not giving him a chance to finish. He rubbed her shoulder awkwardly.

"George?"

Gabe turned to the older man as he stared off into space. "I think I can go back, too."

"Really?" Harry asked.

"Mmm." He nodded thoughtfully. "The hospital I was in was blown to bits during the bombing of London." George frowned. "I must have treated hundreds of people that had survived being trapped in buildings that were hit by German bombs. I suppose I could be one of those that survived."

Gabe saw George's frown deepen.

"Well, that's great!" Marc said. "Don't you think so?"

George shook his head. "I'm not sure I want to go back."

"But, George—"

Gabe held up his hand to silence Marc. "Right now, nobody is going anywhere. We don't even know if McGill's bad guys have a tracker." He glared at Marc. "So let it go."

The table was quiet for some time. Gabe looked around at the faces. They were all deep in thought.

He wondered if they were having the same thoughts he was.

What if he could get his hands on that tracker? Could he go home? No. He knew that wasn't a possibility. In his time, he was dead, officially reported as killed in action. Walking into the UBF headquarters and saying "Hi!" would probably cause some serious PTSD.

Although, there was no rule about him travelling to a *different* time. If he could get his hands on that tracker, he could leave this place — they all could. He looked around the table again. He wasn't sure how he would do it, but he would make it happen.

"So," George said, breaking the silence. "Have we come to a decision about this queen? How do we help her?"

Gabe looked at George. "Harry and I need to talk. I'll fill you in on what we decide."

"Right, then." George stood. "I'm off to bed. Goodnight all." Gabe watched as he put his hand gently on Lilly's shoulder. "Would you like me to walk you up?" Gabe's entire body tensed and he felt his hands clench into fists. The kick to his shins caused him to shift his eyes to Harry, who was shaking his head slightly.

Damn it. When had he developed a jealous streak?

"Okay. Thanks George."

Gabe forced his hands to relax and stood when Lilly stood. He watched her as she passed him, looking everywhere but at him. She said her goodnights to Marc and Harry. Harry, of course, loved how awkward the situation was, and Gabe hated the merry sound to his deep voice as he wished her goodnight.

In the end, she finally turned to him. His chest tightened as he met her gaze. Her dark, innocent eyes looked up at him, and it took all his strength to keep from pulling her to him and kissing the fear out of her. He wouldn't, though—she was already nervous of him, and he didn't want to risk causing further damage. Besides, he had to hold out, wait for her to get over her fear on her own. Instead, he smiled down at her and brushed a strand of hair behind her ear, needing to touch her. "Goodnight."

The tops of her cheeks turned pink as she breathed out, "Goodnight."

* * * *

"What the hell is the matter with you?"

Gabe turned to look at Harry. A dark frown sat where his smile usually was. "Pardon me, Sergeant Major?"

"Don't pull that shit with me. We're friends, Gabe. Tell me what the hell is going on. You looked ready to kill George. Was it because he touched her, or because he was being polite to her?"

Gabe flared his nostrils and turned to look out over the bailey. He liked it up here. He felt at peace breathing in the cool air. He looked beyond the walls into the surrounding country. He couldn't detect any movement. He took another deep breath and inhaled the scent of trees and water, dirt and hay. No Lilly, no roses. "Not sure," he admitted.

Harry moved up beside him. "You know George— he was just being nice. The man is practically a saint. I thought you and Lilly were getting along?"

Gabe rubbed his face. "Lilly's not used to...men like us."

"Men like us?" Harry snorted. "Ye mean handsome and witty, or soldiers with extra abilities?"

"Both, I think."

Harry nodded, fully understanding his meaning. "Then she's a good girl. Not something we're used to dealing with. So you backed off, hoping it would help."

Gabe nodded. "Mmm." He had backed off too much, and now she was distancing herself from him and the others. Lilly hadn't had an easy life, with her mother dying and her own father abandoning her. She had never had anyone she could trust. Even he'd had that—his mom, then his peers, and his buddies in the military. She had been alone from the day her mother died. Pulling away was an act of self-preservation—she was protecting herself from further harm. The question was, how far should he let it go?

"Get Charles to keep an eye on her."

Harry's voice was quiet when he asked, "You think she's going to run?"

"I hope not. It's not safe out there with Eric and whoever else."

"Agreed." Harry looked thoughtful. "Speaking of which, what are we going to do about Eric and his job?"

"We're going to get to Margaret before he does and change her route. If Lilly has read about it, so has someone else."

"Sounds boring."

Gabe gave Harry a wry grin. "Maybe." He shrugged. "Depends on who we run across."

Chapter Seventeen

Lilly looked up at the light blue sky. It was a nice change from the past few days. The rain had seemed never-ending and the days had dragged on endlessly as she had spent her time alone in her room. The only other place to go was the great hall, except the area had a high traffic rate and as the day grew later and later, the room filled with more and more people, including Gabe — and she didn't want to be near him. Her lungs were still closing up on her every time she saw him. This could not go on — this was no way to live. She walked through a small gate and over the drawbridge at the back of the keep. The smaller gate had been specifically built into the wall as a more convenient means of getting to the village, and so the people of the village could get into the safety of the castle walls if the need should arise.

She took her time as she made her way through the village, her mind full of questions about her future.

How would she live here, in 1503, with these men, if she couldn't be in the same room with their leader? The others had noticed how distracted she was, and she was sure they knew Gabe was the reason behind it. How could they not? They saw how he looked at her. She closed her eyes and replayed that one specific moment in her head. The intense stare of his green eyes and his full mouth slightly curled up at the corners. How he casually rested his arms on the table and how his dark shirt clung to his muscled shoulders. Confidence oozed from him, and she didn't want to think about how sexy he looked. How sexy he always looked.

All this because of her stupid fears. Or was it? She didn't know. He had kept a distance from her for two weeks, and to give her that look and then…touch her. She would be better off staying away from him. Leaving was probably her best option, but where could she go? She wished McGill was there — she would ask him if it was possible to send her back. Gabe had said no, that it couldn't happen, but maybe there was some other way. Maybe later in 2012, or she would be happy with 2013. Things wouldn't have changed that much in a year. Or maybe the same year, but in a different location. She didn't have to live in Toronto; she would live anywhere in Canada — it was her home. But she would have to start a new life, with a new name, and she had no idea how to do that. Maybe he could just send her back to the day she was taken…back under the…

She stopped suddenly and closed her eyes. What was wrong with her? Was this what it had come down to? Going back to that day would be suicide.

"No," she whispered. She wouldn't think about it.

She continued walking. Her eyes dropped open and she looked around. Thick, dense forest surrounded her. The only indication that the area had any kind of traffic was the small path she was following. She had been scanning her mind as she walked. She turned in a circle. She had never done that before. She was always conscious of her surroundings—she never allowed herself to scan while she was walking somewhere. But she had this time. Turning in a slow circle again, she saw nothing but green. Now she was alone in the forest—the one place Gabe had told her not to go.

* * * *

"I honestly thought you were overreacting." Harry fell into step next to Gabe as he crossed the inner courtyard.

"Overreacting about what?"

"She's gone." Harry informed him quietly.

Gabe stopped in his tracks. "When?"

"About thirty minutes ago. Charles waited to see if she would turn around once she reached the edge of the village, but she just kept walking. And because you were adamant about him keeping his distance, he found me instead."

The clenching of his jaw pulled at his temples. "Shit." Shifting his direction, Gabe started towards the stables.

"He also said she looked lost, like she wasn't all there."

"Lost?" Gabe stopped and indicated to the stable hands to get his horse ready. Still frowning, he turned back to Harry. Had she been in her own mind as she'd left the village, and walked unaware of where she was going?

"What?" Harry asked.

"She was in here." Gabe tapped his head.

Harry nodded. "You think she's okay?" He called to the stable hand, "Get my horse ready, too."

"No," Gabe said firmly. "I'll go alone." Because when he found her — and he would find her — the ride back would give them time alone. He would use that time to get her used to being near to him. It wasn't the way he wanted to cure her fear, but it would seem they didn't have a choice.

Harry smiled knowingly at him. "All right, I can respect that. But you make it back before dark, or I'll come looking for ye." Harry reached behind his back and drew his sidearm. "Safety's on."

Gabe cupped the weapon in his hand, keeping it hidden from view, and slid it into his waistband.

"Go and get your woman," Harry said, grabbing the reins from the groom.

Gabe swung up, settling into the saddle, and waited as the charger stepped to the side, adjusting to his weight. "She's not mine yet."

"Yes, she is. We all know it. The only one who doesn't know it is Lilly." Harry raised his dark eyebrows. "Why is that?"

* * * *

Lilly froze when she heard hoof beats pounding towards her. She listened briefly for their direction, then ran off the path into the thick forest. The trees would serve as cover as she made her way back in the direction of the keep. At least she hoped it was the right direction. She had come to a fork in the path she had no memory of, and stood looking in either direction for a long time, disturbed that she couldn't remember the area. She never got lost, *never*. But in the end, she'd had to guess which direction to take. That disturbed her even more.

Her heart began pounding in her ears as the hoof beats drew closer and she ducked further into the forest to hide behind a tree. She lowered herself to the ground, drawing her knees up, hiding her face, making herself as small as possible. The hoof beats passed by, but she didn't move. Instead, she closed her eyes, forcing her heart to slow. This was bad — being alone in this time was very dangerous.

"You shouldn't be so far from the keep." The deep voice startled her, but she kept her head lowered as her lungs began to close up, as usual. "Are you all right, my lady?" the voice asked.

My lady? Gabe never called her that. Stiffening, she raised her head slowly and stared into the man's face. He was squatting down about a foot away from her. He had a sharp-angled chin covered with black stubble and a wide, full mouth. A curious smile appeared on his handsome face, making dimples appear at the corners of his mouth. His hair was jet black and kept short, but what really caught her attention were his eyes — he had green eyes, just like Gabe's, if perhaps a little darker.

He stood slowly and briefly stared down at her before stepping towards her and extending his hand. "Would you like me to escort you back to the keep?"

Alarm bells were ringing in her head. This wasn't right. Gabe's voice whispered in her ear. *Do not go any farther than the village. It's not safe.*

The image of Gabe leaping towards her filled her mind. Arrows scattering the battlements. Gabe going away, searching for the one responsible. Was this him?

She wanted to back away from him, but she couldn't, not with her back against a tree. Even if there had been no tree, she still wouldn't have been able to get away. Gabe thought this man was like him. A soldier. A genetically engineered soldier from his time. Her heart pounded in her chest. If she tried to run, he would be on her in seconds. That was, if she even got the chance to run.

His dark green eyes filled with amusement as he studied her. She took his hand and allowed him to pull her to her feet. "Thank you," she breathed, looking him over. He was wearing a light, woollen shirt with brown woollen breeches. She noticed a strap crossing his chest, and realised he was carrying something on his back, but she couldn't see what.

He inhaled and the dimples vanished from his face. "You're scared."

"Of course," Lilly blurted out before thinking. "I'm not familiar with these woods and got lost." She began brushing leaves and dirt from her dress.

"The new Lady Sutherland was out walking unaccompanied? Now, what would your husband say if he knew?"

If she was lucky, he would know by now. "I'm sure he won't be pleased."

He held her gaze as he leaned towards her. "And what would he say if he knew you were here, alone, with me?" There was a ring of amusement to his words.

She swallowed. This was the man. It had to be. He was probing, asking questions to find out about Gabe. "I'm not sure. I suppose it depends on what mood he is in."

"Mood?"

She nodded. "He'll either be annoyed that he had to come and get me or be angry that I didn't order his supper for him."

Cocking his head slightly to the side, he grinned. "You're lying to me." Then he paused and studied her. "I think he will be very upset that I was here with you. Alone. And he won't leave you alone for another minute. He's going to keep you very close from now on."

"Why do you think that?"

He started backing away from her, into the dense forest. "It's what I would do." He smiled at her then, the dimples reappearing. He nodded towards the path, "You're going the right way. Stay on the path — he's coming for you." Lilly watched as he disappeared into the trees.

The moment he was gone, Lilly turned and ran flat-out for the path. She would run all the way back to the keep if she had to. Her heart was pounding in her ears and her legs and arms felt shaky. She had never been so scared in her life.

She broke through the trees on to the path and ran straight into Gabe's chest. Startled, she gasped and pulled away, feeling disoriented, but he caught her and pinned her in place.

"Easy." He wrapped his arms around her.

"I...there...a man...arrows..." she muttered against his chest. Her entire body was vibrating.

"Shhh. I'm here."

"No." She struggled against him. "The man you went looking for. He was here. Talking to me."

There was no outward show of emotion as he slowly released her, just a quiet question. "Did he hurt you?" His green eyes burnt into hers.

Lilly shook her head.

"Show me where." He clasped her hand and they walked into the forest together. She showed him the tree she had hidden behind and where the dark-haired man had appeared, but Gabe was already kneeling down, studying the footprints and the direction they led.

Back on the path, Gabe picked her up and placed her on his horse. He swung up behind her and reached for the reins, encasing her in his arms. They rode in silence until Gabe whispered next to her ear, "Don't ever come into the forest without me again."

She shivered at his quiet command but she agreed. "I won't."

He gripped the reins with one hand and with the other pulled her back until she was resting against him. She was nervous at first, pressed against his large body, but when she tried to sit forward the arm holding her flexed and kept her firmly in place. He held her like that the rest of the way to the keep, forcing the close contact.

By the time they reached the stables, she felt comfortable and safe. Gabe had taken away her fear and replaced it with warmth...and something else. A yearning. Her face heated.

He slipped off the horse and, without looking at him, she allowed him to lift her to the ground.

She shivered. The night air was cool now she didn't have Gabe's body to keep her warm. He reached for her hand and led her inside, to the great hall. The large room was empty except for Harry and George, who stood when they saw them enter. Gabe nodded to the two men but kept moving, his hand tightening on hers so Lilly had no choice but to follow.

Gabe led her up the stairs and down the hall to her room, where he pulled her inside. Thankfully, someone had started a fire, so the room was warm. Still holding her hand, he closed the door and turned her to face him.

As he stared down at her, his green eyes softened. "I'm going to talk to Harry. I will bring you something to eat and drink once I'm done. I won't be long. You should have enough time to change." He stroked the back of her hand with his thumb and her heart had time to jump once before he left the room.

* * * *

Harry had remained in the great hall, and sauntered along behind as Gabe went to the kitchen.

Gabe asked Edna for a plate of food and two cups of ale on a tray. He turned when Harry asked, "Something isn't right. What is it?"

"Lilly ran into Eric."

Harry pushed off the wall. "Is she okay?"

Gabe nodded. "Just shaken up."

Harry could read him. He knew there was more. "And?"

"And now we leave sooner than expected."

"When?"

"Tomorrow night."

"Full kit?"

Gabe nodded.

* * * *

Stopping outside Lilly's door Gabe listened as she paced around the room. Smiling, he knocked lightly and waited for her to open the door.

She stepped to the side as he entered, closed the door and walked around to the far side of the bed.

After placing the tray on the clothes trunk beside her bed, Gabe stood and looked over at her. She was toying with the material of her dress — the same leaf-covered garment she had worn in the forest.

"I thought I gave you enough time to change?"

She looked straight into his eyes. His body began to harden. Coming into her room might not have been the best of ideas. "You did. It's just, I can't get these dresses undone by myself. The lacing…"

Of course, he should have sent Edna to help her. That was out of the question now — he wasn't going to leave until she'd got over her fear of him. He walked around the bed, keeping tight control over his body, and twirled his finger. "Turn around." The tops of her cheeks became pink, but she did as he asked.

It took time, and patience he didn't seem to have, to loosen the lace at the back of her dress. By the time the task was complete he was mildly irritated and, without thinking, grabbed the hem of her cream dress and pulled it over her head.

He froze in place, holding the dress, absorbing her lack of clothing, and almost groaned when he saw the smooth skin of her thighs. At that moment he realised being alone with Lilly was a very bad idea. He looked down at her. She was wearing what looked like a sheer white, oversized shirt. The neckline hung low, revealing her shoulders and upper back, and stopped just below her bottom, leaving the tops of her thighs and long legs bare. Shit. *So much for not scaring her.*

Watching her body stiffen he moved around her and forced himself to look at her red face.

"Lilly." He shook his head, still holding her dress. "I didn't think...it wasn't deliberate." Or had it been? He honestly didn't know, and that concerned him. The one thing he did know was he shouldn't be there, alone with Lilly.

He dropped the dress and took a step back, away from her.

"I know you didn't," she said, looking at his chest. "It's okay."

Gabe stopped. The tops of her cheeks were still pink, her neck flushed, and her pulse was racing. He studied her features. "Why now?"

She stepped towards him and lifted her head to look up at him, and he became all too aware of how close she actually was. "I won't lie. I'm scared, Gabe. I've..." She swallowed her fear. "I've only been with one other person. He was...like me."

"What do you mean, 'like you'?" he asked slowly.

She nodded looking at his chest. "A virgin. We both wanted to not be virgins. So, we...you know."

"I know." He looked at the top of her dark head and smiled at her admission. "And?"

"And it was the only time." She paused, then clarified, "I have no experience."

He felt his smile widen. "And that bothers you."

She gazed up, her face worried. "Yes, it does. I want to do those things...I...I just..."

Before he could stop himself, he reached out and pulled her up against his chest, the need to ease her

212

fears overpowering. "Easy," he soothed. "I don't care if you have experience or not."

"It doesn't bother you that I have no idea what to do?" she asked, stiff in his arms.

"No." he answered her sincerely. "I want to show you. I want to know what makes you hot. I want to see how your body reacts to mine." He lifted her face. "All I want is you."

Chapter Eighteen

Hard, primal need coursed through every nerve in Gabe's body. Now he knew the reason behind her fears, the need to take Lilly, to make her his, was the only thing that mattered. Yet as brave as she had been in telling him her fears, it wouldn't make them disappear.

Holding her face, he smiled down at her. "You have the softest lips." Then he ran his thumb over the scar on her bottom lip. "How did you get this?"

"I fell off my bike," she blurted.

"You fell off your bike?" He looked at her mouth. The scar wasn't big but he could see faint gaps in it. Nodding, she drew her lip into her mouth and he saw her teeth fit perfectly in line with the scar. "You bit your lip when you fell?" He traced the scar for a third time.

"Yes."

"I like it." He said, and lowered his mouth to hers.

Before he kissed her trembling mouth, he traced the scar, in a long slow lick. She sucked in his breath with her gasp and, taking advantage of her open mouth, Gabe slid his tongue between her silky lips.

The kiss was so intoxicating, so sweet, and the way she slid her tongue against his...he barely noticed when she placed her hands on his forearms. Her touch was light at first, but her grip became tighter when he deepened the kiss. Their tongues tangled together again and again in a slow, erotic dance as his hard mouth crossed her soft lips. For a long time they stood like that. Just kissing. His hands on her face. His breathing becoming faster. His body hard and hurting. He was confident he had his need under some kind of control—until she pressed her soft breasts to his chest.

* * * *

Lilly unexpectedly felt cool air on her lips and she opened her eyes. Gabe looked at her, his eyes dark and intense, his nostrils flared and his mouth pulled into a hard line. He ran his hands down her arms as she registered the familiar expression.

Hungry. The word echoed in her head.

Her heart jumped and her breathing sped up.

His grip on her arms tightened as he looked down at her, but she wasn't scared—or was she? All she knew was she didn't want him to stop.

He clenched his jaw, then he slowly turned her so she was facing away from him.

Feeling confused and disappointed, she stiffened. Had he changed his mind? A warm hand brushed the hair away from her ear and Gabe's deep voice whispered, "If I hadn't turned you away, we'd be on the floor right now. And I don't want to do that to you." He paused. "Not yet." His words held a hint of a promise.

"I need to touch you, Lilly. And all I want you to do is enjoy it. Close off your mind and just feel my touch." His mouth lightly brushed her ear and moved to the side of her neck as his hands trailed down her back until he reached her behind, where each hand gently cupped and squeezed.

She hoped he wasn't waiting for an answer, because there was no way she could form a sentence now. He kissed and nipped at the tender skin on her neck and shoulders. Moving his hands around to her hips, he stopped. "This feels right," he said. "My hands belong here."

She nodded helplessly. It did feel right, him touching her.

Continuing his journey, he slid his hand over her stomach and her muscles clenched in response. The sensation tugged all the way between her legs. The anticipation of him sliding his warm hands between her thighs made her legs shake, but instead he moved his hands up over her ribs to her breasts. He brushed the undersides first, slowly moving back and forth, and despite the undergarment she was still wearing, she felt naked beneath his touch. He cupped her breasts firmly, squeezing and moulding them with his palms, then ran his thumbs over her nipples in lazy circles. His mouth ceased its torment, and he rested his face against the side of her head.

"My God," he breathed, slowly massaging her breasts. "Perfect." Then, in a rough voice, he ordered, "Kiss me."

And she did. She didn't think about it, just turned slightly in his arms, twisting her head to the side, and kissed him. A hot, open-mouthed kiss that was all the more erotic with him teasing her nipples through her sheer gown.

Gabe slid his tongue hungrily into her mouth, bringing with it a need so strong it enflamed her own desire. Her entire body trembled as he stroked her with his mouth and tongue. She didn't know how long she could stand this. She was hot and achy and needed more than just his touch and kiss.

With their mouths still locked together, she felt his hand slide around her waist and pull her back against his chest. It felt so good to be pressed tightly against him. He ran his other hand along her hip and slid it under her sheer shirt. Skin on skin, he slid his hand to the top of her thigh and followed the curve of her leg, moving his hand inwards until he eased his fingers between her moist folds.

* * * *

Gabe groaned into Lilly's mouth as he continued to kiss her. Her body was perfect, all soft and curvy. She was pure and natural, untouched by science, and the way she was responding to him... He groaned again. She moved her hips slightly as he took his time rubbing and teasing her sensitive clit, slowly forcing her closer to an orgasm. When he slipped his middle finger deep inside her tight body, her breath caught and she shivered in his arms.

Shit! She was so hot, so wet. He slid another finger in to join with the first and she moaned softly. He cupped her mound, rubbing his palm over her swollen centre, sliding his fingers in and out. Her hands moved restlessly. One gripped his arm where it was locked around her waist, and the other slid down his arm between her legs and gripped his wrist. As he continued to stroke her, Gabe pulled his mouth away, allowing her air. He didn't stop touching her, though—he wouldn't stop.

"Lean your head back," he whispered. "Feel my hands on you."

She did as he asked, and he could see straight down her body. From her flushed neck, to her swollen breasts pushing against the sheer fabric, to his hand between her thighs. His cock twitched. He couldn't take much more of this, and neither could she.

"Gabe." She pleaded. "I can't. My legs are shaking."

"Shhh! You're safe," he breathed into her ear. "I won't let you fall."

He slid his fingers in and out fast, applying just enough pressure to get what he wanted. Her body shivered and she inhaled deeply as the orgasm hit. Her tight core clamped down on his fingers as he continued to pump into her. Her eyes closed and she arched her back slightly, resting her full weight against him. Her breathing was short and choppy, her breasts rising and falling. It was the most erotic sight he had ever seen.

* * * *

Before she could open her eyes, Lilly felt the soft feather bed beneath her. Opening her heavy lids, she looked up at Gabe. He was leaning over her, studying her. Without censoring herself, she asked, "Would throwing me on the floor have been better than that?"

A sensual, almost evil smile transformed his face. "*Much* better." He looked at her neck, his fingers following his gaze. The light pressure lingered briefly, before he slowly ran his hand down her throat to the neckline of her sheer shirt. "This is in my way." He met her gaze. "I think you'd better take it off, before I do."

Take off her last piece of clothing? Her body tensed. With Gabe watching?

She swallowed. No problem. She could do this.

"Lilly?" He asked, studying her carefully.

"I can do it," she said in a high voice.

Reaching for the hem, she began pulling it over her head, but it got stuck under her shoulders. With her back arched, she wiggled and got most of the shirt over her head, but found herself held in place by a warm hand as the fabric tangled around her arms and head.

Gabe's breath heated her skin seconds before his mouth closed over her nipple. He sucked gently, twirling his tongue around the peak, causing it to harden to an achy point. "You can't do that." He pressed his body down onto hers, fitting his hip between her thighs. "You can't move like that and... I won't be able to stop." He groaned, sucking her nipple back into his mouth.

"I don't want you to stop," she gasped, yanking the garment the rest of the way off.

He pulled so strongly on the sensitive skin of her nipple that she cried out, shocked by the erotic sensation, and gripped his hands. He stopped and placed a soft kiss between her breasts. "I'm sorry. I want you so much." He rested his forehead on her chest and took a deep breath.

With her heart pounding, she whispered his name. He raised his head and glared at her. His eyes were clear and hypnotic, deep pools that showed his raw desire. His jaw clenched tight, his face grim. She could see the struggle on his dark face. Was he waiting for her permission? She repeated, "I don't want you to stop." And she arched her body against his, showing him what she said was the truth. "Please." She moved again, brushing her body against his. It was instinct. An instinct she hadn't known she had.

Exhaling, he closed his eyes and kissed the delicate area between her breasts. Gently, slowly, he moved his warm mouth to her other breast. Cupping her, he took his time sucking and licking her nipple until it was hard and rosy. As he ground his thick shaft between her damp folds, Lilly felt something that might have been fear, but she couldn't concentrate on it. Gabe's mouth and hands, tender and loving, were taking over her every thought, creating an ache in her body for him so deep, she wasn't sure it would ever be completely sated.

* * * *

Gabe forced himself to pull away from her. He needed to look at her. See her under him. He pushed up onto his forearm. He looked down the length of her body. Perfect. She was one of a kind—no alterations, and no enhancements. There were no other women with the same body she had, or with quite the same hair colour, and though she tried to hide them, Lilly was ruled by her emotions.

Gabe ran his hand down her body starting at her chest, over her breast, to her flat stomach, past the small patch of dark curls, to her smooth, silky thighs and back up again. There were freckles sprinkled on her arms and legs and the few he saw on her stomach he couldn't help but possessively run his hand over. Perfect.

"Gabe?" Her voice was barely a whisper.

He looked into her exotic eyes. "You are perfect." She was shaking her head before he'd finished speaking. He moved his hand to her chin and forced her to look at him. "Yes, you are."

"I'm not...like you." She hesitated.

He looked down at her. Stunned he repeated, "Like me?"

She nodded.

"You think I'm perfect?"

She nodded again, saying, "I've never seen anyone who looks like you. Who does what you do, or acts like you. Yes... You're perfect."

"Acts like me?" He had never given much thought to how he acted, but he found himself curious.

He watched as she opened her mouth but closed it again. He ran his finger along the scar on her bottom lip. "Tell me." Looking into her glassy eyes, he cupped her cheek. "What is it?"

"You..." She closed her eyes. "You protect people who can't protect themselves. Your strength gives people confidence to believe in themselves. And I'm not sure why, but you put others' needs, *my* needs, above your own." She swallowed and opened her eyes. "And...you are the most gorgeous man I've ever seen." The words rushed out on a sigh.

He was humbled by her praise. A smile pulled at his lips. "I can't help it, it's who I am." He stroked her face, feeling his gut tighten in a nervous knot. Lilly saw only the good—what would happen when she saw the bad?

He felt her shudder, drew her confusion into his lungs. "Don't do that." He curled her arms around his neck as he covered her exposed body with his own. He pressed his mouth to the side of her neck, twirling his tongue over her racing pulse. He took his time, lightly kissing a path back up to her waiting mouth. His hands travelled her body feeling every curve, every mound, until she was moving impatiently beneath him.

Pulling back, he stood and quickly removed his clothes. His cock swelled painfully at the sight of her lying naked before him. Waiting for him. He fell to his knees, roughly pulled her to the edge of the bed , parted her silky thighs. Watching her expression, he stroked the backs of his fingers through her glistening skin. She exhaled a shaky breath and ran her hands over her stomach, reaching for him, desire turning the brown of her eyes into a rich chocolate. He stroked a second time and a third, then eased two fingers inside her waiting body. Her back arched, a soft moan escaping her lips. Gently, he slid his fingers in and out, enjoying the heat her slick body produced. This was killing him. He was pushing himself beyond his normal limits—he would normally have taken her by now, but he loved watching her reaction to him. It was tender and beautiful and something he had never thought he would see in his lifetime. Needing more, he bent his head to her mound of small, dark curls. Closing his eyes, he inhaled her sweet, delicate scent, mixed with the aroma of roses. If he lived for another hundred years — which was entirely possible — he would never forget this moment. He would lock it all into his memory.

Slowly, he swept his tongue against the silky pink folds, tasting her sweet essence. Holding her hips as they jerked, Gabe repeated the sweeping motion again and again until she was pushing at his shoulders, trying to get away from the erotic torment. He clamped down on her hips and held her in place, forcing her to feel every brush of his mouth, every flick of his tongue as it drove deep into her swollen core. Her breathing became fast and her body shuddered as he continued his assault, her cry finally pulling him out of his erotic haze. Letting go, he rose to his feet and looked down at her flushed body. Shivering, she shifted her hips enticingly, ran her hands over her stomach again.

He could taste her on his lips, smell her desire. His body throbbed and jerked, pleading — watching her was just making it worse. He grabbed his erection and squeezed as he stroked his shaft.

Lilly's eyes were glazed, clouded over with passion as he coaxed her further onto the bed. Every muscle in his body was hard and hurting, demanding release. She moved her hands to his chest as he lowered himself between her legs. He rested his forehead lightly against hers. "Raise your legs higher — wrap them around me," he ordered, pressing the tip of his shaft against her slick, damp heat. As she followed his order, he quickly pumped into her wet flesh, using the movement as a distraction. She gasped at his invasion, dug her nails into his neck as she held him tight. He did his best to give her time to get used to him but she was so hot, so tight.

He pulled his hips back, his control gone, but she clamped her legs around in him response. He stopped and whispered against her mouth. "Trust me, angel." Then he covered her mouth in a long, coaxing kiss. He nipped at her lip until she opened her mouth so he could slip his tongue inside. She ran her fingers into his hair as he deepened the kiss, relaxing into him. He began to move then, a slow withdrawal that caused her to suck in a breath and his limbs to tingle. He slid back into her, the sensation increasing in strength as he felt her muscles clamp around him.

Gabe groaned into her mouth. The way she moved under him, lifted her hips to meet him each time he entered her, was intoxicating. He couldn't get enough, he wanted—no, he needed more. More of her tight body, of her light kisses, her tender touch. He pumped into her again and again. Christ, her body was tight, the tightest he had ever felt. So much so, that he wondered if she had lied to him, if she had actually been a virgin.

Still covering her mouth, he slid a hand down the back of her thigh and around the soft skin of her behind. Squeezing, he lifted her leg and held her in place as he increased the tempo. Their breathing sped up along with the pace of their lovemaking and Gabe released her mouth, allowing her to breathe. Closing his eyes, he rested his face against her neck and focused on the way she sucked in a breath when he slid deep inside her tight body. How her stomach clenched in reaction to each thrust. The soft brush of her rosy nipples against his chest and the way she stroked his neck and ran her fingers into his hair. He inhaled her scent deeply, allowing it to fill his lungs. The smell was uniquely Lilly and no matter where she went he would always be able to track her by her scent alone.

As she opened her eyes and stared up at him, his heart seized. He stroked her face, amazed he had been lucky enough to find his own angel. He was far from the perfect man she believed him to be, but he would battle the Almighty himself if that was what it took to keep her. Because he was never letting her go. He couldn't. He *could not* willingly give Lilly up. Not when he knew how rare it was for someone like him to feel any sort of emotional attachment. And now that he had it, he would hold on to it.

Brushing a kiss to her mouth, he repeated the vow aloud for her to hear. "I'm never letting you go. You're mine, angel." With that said, he moved faster and deeper within her, grinding their joined bodies together as he stared down at her. Her eyes were heavy and sexy as hell as she watched him, and he felt the exact moment the orgasm hit her. Selfishly, he bent his head to capture her gasp. He fed on her mouth until his body tensed. The pull of her orgasm was so strong, her hot muscles pulsating around his cock caused such a heated frenzy, that he slammed into her body mindlessly, groaning into her mouth as he finally lost control, coming deep in her welcoming body.

Chapter Nineteen

Lilly sighed, feeling lazy and sated. She'd had no idea that having sex was so exhausting. Fun, but exhausting. Exhilarating, but exhausting.

You're mine, angel. The familiar words echoed through her head again. She had heard them before, spoken in the same order, spoken in the same manner, with complete and utter certainty, but she couldn't place it. She closed her eyes and rewound to the look on Gabe's face. Complete certainty.

Her heart pounded nervously. He had meant what he said — she knew it because he had never lied to her. *I'm never letting you go.*

"Lilly." Gabe's soft, compelling tone pulled her back.

"Yes."

"What were you thinking about that had you so distracted?" He kissed her shoulder.

She stiffened. "When? Now?" She couldn't tell him his words were the most important and comforting anyone had ever said to her. That even though he'd spoken them in the throes of passion and they had most likely been a slip of the tongue, she would always hold them close to her.

He pulled back and she felt his hands cup her hip, forcing her to turn onto her other side, facing him. He narrowed his gaze, studying her for a brief moment. "I meant this afternoon."

"Oh! I..." She shook her head. She didn't want to tell him that, either.

He brushed the hair from her face and gently tapped the side of her head. "You were in here, weren't you?"

She nodded, feeling ashamed she had so little control over her own ability, the thing that supposedly set her apart, made her 'special'.

"Tell me," he demanded softly. "I can't help you if you don't."

She paused, staring at him, then let the words tumble out. "I was thinking about how I want to go home. And how I don't fit in here. How even with my years of studying, I can't pull off a simple thing like being a lady."

"You know you can't go home," he reminded her gently, his hand stroking her hip.

"I don't belong here." Her chest felt tight all of a sudden and she closed her eyes, not wanting to see his expression.

His grip tightened. "Yes, you do." He paused. "Look at me," he commanded in a hard voice. His beautiful green eyes were dark and his face was as hard as his voice. "There is nothing waiting for you there." He gently traced his hand around her behind and pulled her closer, pushing a hard thigh between her legs. "You are alive here. You have a chance to use your skill and knowledge to keep someone from being killed."

She shook her head. "I haven't done anything but wander around in a daze..." She drifted off.

He remained silent, waiting patiently for her to gather her thoughts.

"I know I can't go back, but I want to, so badly. Except I didn't really fit in there, either." She fought hard to keep the tears from her eyes. "I have no place to go. I feel lost."

"Don't go anywhere." Lilly found herself on her back with Gabe's large body covering hers. He smoothed the hair back from her face. "I felt lost and very angry when I first arrived. I missed the life I once had, and then...things changed."

He bent his knees, forcing her legs apart. "What changed?" She could feel his hard erection pressing against her inner thigh, but the only things that moved were his lips. They curved into a smile so tender her heart almost stopped.

* * * *

"My perspective." He looked seriously at her. "It's you. You're what's changed, for me. I haven't thought about the life I used to have since you arrived."

Gabe lowered his mouth to the centre of her chest and pressed his lips to the skin above her heart. Lilly was the reason his perspective had changed. She was the reason he wanted to stay here. Her sweet innocence and natural beauty were only two reasons he no longer craved the life he used to have. "If you left..." He had to be careful how he explained what he felt without scaring her. "I'd be very upset."

"You'd be upset if I went home?"

"You *can't* go home, Lilly."

He sighed when she slid her eyes away from his. She didn't get what he was saying, or rather trying to say. He tried another tactic. "I came from a time when love was unimportant. People were matched together according to their genetic profiles—the goal was to produce a generation without health-related issues who excelled in all academic and physical tests."

"The perfect human?" Her lashes lifted like two small wings.

"Yes, the perfect human. There wasn't any type of attraction or love in my life. I never thought about it, never worried about it—until now. I won't allow you to get lost, out there"—he nodded to the world beyond the room, then touched her temple—"or in here. And if by some chance it happens, I'll find you and bring you back."

* * * *

Lilly's heart leapt. What was he saying? She wouldn't allow herself to think of the possibility. A man like Gabe... It was just too tempting. A dream come true. A dream... Maybe she *was* dreaming.

But she felt the heat of his skin, the weight of his body. No dream—this was the real thing. Her eyes started to burn and a hard lump seem to appear out of nowhere in her throat. How could this be?

"Don't do that, angel." He kissed the skin over her heart again. She felt hot tears clinging to her lashes. She slid her hands into the hair at the back of his neck and held him close to her heart, not wanting to let go. She didn't want to lose this feeling of belonging he had given her. Not one person since her mother had cared enough to want her in their life, until now.

He raised his head and stroked her face. "I didn't mean to scare you."

"I'm not scared. Just..." She wasn't scared, she was *happy*. "I..." Her voice caught. "I haven't felt this way in a long time. Since before my mom was killed." An angry expression crossed his face, but it was quickly replaced by a softer one as he rose onto his forearms. With his face inches above hers, he whispered, "Things change."

The kiss was slow and tender. He brushed his lips back and forth against hers and Lilly sighed as his hands moved over her body. He didn't miss a single part of her. Her breasts were squeezed and nibbled on, her nipples pinched and licked until they were achy and glistening. His fingers circled and teased her clit, enticed her core and everything else, and all the while his warm mouth fed on hers. By the time Gabe forced her thighs wider apart, Lilly was restless, her body throbbing with anticipation.

"Hold on to me." The order was whispered into her mouth as he rolled onto his back, taking her with him. Her hands flew out and she braced herself against the bed, holding herself upright.

With a leg on each side of his lean hips, Lilly felt the tip of Gabe's hard erection pushing into her. Gabe's hands gripped her hips and, while raising his own, pushed her down the thick length of him. She gasped in pleasure as he stretched her body, pressing against her womb. The sensation intensified when he pulled her forward and began rocking his hips in long, slow strokes.

She stayed still for several long moments, breathing deeply. Resting her cheek against his, she absorbed the different sensations. The heat of his body, the prickly stubble on his chin, the tight grip his hands had on her hips, his breath warming her neck, the fullness of him deep inside her.

Slowly, Gabe turned his face until his lips were against hers. "You know what to do." He kissed her. "Now it's your turn. Take from me."

Lilly pushed back so she could see his face clearly, his hard length embedded deep inside her. She looked down at him and felt her face flush, but couldn't look away. Gabe's hard, well-developed body was laid out in front of her. His shoulders were wide, and like his arms they were thick, with hard muscles. She placed her hands on his chest and felt the muscles ripple under her palms, heating her skin.

The grip on her hips tightened as Gabe ordered, "Move, Lilly." And without question, she did as he asked.

* * * *

From under heavy lids, Gabe watched the sway of Lilly's flushed breasts as she rode him. He reached up and cupped one, gently squeezing the fullness, running his thumb over and around the hard, pink nipple. He inhaled her scent again. The fear was still there, but her arousal was overpowering it. He had intentionally forced her to take control of their lovemaking. She needed to put her fears aside and just accept her desire and enjoy the experience.

Although it would seem his plan had backfired — he didn't know how much longer he could do this. She was just too damn tight. His body was trembling as he fought his natural instinct. He needed to take her hard and fast, wanted her to scream his name.

Her soft breasts rubbed against him as her tight body slid slowly up and down his, gripping him in a silky vice.

A low growl was the only warning he gave her before he gripped her behind, forcing their bodies tightly together. Gabe caught her mouth, tangling his tongue with hers, and thrust into her until their bodies shook and she moaned his name.

* * * *

The sudden jerk of her body pulled Lilly out of sleep. Her heart pounded in her ears, her arms and legs feeling shaky as a terrorising chill ran through her. The dream had been so real. Real? Of course, it was real, it had happened the previous afternoon. Except in the dream, things hadn't ended so well for her.

The soldier with the dark hair and green eyes had stood with her in the forest, as he had in real life, asking her the same questions with the same mannerisms. Except instead of backing away into the woods, he had stepped towards her, reaching out with his hand and grabbing her around the throat, squeezing as he moved his face closer to hers. Narrowed green eyes stared at her and for a brief, heart-stopping moment, his face was Gabe's.

Taking a deep breath, Lilly pulled the blanket tight, reminding herself that it was only a dream. The bed shifted as Gabe's arm curled possessively around her, pulling her back against his chest, their two bodies fitting together perfectly. "All right?" He asked.

She could feel the hard muscle of his thighs behind hers. The heat from his chest warmed her back and the hair on his arm tickled the underside of her breast. She felt warm and safe all of a sudden. "My memory was reminding me of what could have happened this afternoon."

He tightened his arm around her, kissed her shoulder. "What did he say to you?"

"He asked about you. And what would you think if you knew I was alone with him."

"What did you say?" He kept his voice casual, but she wasn't fooled.

"I tried to lie, to make it look like I was more of a bother to you than anything. But he knew I was lying."

"What makes you think that?"

"He looked at me kind of weird and then said, 'You're lying to me.' He knew I was scared, too."

"Did he?"

"Yeah. It was weird." She covered her mouth as she yawned. "He stopped and took a deep breath and said I was scared. Could he have sensed it?"

Gabe left her question unanswered and instead asked, "What did he say after that?"

"He said that he thought you would be very upset that I was alone with him. And that you wouldn't leave me alone for a minute, that you would keep me very close."

"Mmm. What else?"

Lilly stilled at hearing his comment. It sounded as though Gabe might be impressed.

"What else did he say, Lilly?" Gabe asked. "I need to know all of it."

"I asked him why he thought that and he said it was what he would do. Then he told me I was going the right way and that you were coming for me."

* * * *

Gabe kept his body relaxed, but clenched his jaw tightly enough to feel the pull up into his temples. Lilly had no idea how right she was. There was no doubt that Eric had sensed her lie, and her fear. The UBF had been working on training those few special soldiers with enhanced hearing and sight how to pick up the signs when they were being told a lie. Any soldier with an enhanced sense of smell could easily pick up her fear. Which meant not only was Eric indeed from the future, but he seemed to have all the same skills as Gabe. This new intel, although retrieved in a manner he would have preferred to avoid, was good all the same, and because of her photographic memory Lilly had just helped him more than she could comprehend.

Lilly lay curled into his body, unmoving for some time. He liked holding her like this. He nuzzled the top of her head. "Thank you for answering my questions."

She yawned again. "You're welcome." He smiled at her soft, drowsy tone.

The sudden, overwhelming urge to tell her how much she meant to him, caused his chest to tighten. She had become the most important person ever to have entered his life. The circumstances weren't normal, but then he wasn't normal, Lilly wasn't normal—none of this was normal. The more he thought about it, the more he thought it was completely fucked. Lilly had been born, lived her life and died sixty-two years before his birth. He closed his eyes. A person could go crazy trying to make sense of it.

He was very lucky. Men like him did not get women like Lilly. He had a job that didn't allow any type of attachment. No wives, no children, no lovers—no one. UBF soldiers were trained to be the best, and that would not be the case if they were distracted by other areas of their lives. The job also had a certain degree of violence, with which he coped well. The downside was it had made him hard and detached. Compassion and kindness were not in his nature—he had to work at them. Yet when it came to Lilly, he was protective and gentle, the compassion and kindness followed, and he didn't have to force it—it happened naturally. His chest tightened again. She had brought out a different man in him. A man who could...love.

He nuzzled her head, listening to her slow, even breaths as she slept. His pulse started racing, adrenaline pumping through his veins. He knew she would remember his words when she woke, but he whispered them anyway. "Love you, angel."

Chapter Twenty

"How many women were you matched with?"

Gabe smiled as he moved to the deep, wooden chest and opened the lid. He was getting used to Lilly's sudden questions. Looking over his shoulder, he raised an eyebrow. "Are you sure you want to know?"

He watched her chew on her bottom lip. "No." Then she shrugged, "But I asked, so I guess I do."

"You guess, do you?" he asked, eyebrows still raised.

She nodded, so he told her the truth. "I was matched with fifty different women."

"Wow!" She turned and walked to the large window in his chamber.

He carried on pulling his kit from the chest. "Those women were selected as a good match for my genes."

She nodded, staring out of the window.

Shit! Why did she have to ask him that? She knew he wouldn't lie to her. He placed his standard issue, armoured tactical shirt on the bed and went to her. Standing directly behind her, he carefully explained, "I didn't sleep with all of them. I never exchanged personal information, and I didn't socialise with them anywhere else. We were there for a purpose, and that was it."

She nodded again. "What happened to them?"

"I don't know. I didn't ask." Her brow creased. He continued, "I wasn't allowed to get to know them—as a UBF member, I wasn't allowed to have any type of personal relationship. I did what was expected of me and followed orders." He could see the tension in her shoulders and spine. "Lilly, I told you you wouldn't like some aspects of my time."

"I remember. What about..." Her frown deepened. "Do you have any children with any of these women?"

What a question. When he was younger and had first joined the UBF, he had been careless and enjoyed the many women assigned to him. As time went on, he'd begun to understand why the military saw to his needs. He didn't agree with their methods of creating the perfect soldier, yet he wasn't in a position to disobey orders either. To this day, he honestly had no idea if he had any children as a result of his sexual encounters. He looked her in the eye. "I don't know. They wouldn't have told me if I had."

* * * *

Lilly could hear the regretful tone to his words. Her heart suddenly ached for him. To be used in such a way. Never knowing if he was a father or not. Yet, how much worse would he feel to know he did have a child, only for it to be taken away from him? "It sounds so cold and scientific."

"It was. Why do you want to know all of this?"

She didn't know why. Since Gabe had announced he and Harry were going to intercept Margaret's entourage, a weird, almost nauseous feeling had plagued her, like a warning, and her mind had kept replaying the dream she'd had during the night. She didn't know why. And she certainly didn't know what had possessed her to ask Gabe questions about his sex life.

"I'm not sure. I feel like something isn't right, but I don't know what."

He focused on her face, "What kind of feeling?"

She pressed her hand to her breasts without thought. "I feel nervous every time I think about you going to protect Margaret. Like something bad will happen. But I don't know what."

Gabe narrowed his eyes as he closed the gap between them and pulled her to his chest, wrapping his arms around her. He rubbed his chin on the top of her head. "I'm coming back, Lilly. I promise."

Her voice was a little high when she replied, and she stumbled over her words. "Okay... I would... Good."

She sighed, closing her eyes. He had promised to come back. That was good. That meant he must like her, or maybe even... *Love you, angel*. Was it true? Had he said that to her last night? Or had it been another dream she'd conjured up?

Pulling back, Gabe lightly cupped the sides of her face. "You are the first person that has ever worried about me. Thank you." He pressed his lips to hers and she felt his heat melt away the fears that surrounded her heart. He kissed her until her knees felt weak, releasing her just when she thought she couldn't handle another second of his torment, then dragged her to the bed, where she expected him to make love to her. Instead, he helped her climb up and, as she sat on the bed, began preparing his equipment.

"Tell me more about Queen Margaret. Do you have any idea what she would look like?"

She paused, then nodded, then shrugged.

Gabe looked at her confused. "What does all that mean?"

With her shoulders still raised, she answered, "Kind of."

"Kind of?"

"Well, I've only seen pictures of paintings of her."

He gave her a confused smile. "Say again?"

"I've only seen books that have pictures with paintings of her. I've clearly never seen her in person and the paintings are in England..." She shook her head, "I mean here. I've never left Toronto."

Gabe smiled as he continued pulling his gear out of the large trunk. "Then can you tell me—"

"Wait, that's not true." The words rushed from her mouth.

Patiently, he asked, "What's not true?"

"My dad, he took me and mom to his parent's house where he grew up."

"Where was that?"

"In Montreal." Why was she telling him this? He probably had no idea what she was talking about. She looked away, feeling like an idiot.

"Montreal."

"Yeah, it's in Quebec."

"I know where Montreal is. Your father's French Canadian, then?"

Her head shot up. How did he know that?

Gabe smiled and answered the questions in her head.

"Reconnaissance teams were sent over after Canada separated." He shrugged his broad shoulders. "I studied the reports they sent back. The cities in your time are the same cities in my time." He winked. "Now, can you remember what these pictures of paintings looked like?"

Lilly's vision became blurry as she searched through her mind. There was a book with detailed photos...when had she seen that? First year university, or second? She scanned both and found it at the tail end of her second year. Once found, the photos of Queen Margaret flew around in her mind. She picked the clearest and stopped it before her eyes. Blinking, she brought Gabe into focus as he leaned on the bed. "That was fast." His green gaze burnt into hers. "Were you talking to me or to yourself?"

"Wha... I was talking?"

He nodded. "You found the book you were looking for?"

"Yes." She had no idea she talked when she was scanning. Was that new?

"And?" He pushed back from the bed, resuming his task. Lilly was about to answer him when he knelt on the floor and reached with both hands under his bed.

Lilly watched, stunned because she had been sure the bottom of the bed was a solid piece of wood.

"False bottom," Gabe explained. "This is where I keep my kit. Your audio device, wallet and watch are also under here."

"Okay."

It took less than a minute for him to pull a long, odd-looking item from beneath his bed. He unwrapped the blanket and Lilly found herself leaning away when she saw what it was.

A gun.

She'd had no idea he had brought a gun here, to this time. She stared at it, then at Gabe.

She opened her mouth in shock. At first, nothing came, out until he said her name.

"They don't have guns" — she slowly shook her head — "in this time."

He picked up the long, sleek-looking rifle and cradled it in his arms. Lifting it, he nestled it into his shoulder and bent his head to look through the scope that sat on top. "I know. That's why I hid it."

She nodded and traced the length of the gun with wide eyes, then looked back to Gabe.

Holding the rifle, he shifted his eyes to her, sensing her discomfort. "I was in the middle of an operation, Lilly. The gun came with me."

Very slowly, he ran his hand down the black barrel. It looked like the guns she had seen on TV and in movies, but there was something odd about its shape and the flat paint covering it. It looked like the entire gun had small, black squares painted on it. It reminded Lilly of the digital pixel squares on high-definition pay channels.

Gabe ran his hand back along the underside of the barrel. The way he held it, touched it, looked personal. Like he was stroking a lover. That particular idea unnerved her.

He lowered the weapon back onto the blanket. "I was first taught to disassemble, clean and reassemble my weapon when I was fourteen. I haven't used it since the day I was shifted here and yet I could still do it with my eyes closed." He looked up at her with a slight smile that turned wary. "Lilly? What's wrong?"

"I...you looked..." She stopped herself. She didn't want to know why he stroked his gun like that. Instead she blurted out the description of the Queen of Scotland. "Margaret had—I mean, *has*, light brown or auburn hair, and either light brown or hazel eyes." The words flew from her mouth. "The pictures aren't that clear, but she was fair-skinned for sure."

He remained silent as she babbled out the rest. "She has a high forehead, long nose and almond-shaped eyes."

Gabe was not easily sidetracked. "I looked what?"

"You were *stroking* that gun."

Lilly pointed to the rifle where it lay on the bed.

He shrugged. "No, I was wiping the lint off it. But I can see why you would think that. I take good care of my weapons, so when the time comes to use them, they won't fail me."

* * * *

She looked up at him from the bed and licked her lips. From the moment she'd entered his room, he'd been trying not to throw her on the floor and make love to her. He'd been doing pretty well so far, but if she kept licking her lips like that, they were both in for a sweaty afternoon.

A simple blink of her dark exotic eyes and he almost crawled across the bed to her. Yet he was able to stop himself and instead leant down onto the bed, keeping eye contact with her. "The only thing I stroke is you. Understand?"

Nodding, she ran her tongue across the scar on her bottom lip.

"Damn it," he hissed between clenched teeth. "Stop doing that." His body was suddenly hard, aching, demanding.

A low, throaty groan escaped as he stared at her. He was so close. Close enough that he could reach out and take her. She wouldn't fight him, she would come willingly, and Gabe knew this because he could smell her how turned on she was. At first, it had been hard to identify. Her scent was very subtle — sweet, even. But he recognised it now, would recognise it anywhere.

Clenching his teeth, Gabe closed his eyes and lowered his head, trying to attain some control. But it was so hard with her scent filling his lungs. It called to him, pleaded to him, made his body spring to life. His jaw squeezed tight. He couldn't let himself get distracted — he needed to get his kit ready. He couldn't allow Eric to continue to attack the keep and put her at risk.

The bed shifted and her voice was soft when she apologised. "I'll go. I shouldn't have interrupted you." He raised his head in time to see her moving towards the door.

Clearing the width of the room in a single move, he landed in front of her, blocking the door. Gripping her by the shoulders, he gave her a little shake. "Look at me, Lilly. Do I look upset?"

Her dark, delicate eyebrows pressed together. "I'm not sure."

Gabe patiently explained. "When you're near me my body has a mind of its own." He circled her wrist and moved her hand to the hard proof. "This is what happens when you lick your lips and stare at me with your sexy eyes." He rubbed her palm down the rigid length. Holding her wrist, he repeated the stroke once again, then released her.

The next stroke was all Lilly. She moved her hand slowly down, lightly squeezing. The pressure from her hand through the rough material of his breeches intensified the touch and he gripped her shoulders again, only this time using her as an anchor.

The blood pounded in his ears, raced through his veins. His nostrils flared as his breathing sped up. Lilly repeated the stroke again and again, until his knees almost buckled.

"Stop." The word came out harsher than he'd intended.

Grasping the sides of her head, he buried his fingers in her hair, pulling her closer. He pressed his lips to her forehead inhaling her sweet scent.

"I want to finish this, but I know if I do, I'll get lost in you and won't get anything else done."

She nodded, pulling away. "I understand. I'll go to my room and write down Margaret's description for you."

"Thank you." He paused, tucking a strand of silky hair behind her ear. "I'll be done before supper. Wait for me and I'll walk you down."

Her breathy, "Okay," made him smile. Searching for her mouth, he selfishly drank in the sweet taste of her. His body shook. God, he wanted her. Wanted her pinned beneath him. Soon. His erection swelled at the thought.

Placing one more hard kiss on her soft lips Gabe reached for the door, opening it for her. Watching as Lilly moved down the hall, Gabe impulsively called out, "Lilly?"

She turned back to face him.

"How do I look now?"

She hesitated, but there was laughter in her voice as she answered, "Hungry."

Gabe went back to work preparing his kit. His actions were automatic, having performed the task so many times over the years. His mind wandered as he disassembled and cleaned his rifle. The image of Lilly safe in her room came to mind.

Lilly safe in her room. She was safe in there. He frowned. As long as he was here. His frown deepened. Would she be just as safe when he was gone? A number of scenarios flashed before his eyes, and none of them pretty. They were in 1503 for God's sake. The odds of the keep being attacked were high. The odds of Lilly being kidnapped or killed in the process were even higher. She was his weak spot. He knew it. Eric knew it, too, and wouldn't hesitate to exploit it.

The idea of her being alone here, without him or Harry to protect her, did not sit well with him. He had to find a way to keep her safe while he was gone.

The simplest answer was for him to post guards on her. They would follow her closely during the day, ready to protect her if needed, and he would post guards by her door and at the end of the hall at night.

Guards were good, but guards and her sleeping here, in his room, was better. His chamber was in the centre of the keep, with other rooms surrounding it for protection. The door was made of heavy, reinforced wood that locked from the inside with strong metal brackets on either side of the door meant to hold a long piece of wood. It turned the door into a heavy barrier, capable of keeping outsiders out. It wasn't ideal, but it would have to do until he got back. He should move her in now. Just to make sure she was safe...

Shaking his head, he swore. "Selfish bastard."

He was selfish—he had no problem admitting it. And he wasn't motivated solely by her safety. He wanted her in his bed, surrounded by his scent. He wanted her sleeping in his bed, so when he came back he could crawl in next to her and wake her by making love to her.

She would be safe in this room while he was away—or safer, anyway—and until he left, he would keep her safe in his arms.

Chapter Twenty-One

Lilly stepped into her chamber. It was black. Not even a candle was burning. Taking a few steps inside, she jumped when Edna came in the room behind her. "My lady, I'm sorry I didn't catch you before you came up." She held out a lit candle so Lilly could see.

"Thank you, Edna. It's so dark in here I can't see a thing." With the candle held out in front of her, she stepped further into the room and stopped again, frowning. "Where is the large trunk and my knap—?" She quickly caught herself. "My belongings?"

"Lord Sutherland has had your belonging moved into his chamber, of course."

What? Why? Her head began to spin. Why had he done that? This room was her only sanctuary. The one place she could go and have no fear of being herself. In this room she was...free.

"Is something amiss, my lady?" Of course, Edna and the others would assume Lilly was aware of

Gabe's decision. They were in the sixteenth century. Men made the decisions, and women did as they were told. She would have to go along with it—she didn't have a choice.

"No, of course not. Thank you for reminding me, Edna."

Retracing her steps, Lilly entered the dimly lit hall and started for Gabe's chamber. Step by step, she closed the gap, and with each of those steps, her annoyance grew. At this rate, she would be furious by the time she reached his door.

"My lord requested a bath for you." Edna said from behind her.

Staring at the dark wood, Lilly breathed, "Did he?"

She opened the heavy, wooden door.

She was greeted by a warm, glowing fire and nothing more. A weird combination of disappointment and relief ran through her as her anger fizzled a little.

The room was neat and orderly. Gabe's gun and the rest of his belongings were nowhere in sight. The trunk full of dresses was resting against the end of Gabe's large bed and her knapsack was nowhere to be seen. Where was it? She looked at the bottom of the bed and wondered if he had hidden it with his belongings in the secret compartment.

She stared at the large, wooden tub. It was full of steaming water and angled towards the fire for additional heat. The day had been damp and grey, raining on and off, and the bath looked so inviting that Lilly relaxed at the idea of sitting in the warm water.

Once Edna had helped her with the lacing of her dress, she said goodnight to the older woman. She stepped into the tub and sighed as she slid down into the water.

Steam rose all around her. Heaven. All she needed was a good book, and this would be perfect. She could pull an old favourite out of her mind, but that would be too much effort. She sighed and enjoyed the warmth of the water. The tub was big enough for her to stretch out, so she laid back and ran her fingers through her wet hair. Then, using a small cloth strip, she scrubbed her body until she felt clean. Resting back against the end of the tub, she stared at the fire and tried to relax. Not an easy task, and before long her thoughts travelled to the most recent turn of events.

Why had Gabe moved her stuff in here? She'd been fine where she was. Her room was small and cosy, and she liked that. Gabe's chamber was nice, too, but it was Gabe's. This was his space, not hers.

More to the point, why hadn't he even bothered to tell her? Irritation rose in her and so did an inexplicable fear.

She sat up, looking around. She could make her own decisions, and her decision was to go back to her own room, to her sanctuary. She needed to be on her own. She was safer that way. She gripped the sides of the tub and started to pull herself up, when heavy hands gripped her shoulders, holding her in place.

"Easy," Gabe's deep voice soothed. "There's no need to get out yet. Enjoy." His voice vibrated through her body, and she felt her irritation begin to melt away.

He held her still until she slid back into the water, and began rubbing her shoulders, relaxing her suddenly stiff muscles. She forced her eyes closed and concentrated on the feel of his hands on her. Gabe had her best interests at heart. Gabe always had her best interests at heart. He would have a good reason for moving her into his room.

Gabe withdrew his hands, then softly commanded, "Scoot forward."

The water level rose and Lilly felt Gabe's hard thighs circle around her as he lowered himself into the tub behind her. Heat pulsated through her. It looked like her fantasy was about to come to life.

* * * *

Gabe pulled Lilly back so she rested against his chest. He watched without a word as she crossed her arms, covering her flushed breasts. He knew she was annoyed with him and not because he could smell it but he heard it. Her agitated sighs and tongue clicks were a dead giveaway. He should probably apologise. He wasn't used to consulting anyone else when he made a decision—he was used to giving orders, and having them obeyed.

Rubbing his hands down her arms, he folded his arms over hers. He hadn't intended to join her, but when he'd seen her lying there with her breasts swaying just below the surface of the water and her bare limbs stretched out, he hadn't been able to help himself.

After a deep breath, Lilly slowly relaxed, and he took it as a good sign. Gripping her hands, he unfolded her arms so they floated in the water with his. His fingertips began to itch at the sight of her flushed skin. He wanted to cup her breasts and feel the weight of them, run his hands over the freckles on her stomach, but he held back. There would be plenty of time for him to touch her before he left, and right now, he was enjoying this too much for it to end.

"This is a first for me. I've never had a bath with a woman before." He laced his fingers with hers. "How about you?" he asked, although he knew the answer.

"Is my knapsack under your bed?" Gabe tilted his head back. He wanted to laugh at her abrupt change of subject, but he smiled instead and answered her question.

"Yes. Do you need it?"

"Yes…" She paused, and conceded, "Not right now. I was just wondering."

"I'll show you how to get at it before I go."

"Thank you." Then she said, "This is a first for me, too." Gabe smiled again. He waited for what he knew was coming, and watched the beads of water that trailed down the rounded sides of her breasts. He gripped her hands tighter before he gave in to the urge to cup and squeeze her body.

He felt the sudden tension in the muscles of her back and in her shoulders and spine. "Why did you have my things brought in here?"

"My chamber is in the centre of the keep. It has a heavy, reinforced door that can be barred from the inside, as well as a lock."

"But why did you have my stuff moved in here?"

"Because you'll be safer in here than your old chamber while I'm gone, and" – he might as well tell her – "because I want you in here."

"Oh." She appeared to think this over. "I'm not one of your soldiers, you know."

"I know. And I appreciate that fact on a daily basis." He rubbed his cheek against the side of her head. He wouldn't apologise for trying to keep her safe.

Gabe looked down her body, noticing goosebumps covering her skin.

"Cold?"

"A little." It was a lie. Smiling, he swept the warm water up her chest, covering her stomach and breasts.

"There will also be guards placed outside the door at night, and you will have an escort if you decide to walk to the village." He swept the water up her body again. "Please don't go into the forest. It's not safe. I don't know where Eric is right now."

"Is that his name?" Lilly asked. "The person you went after?"

"Yes."

Gabe swept the water up her chilled body again, but stopped and covered her breasts with his hands. He swirled his palms over her rosy nipples before pulling his hands away.

"Gabe?"

"Mmm."

"There is something about Eric that worries me."

"What's that?" he asked, moving his hands slowly over her soft flesh again.

"I don't know." She sighed, frustrated, "There's something... I just can't seem to pull it from my head."

"You will." He pressed his lips to her shoulder, then sucked the smooth skin into his mouth, leaving a mark. He watched as she clasped her hands and twisted her fingers together. Something else was bothering her. He slid his hands down, covering her stomach, while he waited for her to ask her questions.

Running his hand over her stomach, he said, "I like these freckles."

Gabe smiled at her sudden deep breath and waited for her to blurt out a question.

"I'm not sure I should be in here—this is your space."

"I'm a soldier, Lilly. I'm used to sharing quarters with other members. And you're much prettier than any of them," he teased, keeping his tone casual. "This is the safest room in the keep. I want you in here at night while I'm gone."

"Maybe I should just go with you—"

"No." He cut her off. "You won't. You will stay here. What's the problem, Lilly? I'm sorry I didn't tell you, but that's not all that's bothering you."

"I'm just...so used to being by myself. I value my personal space, so I try not to invade others'. If I'm in here, I'm invading your personal space, and I don't want to do that."

He could see her pulse pounding in her neck.

"Are you more worried about me or yourself?"

She remained silent as she gripped her fingers together.

"Mmm. I have a feeling there is more to it than you invading my personal space." He swept the warm water up her chest when he felt her shiver.

This time Gabe wrapped her arms across her breasts, covering them with his own. Holding her close he pointed out, "I've been close to you in one way or another since you first arrived."

Wanted to be close to her was more accurate. He kept that thought to himself. "I never expected to be this close." He rested his cheek against her head as he spoke. "I do know that you like it, and I also know it confuses you that you like it."

"You know?" He nodded against her head. "I can't help it," she said. "So much has happened. It's all new to me. I've always depended on myself—I've never had anyone else *to* depend on."

"Remember the time I came from. It was against orders for me to have any sort of relationship," he reassured her. "I don't know the first thing about having a relationship. Unless you can call the strange symbiotic attachment I have to Harry a relationship. But I can tell you without a doubt, I do not want to share a bath with him."

Her laughter made him smile. "This is new for me too, Lilly, and I can honestly say that I like it." He pressed his lips to her ear and whispered. "Very much."

A shiver ran though her again. Gabe was right—she was confused. She had been alone for so long, struggling to survive, and nervous of any type of close relationship. It was different here with Gabe. Never before had she felt that she needed someone, until she had realised she needed Gabe.

He was very easy to be around. She didn't have to hide her photographic memory for fear he would freak out. He was easy to talk to, and he was patient when she jumped from subject to subject. Then there was the demanding, passionate side of Gabe. Never in her life had she felt the overwhelming sensations Gabe caused in her. She felt sexy and lustful, beautiful and free. Emotions she had never experienced before. It was still somewhat difficult to get used to the fact that a man like Gabe could want her. The idea made her giddy, but she was still nervous being around him and not entirely sure why. Even now, laying with him in the bath, she hoped he would pull her out and make love to her, but was afraid too. She closed her eyes. God she was confused. What was she so afraid of — that he would leave?

She shivered again.

"Are you that cold?"

She didn't want to lie to him, but she didn't want him to know the truth either. "Yeah. I think I'll get out." She pulled herself upright and reached for the linen cloth Edna had put near the tub.

Keeping her back to him, she stepped onto the cool floor, wrapping the cloth around her back, and concentrated on drying off. She tried not to think about Gabe sitting behind her naked, or the fact he was fully aware of her feelings of unease about becoming too close to him. She really wished she had the ability to hide her emotions — the thought of him knowing her fears made her cringe.

Sweeping the cloth down her legs, Lilly tensed when Gabe trailed his fingers down her spine. He gripped her hips, pressing himself against her behind, his hard arousal evident. She would never have believed, until she met Gabe, that such a big man could move so quietly. She hadn't even heard the water stir.

"Why is it, when you perform the simplest of tasks, it turns me on?" She wanted to stand up straight, but his damp body pressed against hers, keeping her bent forwards. He curled his arms around her waist as he trailed small kisses up her spine. She clutched the cloth to her chest as he heated the skin on her back. She shivered again, but not from the cold.

He pulled her upright, turning her so she faced him. Tiny lines appeared at the corners of his eyes as he studied her. "You're not still nervous of me, are you?" He tugged the damp cloth away from her breasts.

"Of us," she whispered back, ashamed of her stupid fears.

Gabe, the perfect man, stood before her, his strong, well-muscled body still glistening from the water and she had an urge to lick every drop of water from his chest. *Oh God!*

"We made love twice last night and I slept next to you."

She shook her head, "I know. I'm sorry. It's not what you think. I'm not nervous of you—I'm nervous of how you make me feel. I'm not used to this."

He pulled her closer and nudged her chin up, searching her face. "Used to what?"

She couldn't do it. What would he think of her if he found out she was a total control freak?

"Tell me," he said.

"I always know the answer," she blurted. "I read about stuff and know what to do, because it never leaves..." She touched her head. "But this is something you can't learn from books, not really. Not that I've even read those kinds of books. I don't know what to do, how to act." She sighed. Why couldn't she get past this? Why did she have to know everything about everything? Why hadn't she studied sex manuals, instead of the medieval era?

"You're nervous because you haven't read up on what to do during sex and you think you'll get it wrong somehow?"

It sounded so absurd when he said it.

He raised his eyebrows and a slow, sexy smile covered his face. "This is really bothering you, isn't it?" He cupped the side of her face, his thumb stroking her cheek. "A book can't teach you how your lover wants to be touched or kissed. You have to experience it," he began gently. "There is no right way to make love—there are many ways. The most important thing is to do what feels good, what feels natural. Enjoy the moment." He tunnelled his hand into her hair and cupped the back of her head, pulling her closer to his chest.

"Don't think, just do it?"

His hands fell to her waist, and he stood waiting for her to choose.

Could she just stop thinking and let her body take over? He had told her last night to take from him. Now she had the opportunity, and she was hesitating.

"Stop thinking," he ordered softly.

So she did.

She swept her tongue over a single bead of water that was sliding down the centre of his chest. She could taste the rosewater Edna had put in the bath, but Gabe's own taste overpowered it. He tasted hot, rich and very male.

Another droplet made its way down his heated skin, sliding over his nipple. Lilly flicked her tongue across the tip, catching it. Before she knew what was happening, the droplets of water were forgotten and she was lightly kissing his chest. She felt his hard muscles flex each time she pressed her lips against his skin. She trailed kisses across to his other nipple, brushed her lips against it and slowly circled the hard peak with her tongue.

Gabe's groan was soft as he rested his face on the side of her head and, as he had done earlier in the afternoon, he grabbed her wrist and placed her hand on his thick shaft. Slowly, keeping her mouth pressed to his chest, she stroked the hard length of him. It was like gripping hot, silky steel. She pumped her hand down again, loved how her palm heated from the touch. His muscles contracted and released with each stroke of her hand. The grip he had on her waist tightened, became almost painful when she closed her mouth over his hard nipple at the same moment she ran her hand down, squeezing his erection.

His chest heaved with each breath and a sound, more growl then groan, escaped as she repeated the torment. She looked up at his face while she increased the pace. His eyes were open staring back at her, the muscles in his jaw flexed and air hissed through his teeth with each breath.

He looked dangerous and sexy. A rumble came from his chest as he gripped the sides of her head, pressing his mouth to hers. "I told you not to look at me like that."

His mouth came down hard on hers when he kissed her. His teeth pulled on her bottom lip until she whimpered from the slight twinge of pain it caused and opened for him. He swept his tongue fast and almost aggressively into her open mouth, caressing her tongue with his. He wrapped his arms around her, pinning her arms to his chest as he lifted and carried her to his bed.

Lilly enjoyed the way Gabe's passion took him over and she loved that she was the reason behind that passion. Sighing, she ran her hands through his hair as his hard body pressed her into the soft bed. Her lips cooled when he pulled away. "I want you," he bit out between clenched teeth, his perfect face a mask of dark hunger. "I can't wait any longer."

Gabe stared down at her, his chest heaving, and Lilly realised, astonished, that he was waiting for her. He was waiting for her approval. Even in this passionate haze where he seemed aggressive and controlling, he was willing to wait for her consent. Her chest suddenly began to ache and her heart swelled. To go so against his very nature, to allow someone else to take the lead, took greater strength than giving orders. Even now, he was putting her needs above his own.

Take from me. His words from the night before replayed in her head.

"I can't wait, either," she confessed, her heart fluttering as his mouth covered hers.

Lilly felt Gabe's hands travel down her ribs and waist and stop, clutching at her hips. He pulled his mouth away and bent his head to her breast. His mouth closed over the tip and he suckled hard, pulling the achy tip deeper into his mouth. She sucked in a breath as her hands gripped at his hair, her hips arched up as if pleading for more.

Releasing her breast, Gabe pushed away from her, still holding her hips, and with a flick of his hands she found herself face down on his bed, her arms spread wide and her hair in her face. His grip remained on her hips as he proceeded to pulled her off the bed until her feet touched the floor.

Her body felt open to him and the position she suddenly found herself in made her feel exposed and vulnerable. She couldn't see what he was thinking or doing.

"Gabe?" His name came out as a plea.

* * * *

Gabe felt her tense as his hands moved up her body, tracing the curves of her hips, the tuck at her waist, then up her ribs until he cupped her breasts.

He kissed her back, and at the same time he rolled her nipples between his fingers. "Trust me, angel." Even as the words rumbled from his chest, he wasn't sure she *could* trust him. The way he felt when he was with her...it was as if he didn't have control of his own body. All he could think about was Lilly—her mouth, her body, her taste.

He made a conscious effort to slow down and took his time kissing and stroking her body, getting her used to him bending over her in this manner. He kissed her shoulder blades, sucking her sweet-smelling skin into his mouth, marking her again. He had never done that before—left a mark on a woman. The thought had never occurred to him, but now he wanted everyone to know Lilly belonged to him.

She shifted her behind against him, causing his cock to slide between the soft crease of her behind. He clenched his jaw, fighting the strong instinct to take her hard and fast.

His voice was rough when he finally spoke. "Brace yourself on the bed." She did as he asked and he kissed the soft skin on her back until he was standing up behind her. He ran his hand over her behind and slid it down in between her legs, where he felt her slick lips. He inhaled her scent. Her body was ready for him. She sucked in a breath when he slid a finger deep inside her tight opening, testing her readiness for him.

"You're so wet," he groaned, and bent, placing another kiss on her spine, slowly sliding his finger in and out. He teased her sensitive core. She was so wet, so hot and so perfect.

Her scent was driving him crazy. He slid his finger in and out in quick succession. Her groan mixed with his when he removed his finger. Shaking with need, he gripped her hip with one hand and his throbbing shaft with the other. "Spread your legs a little wider for me," he said, already easing the tip of his erection inside her.

When she did as he asked, he couldn't help but surge forward, plunging himself deep. Her muscles clenched tight when he pulled back, and he heard her suck in a deep breath. He plunged in again and began a slow, steady pace, stroking her body as he took her. Bending over her, he reached forward and teased her breasts, while lightly nipping and kissing the smooth skin of her back.

Moving his hands lower, he slid his fingers into her soft folds and once again purposely stroked her sensitive clit. He had watched her reaction the night before and applied the precise amount of pressure she needed. She began to move restlessly and her hand reached down and covered his while he continued his assault. Gabe groaned again. He loved that she held his hand in place—it proved he was pleasing her.

Her nails dug into his hand and her breathing sped up. He grabbed her hips, driving forward as she pushed back. Their heavy panting filled the room, only to be drowned out by their fervent loving. Each time he entered her it felt deeper, stronger, Lilly's hot core welcoming him, squeezing him with each stroke. He felt her tight, hot muscles grip his shaft at the same moment he exploded inside her. His head rolled back and he groaned as the euphoric sensation raced though his body, every muscle burning with ecstasy.

Possessively wrapping his arms around her, he pulled her up towards his chest, his body still buried deep within her. He moved slightly and felt Lilly's sensitive muscles tighten around him. He kissed the side of her neck as she panted and trembled.

Pulling away, she crawled onto his bed and Gabe followed, stretching out next to her. They lay together for a few minutes, not touching, just trying to catch their breath. He looked over at her. She was staring at the ceiling, a sexy, sated look on her face. He hadn't realised until that moment how much she trusted him. Trusted him not to hurt her, which he knew was difficult for her. He felt humbled and guilty.

Rolling onto his side, he grabbed her hand and brought it to his mouth, kissing her knuckles. "Thank you for trusting me."

She gave him a soft smile. "Thank you for being patient with a born-again virgin."

Startled by her comment, he laughed, tugging her with him as he rolled onto his back. She curled into his side and rested her head on his shoulder.

After a few moments, she spoke. "Gabe?"

"Yes?"

"This is rare, isn't it?"

"What's rare?" Gabe asked, stroking her arm.

"Us. It doesn't happen this fast normally, does it?"

"Our attraction for one another?"

"Yes. It's not normal, is it?"

He shrugged. "Maybe it's normal for us." Okay, Lilly agreed that they were attracted to each other. But was she feeling what he was feeling? For the first time in his life, he was actually nervous, and second-guessed his own instincts.

"We're not normal," she said quietly.

The worried tone in her voice had him concerned, so he kept the conversation light. "True, but that's good. Normal is boring, and boring makes me cranky."

"Oh!" She laughed. "I guess I should keep that in mind."

* * * *

Gabe lifted his head and rested his hand under it. The casual movement was smooth, his muscles flexing and releasing with the simple task. Lilly stared at his chest, then placed her hand in the centre. The steady rhythm of his heart beat under her palm. Strong. Alive. As usual, her mind was flooded with images and questions at the slightest trigger.

"When do you have to leave?"

"In a while. We still have some time." He rubbed his thumb along her arm.

She didn't want him to go. He could get hurt, or worse. But if he didn't go, what would happen to Margaret? She was so young—just a child, really. The future depended on Gabe keeping the young queen safe. But what was he saving? What was in the future that was so important?

"Lilly?"

She tilted her head and looked up into his questioning eyes.

He knew she was scared. How did he do that? "It's nothing."

"That wasn't very convincing."

She sighed. "It's this thing with Margaret."

"I won't let anything happen to her." He ran his finger over the scar on her lip. Gabe had repeated the stroke so many times since she'd arrived that she'd become used to the touch, found it comforting.

"I know. But it's not that."

"Then what?"

"I wish I knew what it was you were helping with. Why are you protecting the future? What will happen if you don't?"

"Without actually participating in the plan, we'll never know." He paused. "Unless I get hold of Eric. But even that wouldn't guarantee us an answer."

"I just..." She trailed off, shifting her eyes away from his. What if she was wrong? What if Margaret wasn't the one in danger?

He turned his muscled body towards her, protectively pulling her closer. "Tell me."

She met his green stare. "What if I'm wrong? What if you go all that way and it's not Margaret who's in danger?"

"If that's the case," he began patiently, "I deliver Margaret to her husband, come back here, we sit down and start from the beginning." He brushed the hair back from her face. "I know you feel out of your comfort zone, but it's okay to be wrong sometimes."

"Not with this." She shook her head. "Someone could die."

"Lilly." Gabe's warm hands cupped her face. "You are doing more than most. If someone does die, it's not your fault, it's not my fault—it's not even

McGill's fault. The blame belongs solely with the person responsible for the act."

She nodded. He was right, and she knew it. There really wasn't much she could do—what she did to help was mild in comparison to what Gabe and Harry still had to do. But the doubt was still there, lingering, and for some reason she just couldn't shake it.

She changed the subject. "How far from the east coast are we?"

He studied her briefly, then answered. "Two, maybe three days of hard riding. Depending on where she is."

She placed her hands on the hard muscles of his chest, absorbing his warmth. "She won't be hard for you to find, will she?"

"If she was alone, or had a smaller party escorting her, it might take a little longer." He sighed. "But if her entourage is as big as you say, then the locals in any area she travels through will know she's there."

"So, anyone could find her?"

"Yes."

"It would be even easier for a soldier like you."

He nodded.

That meant Eric could find her just as easily. He might already have found her. "Do you think that's why Eric is here?"

"If what McGill says is true, it would make sense. But..." Gabe hesitated. "He's still in the area."

"That's good, isn't it? He hasn't left to find Margaret."

"I'm not sure. If I knew my target was travelling in plain sight, I would already have finished the job. Unless he wasn't informed of her location. Still, he should have tracked her down by now and be en route."

"Is he waiting to follow you?"

"Maybe," he agreed. "But it doesn't matter right now. The only thing I want to concentrate on is you and how you feel." His hand ran down her side until it reached her behind. She sighed as he massaged her gently. "And the noises you make when I make love to you."

"I make noises?"

"Mmm. Good noises."

She sighed as he brushed his lips over hers. The distraction sounded pretty good — she didn't want to think about what lay ahead for him, either.

Gripping the back of her leg, he lifted it onto the hard muscle of his thigh and pulled her closer, their bodies now glued together. He nibbled at her lips as he pressed his thick shaft against her sensitive core.

"This is another way to make love." The words came out mixed with her ragged breath.

"Yes, it is. But this time, we go slowly. I need you like this, so I can feel every part of you." He ran his hand over her hip. "See the look in your eyes." He wrapped her arms around his neck and brushed his mouth over hers. "Feel your mouth on mine, feel you surround me." He thrust into her, and then began grinding against her in slow, tantalising circles as he pressed his lips to the frantically beating pulse in her neck. "Because this will have to last me, until I get back to you."

Chapter Twenty-Two

Gabe motioned silently for Harry to move up the right side of the small group of men while he moved up the left, into a flanking position. They had been watching the entourage for less than a day and had easily picked out the soldier in command of the queen's — as well as her entourage's — safety.

Keeping to the shadows, Gabe moved closer to the group. He rolled his eyes as he listened to the instructions given to the small group of soldiers. The commander's strategies were pathetic. They might work against others from this time, but they were no match for Eric and his crew. And Eric was in the area. Gabe was certain of it. The trail he'd left had been intentional, and would be easy to follow. He didn't want Eric's small group near the keep, or Lilly.

After receiving their instructions, the group of soldiers dispersed, leaving the commander alone with his second-in-command. Gabe caught Harry's gaze, then nodded, signalling the go.

From his position in the forest, Gabe could clearly see Harry step out into the opening, his long, black, woollen cloak covering him from head to toe. Slowly approaching the two men, Harry held his hands out, palms up, away from the sword he carried—the sword he was capable of using, but wouldn't. Harry had being training with the weapon since the moment he'd arrived, and Gabe had followed suit, but neither of them enjoyed using swords. They were clumsy and heavy and weren't easily concealed.

The soldier standing next to the commander stepped forward, drawing his sword. Gabe shifted slightly in response, adjusting his aim accordingly.

"Halt." The commander addressed Harry, "Who goes there?"

Harry carefully raised his hands, pulling back the hood and intentionally exposing the tartan he was wearing.

Both men stilled, eyeing the kilt Harry had 'borrowed' from a member of the Stewart clan. The tartan had been a pain in the ass to get, but it should prove worth the extra days' ride.

Harry nodded his head. "Harry." His accent was thick and rough. "I've come tae deliver a message to ye, concerning our new queen."

"A message?" The commander put his hand on the shoulder of his second, in silent command. The soldier lowered his weapon.

"Aye. Sent by the King of Scotland himself. He sends a warnin'."

Gabe rested his finger lightly along the side of the trigger as he watched the second-in-command tighten his grip on his sword.

Harry crossed his large arms, eyeing the second. "The king was informed of a plan tae kidnap his bride. I was trusted tae deliver th' message without…" Harry looked in the direction of the entourage. "Without alarming Her Majesty."

The commander stared at Harry, deep in thought, and asked, "You are all the king sent?"

"Aye," Harry confirmed. "He thought it best, nae tae draw unwanted attention. It wouldnae bode well for my laird if he sent his men marchin' intae England, even if it was tae protect his English bride."

Gabe kept the second in his sights, even though the man relaxed the grip on his sword.

The commander nodded. "Who is behind it?"

"I wasnae privy tae my king's thoughts. Though, he is anxious tae have his bride at his side an' is awaitin' yer arrival at Lampton Kirk."

"He is awaiting us at the border?" the second asked.

"Aye. He asks that ye bring Queen Margaret tae him without delay."

The second turned, catching his commander's attention. "My lord, if this is true, we must keep the queen moving. Stopping for any period of time would put her at risk."

Harry nodded at the second-in-command. "I agree—keeping the queen movin' would prove to be a safe option. However, a safer option would be tae keep the queen movin' *without* her entourage. A smaller party is faster—harder to track." Harry winked at the second. "Why dae ye think we Scots

can get intae and ootae your lands without gettin'
caught?"

* * * *

Eric knelt down, scanning the tracks. The attempt to
cover them was either poor or planned, depending on
how one thought.

"I'm a rookie, and even I can cover my ass better
than that," Jason said.

John stepped up next to Eric and looked down at
him, clearly enjoying the fact he was in the dominant
position. "Looks like Sutherland's skills are all
physical. The intellectual needs some work."

Eric rose to his full height, an inch taller than John's,
and gave him an evil grin. "If you say so, sir."

John stood toe to toe with Eric. "I do say so,
Sergeant. Keep tracking him."

Eric nodded curtly and turned. They were following
a man who wanted to be followed, and it would be
used against them. He was certain of it, because it
was exactly what he would do.

* * * *

Lilly was making her way back through the village
when she caught sight of George talking to someone.
The smaller man, covered in a brown, woollen cloak,
constantly shook his head at George. She frowned,
watching, wondering if George was all right—until
she noticed it. The person in the brown cloak shifted
from side to side, as if he was compelled to do so. She
stopped dead as the image of Professor McGill

flashed before her eyes. He had worn a brown cloak last time she had seen him.

Her eyes met George's faded, blue ones. A frown sat heavy on his brow. She mouthed the name 'McGill', and he nodded, confirming her guess.

George directed his attention back to McGill and nodded towards Lilly. Her chest became heavy as McGill turned to face her, an overwhelming fear rocking thorough her body as she stared at his grim expression.

She continued towards the two men, her heart beating wildly. She'd been sad when McGill had first left. It had felt like her old life was slipping away with him. But now he was here, she didn't want him to be. She was happy for the first time in her life, and with McGill reappearing, she wondered if he was here to take that happiness away. Why was he here? What was the news he had to deliver that caused that look on his face?

Stopping before the two men, Lilly kept her hands hidden under her cloak, her hands squeezing into fists at her sides.

She did a double take when she noticed McGill wasn't wearing his glasses, but quickly managed a smile. "Hello, Professor."

"Lilly." He nodded, returning her smile, though his seemed filled with genuine affection. "You look wonderful—much better than last time I saw you." His nervous shifting stopped as he spoke to her. "Gabe and the others have been taking good care of you, I see."

"Yes," she answered honestly. "They have." She hesitated briefly, feeling uneasy. Ignoring it, she asked point-blank, "Are you here to tell us whether Margaret is the one in danger?"

"Partly." He began nervously shifting back and forth again. "I need to speak with all of you about what I've found out. But George has just informed me Gabe and Harry are gone."

"Let's take this inside, to a more private area," George suggested. "Lilly, go and find Marc, and we'll meet you in your old room?"

* * * *

Marc followed close behind her, nodding to the blond soldier who stood waiting outside the room. Lilly had thought it strange at first when Marc had asked the man to accompany them upstairs, and when she asked why, Marc had simply shrugged and said that Gabe would want him to.

"Right, now," George said after the door was closed. "What's this all about?"

Lilly turned to McGill as George and Marc each took a spot on either side of her.Together, the trio watched as the professor fumbled with his glasses, sliding them up his nose, and began his nervous pacing. "First, let me answer Lilly." He turned to face her. "Yes, Queen Margaret is the one in danger. I knew you would figure it out." There was a hint of pride in his voice. "Your knowledge of this time period is unsurpassed. I'm sorry I was of no help." He shook his head sadly. "But I have been given some important information."

"Which is?" Marc asked, in his normal, sarcastic tone.

"That Queen Margaret is being used as bait," he said.

"Bait?" George asked. "To catch who?"

Chapter Twenty-Three

Gabe studied the dense forest surrounding the small group. They were being tracked. He had been right. Eric and his team had been following them for some time now.

The queen had been reluctant to separate from her entourage, but had finally given in on the understanding that her maid would accompany her. Gabe looked over at the girl sitting side-saddle on a gleaming, white mare. This small, nervous girl was a queen, and would soon be the wife to a king. What kind of father sent his child to a man she did not know, and who at one point had been an enemy? The idea had him squeezing the muscles in his jaw.

"Stop it," Harry hissed low. "She's already nervous. Don't make it any worse for her." The young queen looked in his direction at that very moment, and Gabe couldn't help but smile at her. She smiled back and quickly looked away.

"I knew you could be charming if the situation called for it," Harry chuckled next to him.

"So," Harry demanded some time later. "How many have you picked up? I've noticed one so far."

"Three." Gabe casually looked around. "Plus your one. If it isn't one I've already smelt, it'll bring the total to four." Gabe glanced sideways at Harry. "Two shy of a full team. How much do you want to bet there are two ahead, waiting for us?"

"No bet." Harry shook his head. "This reeks of a standard interception. The four behind, driving us forward into the two waiting ahead. Not very original."

The two men rode in silence for a few minutes, watching the forest around them.

"Well?" Harry asked. "You want me to go?"

"No. I'll go." Gabe swayed back and forth with the motion of his horse as he glanced around. "Stay here with the group and keep them moving."

"You sure? I don't mind going. You haven't kept me busy enough — I'm starting to get bored."

Gabe smiled. "You'll get your turn — there are still four behind us."

"Yes, there are." Harry smiled, nodding his head, then raised his eyebrows. "How long should I give ye?"

Gabe paused, calculating the time it would take. "Locate their scent, track and then eliminate..." He shrugged, gathering the reigns of his horse. "Thirty minutes." He began urging the horse to the outside of the small group. "If I'm not back in thirty, get her the hell out of here."

He frowned as he passed the half-assed circle surrounding the Queen. Catching Harry's attention, Gabe gave a quick command. "Tighten up that circle." He indicated with his chin. "And give her your cloak."

Harry nodded.

Gabe moved alongside the small group of soldiers surrounding the Queen and her maid. Something was not right. Queen Margaret wasn't any ordinary woman. With her rich-looking dress and cloak, she was the perfect target, and regardless of their attempt to shield her, she was still exposed. What were they waiting for? Why hadn't this team made its move?

Gabe hadn't travelled far before he caught the first scent. He had left his horse on the trail for Harry to find and, without much noise, moved quickly into the forest. He silently crept closer to his target. The man's scent—a mixture of sweat and the excitement of a kill—was easy to spot.

The idea that a soldier of the UBF was excited to make a kill disturbed him. What repulsed Gabe even more was the fact that this man wanted to kill an innocent girl. The king's army did not kill children. These men would have stood before high-ranking officers and pledged their service to the king, agreed to uphold the ideals of the Royal Military. Rage swelled inside him. He was going to have to remind these bastards of their oath. Quickly taking the emotion under control, he focused it on the target. He could not afford any distractions. Lilly was waiting.

Gabe's nostrils flared, the soldier's scent overpowering now. He was almost on top of him. The slightest of movements next to a large oak tree caught his attention. Gabe made out the outline of a man lying on the ground, covered with leaves and twigs. He swiftly judged the distance and, without hesitation, covered the expanse in one fluid movement, landing directly on top of the assassin, driving his knee hard into his back. The sound of snapping bones travelled only as far as the bushes that surrounded them.

Instantly locking on to the soldier's throat with one hand, Gabe used the other to close over his mouth and nose, muffling any sound. As the soldier struggled against him, Gabe put his full weight onto his back and dug his fingers and thumb into and around the man's airway. Speaking softly, Gabe reminded the soldier of the promise he had made — "The King's army does not kill innocent children." The soldier shook his head and clawed at Gabe's hands, trying to free himself, but was rapidly losing consciousness. The struggling stopped when Gabe felt the airway collapse and the man went limp.

After collecting the soldier's kit, Gabe patted down the man's legs, finding a wicked-looking blade with a serrated edge tied to one leg and a field log in the pocket on the other leg. He stuffed the log, knife and extra rounds into the soldier's pack, along with any other evidence that the body was not from this time, and shouldered the standard issue rifle along with his own.

After a quick attempt at covering the body back up with leaves and fallen branches, Gabe doubled back, headed across the trail to the opposite side, and moved fast through the dense forest until he located the next target farther down the trail. This one was more difficult to pinpoint — the scent was similar, but not as strong. This man's excitement was restrained.

Gabe crouched low behind a thick bush, shrugging off his pack and the dead soldier's rifle. Then, flattening himself to the ground, he inched out into the open.

* * * *

McGill pushed his glasses up his nose and looked curiously around the room, then turned to face Lilly. "To catch Gabe."

"Gabe." Lilly caught her gasp before it left her mouth. Her stomach clenched into a hard knot. "Why?"

McGill stepped forward, worry covering his face. "Gabe was the best soldier of his time, the top of an elite group. In my time he is notorious—his skill and ability in combat situations is legendary."

Lilly nodded. She knew all this. "Yes, you mentioned this before. What does it have to do with anything?"

She scanned McGill's face. It was covered with a light sheen of sweat.

"I was very careful when I decided to bring you all here. I deleted all the files on the computers, and on the main TSIS system. Any paper trail that was left, I shredded then burnt. I forged the log entries to make it look like I was travelling back and forth to Toronto, gathering information. But somehow, someone—I'm not sure who—figured out what I was doing."

"You mean this, us coming here, was all you? Nobody else knew what you were doing?" Marc asked, shock in his voice.

McGill nodded. "It was a side project of mine. A personal project."

"That your superiors wouldn't have agreed to?" Marc guessed.

"That's correct."

A side project. Lilly felt sick. He made all five of them sound like cold, inanimate objects — or like rats in a lab.

George shifted his weight next to her, then clasped his hands behind his back. "And just who is after Gabe?" he demanded, his normal calm and gentle mannerisms replaced by obvious displeasure.

"I was informed by members of a UBF team about a group of soldiers responsible for the security of the TSIS lab. They found out I had shifted Gabe back here to 1503."

"Informed you?" Marc asked suspiciously. "I can't see anyone like Gabe or Harry just giving away information like that."

"Well…the truth is, I woke to find six men in my bedroom, and they demanded to know why I was sending some of their men back to 1503." He pushed his glasses up his nose.

"That sounds more like it," Marc snorted. "But if you didn't send them…who did?"

"It was Dr Penner, my supervisor." He looked at Lilly. "With an agreement for a *very* large sum of money, not only did she show them how to operate the TSIS trackers but also the main terminal in the lab. And when she had finished her lessons, they killed her. The UBF team I spoke with confirmed the method by which Dr Penner was murdered. It was a typical UBF kill."

"What's a typical kill?" Marc asked.

"One shot to the throat to silence, one in the heart to kill and one in the head so no memories can be extracted of who made the kill."

Marc went pale. "Whoa! I really didn't need to know that."

Lilly turned back to McGill. So that was why he had sounded off when he'd mentioned his supervisor on his last visit—she had been murdered. The thought caused her heart to pound in her chest. "Why do they care if Gabe was shifted back here?" she asked, afraid to know the answer. Because, whatever the reason, she had a feeling Gabe would be the next target for the men who had killed Dr Penner.

"Apparently, one of the men shifting back here let it slip they were going to finally see the legendary Gabriel Sutherland in action. The UBF team that paid me a visit told me not all of them enjoy having Gabe's talent thrown in their faces. They're here to see if he lives up to his reputation."

Lilly felt suddenly cold and her stomach lurched.

Chapter Twenty-Four

From his position on the ground, Gabe could just make out the tip of a rifle barrel. If he hadn't picked up the man's scent, he would have missed him lying flat against a thick tree branch.

Gabe never took his gaze off his target as he stopped breathing and just listened. Birds in the trees, leaves rustling, something small running along the ground, a breath. He cocked his head slightly in that direction, concentrating.

Another breath. It was slow, controlled.

Sniper.

He was wearing a ghillie suit, with added extras of local vegetation. Along with the smaller branch and leaves of the tree where he had made camp, it was excellent cover.

There was one sniper for every UBF team. In some cases, other members of a team were also sniper-qualified, himself included, but a truly gifted sniper was always a blessing to any team. Except in this case, the man was a curse. When the group of men protecting the queen travelled within range, the sniper, from his elevated position, would be able to watch and control the situation — or he could simply pick off his target and go on his merry way.

Gabe looked up. The branch the sniper was resting on was a good fifteen feet straight up. He ran through different scenarios in his head. Climbing up was out of the question — his weight against the tree would draw the sniper's unwanted attention. He could try drawing the man's fire and then shoot him, but the gunshots would draw attention from the rest of Eric's crew. He sighed, not liking his final option. He was going to have to knock the bastard out of that tree.

Still on his stomach, Gabe inched his way towards the tree. Without a sound, he pulled himself up tight against the thick trunk and edged around until he was standing under the branch the sniper was resting on.

Crouching low, he silently reached for the knife sheath strapped to his calf and slid the blade free. His muscles became tense as he centred himself. He took a deep, quiet breath, then launched himself straight up, arms stretched out above him.

The sniper had anchored himself to the tree, his legs straddling the branch. As Gabe leapt, he grabbed the man's thigh, locking on, and drove his knife deep. With Gabe's full weight on his now-wounded thigh, Gabe easily pulled him from the branch and the two men fell back to earth.

Pulling his knife free, Gabe landed first and rolled away before the sniper hit the ground. Clutching his thigh, the man landed hard on his side, his shoulder taking most of the impact, then groaned as he rolled onto his back, sucking air into his lungs.

Straightening, Gabe readied the knife as he walked towards the man and stood over him. The soldier looked up, confused one second, in shock the next. He started to struggle to his feet, groaning as he did.

Gabe placed one foot on the man's chest, holding him down with his weight. "You know me?" Gabe asked, puzzled by the man's obvious shock.

"Yes," the man heaved.

"How do you know me? Have we met?"

"No." The man's face was turning grey. He was losing blood fast.

Gabe increased the pressure on his chest. "How?"

"I'm UBF." His voice crackled with pain. Gabe eased back, taking some of his weight off the man's chest.

"I know what you are. It's the one thing keeping me from killing you. Now tell me how you know me." The words rumbled like a warning in his chest.

"All UBF members know you." The man clutched at the wound on his leg. "We're taught about you during the first few weeks of training. It's you—you and your fucking skills—that all UBF members are judged by."

Frowning at the man's statement, Gabe took note of the amount of blood flowing from his wound and its location on his thigh. The femoral artery had been severed. He was bleeding out. There wasn't much time.

"You came with a full team?"

"Yes." The sniper released his leg, groaning, and fell back, his breaths becoming shallow.

"What's the reason for targeting Queen Margaret?" Gabe took his foot off the man's chest and stared at him, unblinking.

"She's not the target." The soldier said with a bite. "She's the bait."

Gabe squatted down, holding his knife tightly, and studied the man.

"Who's the target?"

The sniper took a deep breath, his eyes glassy. Gabe nudged his shoulder. "Tell me who the target is," he commanded.

The sniper breathed the words out, closing his eyes. "You are."

* * * *

"Wait, what are you saying?" Marc asked.

"Why would they want to kill Gabe? You took him before any of these men were even born," George said, clearly appalled at the idea.

"It was always assumed Gabe was killed in action, and from that day, his legend grew." McGill paced around the room. "His scores on tests, his accuracy at the firing range, his reaction time and speed were all recorded. The UBF base their members' training on the standards Gabe set. And he set a very high standard. So high, in fact, that only a small percentage of UBF members have ever come close to it." He stopped in front of Lilly. "It would seem these men want to judge for themselves if they are up to snuff."

Lilly's heart squeezed in her chest as her mind filed the information.

No. This couldn't happen! She had just found Gabe. He'd said he would come back to her. Her lungs began to burn. She placed her hand on her chest and took a deep, ragged breath.

"Lilly," Marc said, wrapping his arm around her shoulder. "Weren't you listening? He said Gabe was the best." He gave her a little shake. "So good that the other soldiers can't keep up with him. He'll be fine."

Deep down, she knew he would be. She had only seen a small fraction of Gabe's abilities, and he was good.

But good or not, he was only one man, and there were six of them. Until she saw him again, she would be afraid for him.

"Lilly?" Marc's concern for her was touching, but she didn't trust her own voice. Instead, she nodded.

She caught McGill studying her, a sombre look on his face, and she got the distinct impression that he had just been hurt.

He nodded and looked at the floor. "I thought this might happen. I shouldn't really be surprised. Especially after I told you Gabe would take care of you. I just didn't think it would happen so fast."

Lilly knew instantly that *she* had hurt him. She'd never thought...

She'd had no idea McGill had feelings for her other than the friendship he'd mentioned. That didn't change the fact she'd hurt him, though. She stepped forward, wanting to give some sort of comfort, but still looking down he turned away from her, unaware of her intentions.

George caught at her arm, shaking his head at her. Fully understanding his meaning, Lilly stepped back between Marc and George.

"So," Marc changed the subject. "Do you have any idea who these men are?"

"The other UBF team gave me their names, but nothing rang any bells. They are just a group of soldiers who want to prove their worth."

"And by killing Gabe it will prove they are worthy?" Marc asked.

"Yes. Apparently they think so."

Chapter Twenty-Five

He was the target.

Why?

That single word had rebounded around his head since the sniper had told him. The man was dead, so there was no way to confirm it until he got his hands on one of the four still following them. He would have to wait to get his question answered. And he really wanted his question answered.

As they entered Lampton Kirk, Gabe and Harry put a greater distance between themselves and the small group once they spotted the king and his men waiting.

King James stopped in his tracks as he watched the group approach him. At first, he looked shocked to see his bride. Gabe wondered if it was that she had arrived sooner than he expected, or because she was so young. Regardless, the King of Scotland didn't hesitate and crossed to her, where he bowed formally, even going so far as to gently lift her off her horse.

"Well?" Harry asked, stopping his horse next to Gabe's. "Satisfied?"

"Yes." He had intentionally waited to see the King with his young wife. The idea still rubbed him the wrong way, but the King's initial reaction to Margaret seemed genuine, and the way he handled her gave Gabe the reassurance he'd been hoping for. "Let's go home."

Home. Back to Lilly.

Gabe turned his horse and urged it forward. He had never thought of this time as his home before. He had just thought about it as another mission, something else he had to survive. Lilly had done that, made him feel this way, and all because she was waiting for him to come back. He pictured her face every time he closed his eyes. The look she had given him as they made love the last time. The tender touch of her hand on his cheek.

Love? God, he hoped so.

* * * *

There were only four of them left.

A six man, highly trained UBF team had come to this time with their top-of-the-line weapons and two of them were already dead, without a single shot fired.

Sergeant Major Eric Graves smiled to himself, silently listening as the other three members of his team debated the best course of action. Sutherland really was good. But then, he had never been among those who doubted the man's skill.

"We only have a short window. His keep is no more than a full day's ride. We have to hit them now," Corporal Jason Hardy suggested.

Eric looked over at the kid. He had joined their team only a few short months ago, and was an easy mark for their officer-in-command, Lieutenant John Patterson, to dig his claws into.

"I agree," said Corporal Jill Norris. She was one of only five women who had proved themselves physically strong enough to qualify for the UBF. She was smart, funny and not hard to look at, but she, too, had fallen for John's way of thinking. She had also fallen for John.

Love. The ultimate weapon.

"Our chances have dropped significantly now that he's killed Gord and Paul. Paul's not such a big deal, but Gord would have upped our chances. And I assume we can all agree that once he's in that castle, it's going to be a bitch trying to get at him. He has his soldiers on an irregular patrol—their patterns change constantly."

"We've completed missions before without a sniper. Gord was a good asset, but not essential. We will complete the mission as agreed," Lieutenant John Patterson declared.

The officer-in-command of the UBF team was tall and lean, with ice blue eyes and blond hair, a long, straight nose and concave cheeks. Yet what he lacked in physical appearance, he more than made up for in skill. He had been the one to plan this mission—a mission John believed would redeem them in the eyes of the other teams. Eric knew better. All they had to do was finish their time babysitting the TSIS and get the hell out of there.

Boring but easy.

Then John had become friends with Dr Penner and set this plan in motion. It was a bad plan, but Eric couldn't just walk away.

Keeping his eyes forward, Eric felt the weight of John's glare. "I think Jill is right, we should hit them before he enters the keep. What do you think, Eric?" John rubbed his pointed chin.

Inhaling deeply, Eric looked around the surrounding forest and, with an evil smile, turned to face his three team mates.

"What are you smiling at?" John asked, annoyance in his ice blue eyes.

"You don't have a choice anymore." Eric leaned to the side just as a bullet flew past his head.

* * * *

Harry lowered his rifle and smiled. "Oh, he's good. Did you see?" He squinted. "He knew right away we were here."

Gabe nodded, lowering his infrared scope. Frowning, he studied the man with the dark hair.

"What is it?" Harry asked cradling his rifle in his thick arms.

"Not sure. I still get the feeling I've seen him before." There was something familiar about him, his casual confidence, the almost evil smile he gave his OC. What sparked the feeling of awareness were the dimples that appeared when he smiled. He had seen those dimples in the same location on another. He just couldn't remember who that person was.

Harry raised his rifle and tracked the man through his scope. "Mmm. He does look a little familiar. Can't place it, though." Harry scanned the area, locating the three remaining soldiers.

"Two stationary, in front, a hundred and twenty-five feet. Two moving fast on each side." Harry lowered his rifle. "Oh no! I think they're going to box us in." He turned to Gabe with raised eyebrows. "Is it time to panic yet?"

Gabe chuckled.

"Maybe we should let them." Harry gave him a wide smile. "Make things a little interesting."

Gabe slapped his friend on his shoulder, giving him a wicked smile. "It's scary, how much we think alike."

Harry chuckled.

"Let's take the two flanking us first, then move on to the OC and his sergeant major. I want one of those two alive—I have a few questions I need answered."

"Roger," Harry answered, before moving swiftly into the dense forest.

Gabe froze, listening. The soldier who was flanking him was close. Gabe could hear the softly placed steps. He closed his eyes and inhaled. He was upwind from the soldier, but the scent was very close, and there was an unusual subtlety to it. The light brushing of fabric against fabric caused Gabe to tense, and the sound of hands tightening on a gun had his eyes snapping open.

Gabe whirled to face the soldier stalking him, stepping to the side just as the man took his shot.

Gabe blinked. Not a man.

A woman.

With his body already in motion, he continued with his attack and grabbed the barrel of the gun, forcing it up.

Another shot.

Gabe used the full weight of his body to slam the soldier into the ground, briefly knocking the wind out of her. She recovered quickly and struggled under him. Fighting hard, she managed to get an arm free and slammed her fist, followed by her elbow, into the side of his face. Woman or not, Gabe wasn't taking that, and slammed his body hard down onto hers a second time, knocking her head back on the ground. She was dazed by his blow, and Gabe was able to grab her hands and pin them over her head.

She glared up at him, hate in her amber eyes. Gabe gazed back calmly and asked, "Having fun playing with the boys?"

Her nostrils flared as she glared up at him, but she remained silent.

He hadn't been a big believer in women being able to join the UBF, until he'd had a woman in his first team. She had been fast and agile, could handle herself in a fight and was good with a gun. Not to mention, she could fit into small places that he and the other men couldn't. His opinion had changed after that.

"Did you really think I would stand still and let you shoot me?"

She shrugged. "It would have been the polite thing to do. But I'll still get my kill. I always do."

Gabe studied her face, watched her pulse. She wasn't lying. She would try to kill him again, and keep trying, until either she succeeded or he killed her. That was something he would rather avoid, but if it came down to it, he knew he wouldn't hesitate.

Gabe gave her a smile that didn't quite reach his eyes. "That makes two of us."

A shot rang out, and the woman took advantage. Planting her feet, she thrust up with her hips with such force that Gabe went flying over her head. Letting go, he rolled onto his side, pulling his knife free, and quickly came to his feet, knife at the ready.

The woman chuckled as she took her aim.

"You'll never make the kill. And I don't care what we were taught—Gabriel Sutherland is not faster than a bullet." She blew a strand of her cherry-red hair away from her eyes. "Why bother trying?"

Gabe studied his target, looking for the best point of entry. She was wearing a slightly modified version of his armoured shirt. From what he could see, she had upper vital protection only, leaving the rest of her body open.

He inhaled slowly, keeping his adrenaline under control, then smiled, cocking his head to the side.

"What are you smiling at? I'm going to kill you," she gritted out between clenched teeth. Gun raised, her finger rested lightly on the trigger.

"You shouldn't have hesitated." Another shot rang out, and Gabe threw the knife at the same moment the woman's gun was struck by Harry's bullet. A searing pain pulsed in Gabe's arm, but his aim held true. The woman dropped to her knees, clutching at the knife in her throat, and fell to the side.

Harry stepped up beside him, looking at his arm. "All right?"

Gabe looked down at the blood soaking his shirt. He moved his arm, flexing the muscle. "Just a nick."

Harry nodded, then stepped over the body lying on the ground and squatted next to it. "Shit. I thought mine was bad. Fuck, I hate these ones."

Gabe nodded. He hated them, too.

A woman. A being who could bring life into the world. His stomach rolled. Ignoring it, he concentrated on Harry's statement, instead. "What was yours?" he asked, eyeing Harry as he stood.

"A kid, early twenties. Had some skill, too. A bloody waste." He shook his head.

"A waste. Both of them," Gabe agreed.

"Although," Harry raised his eyebrows, "yours looks as though she gave you a run for your money. That eye sure looks pretty."

Gabe touched the tender skin under his eye.

"I don't know about you, but it really pisses me off that these two soldiers were wasted on us." Harry slid his gun into his chest holster hidden under his cotton shirt. "Shall we go and take out our aggression on their OC?"

Gabe smiled, flexing his shoulders. "Sounds good."

Reaching for the reins of his horse, Gabe saddled in a quick, fluid movement and turned in the direction of the remaining two men.

"Gabe," Harry called. "Your knife."

Gabe turned to the woman lying on the ground, his knife buried deep in her neck. "Leave it." His stomach rolled again. "I have another."

Chapter Twenty-Six

The warm glow of the fire caused shadows to flicker across the ceiling. Lilly waited for her eyes to adjust as she stared up at the shadows. She was so tired her eyes burnt and her head pounded. She should have taken George's advice and drunk Edna's sleeping tea. She would have, too, if her stomach didn't feel so upset. She couldn't even look at food — there was no way tea would stay down.

She had felt sick ever since McGill had told her that there were men here trying to kill Gabe.

Gabe.

She missed him. So much, it scared her at times. All she'd been able to think about for the past few days had been what her life would be without him. This was the direct cause of her nauseous stomach, the pounding in her head and the overall feeling of wanting to curl up into a ball and fade away.

She rested her hand on her forehead. This was not good. She felt like she was about to break apart. She knew if something happened to Gabe she *would* fade away. She would go into her own mind and stay there, replay their time together over and over until she died from old age. That, too, scared her. The feelings she had for him were so profound that without him she would simply disappear from life.

A high-pitched laugh echoed in her head. Who was she kidding? She'd been halfway there before she'd even met him, and now she'd had a taste of what being loved was like, when the time came for it to be taken away, she would be a goner. And it was always, always taken away.

Closing her eyes, she rolled onto her side, groaning from the pain in her head. Her heart jumped when the bed shifted slightly. A faint scuffing sound trailed softly around the chamber. She held her breath, feeling her heart pounding in her chest. Who was that? How had they got in here? The bed moved again and she heard the sound of water splashing into a bowl. With her curiosity getting the better of her, she pushed up onto her elbows to see the intruder.

Lilly stared in disbelief at the sight of Gabe resting against the wooden trunk at the end of the bed.

It *was* Gabe. It *had* to be. She watched, as he wrung the water out of a cloth and began patting his opposite arm. His shirt was off and Lilly could see the hard, well-defined muscles of his back and shoulders. Her eyes became blurry from staring for so long, and she blinked again.

Gabe. It was him.

Slowly pushing herself into a sitting position, she threw the covers aside and swung her legs off the bed, keeping her eyes glued to him the entire time.

Her heart stopped beating as she rounded the end of the bed.

She needed to see his face, so she could believe it was truly him.

Gabe looked up as she stopped at the corner of the bed, his intense, green eyes glowing at her.

Gabe.

He was back. But how?

"There were six soldiers! They were going to kill you! McGill said—"

"Yes, there were six," he interrupted her. "And they did try, but they were unsuccessful." He put the cloth into the bowl, and said, "I made you a promise. Tell me what it was."

Lilly didn't even have to think—the answer came out the instant she opened her mouth. "That you would come back."

He nodded. "I don't break my promises. Now." He looked her up and down, a hungry smile curling his lips.

Lilly became acutely aware she was wearing only the sheer undershirt. "Come here."

Her first instinct was to throw herself at him, but she hid her weakness from him and stepped in front of him.

"Lilly." Her name came out a rumbled warning as his hands locked onto her hips. He roughly hauled her against his chest and fastened his mouth over hers.

Lilly allowed the heat to race though her and impulsively stroked her tongue along his bottom lip. He tasted wonderful—erotic and hungry. Her head began to spin.

Gabe.

Her heart swelled with such love for him it felt like it was going to burst. She pulled her mouth away and ran her hands into the hair hanging low down the back of his neck.

She stared into his dark face and bit her lip, trying desperately to keep her feelings inside. And the harder she tried to keep the feelings to herself, the stronger the desire was to tell him. She needed a distraction and lightly touched the darkened skin around his eye.

"Your eye."

"It's fine." He continued to watch her until she couldn't hold it in any longer.

"I... I..." she whispered, choking, trying to get the words out. Tears blurred her vision.

"What?" He tightened his grip on her hips.

She focused on his chest and quietly finished, "...love you."

Before she could blink, his hands flew up and cupped her face, forcing her to look at him. "Do you mean it?" His grip on her face became almost too tight. His chest muscles tensed under her palms, as though he was preparing himself for a blow.

Of course she meant it. She loved him. Her brows pushed together, and her chest heaved as the words rushed out. "I wasn't sure at first if what I was feeling was love, because I've never been in love. And everything has happened so fast... And I never thought... But when you were gone and McGill told us about the other team..."

Gabe's glare was so severe, but he said nothing and continued to listen to her ramble on. He had never looked at her like this. She knew right then she had made a huge mistake in telling him, but she just couldn't keep her feelings in any longer. She closed her eyes and tears slipped into her lashes.

"All I could think about was how empty I would feel if something bad happened to you. It felt like part of my heart was missing."

Gabe exhaled slowly. Lilly loved him. It was there on her face, in her tears, laid out for him to see. His chest constricted and his heart swelled. She shouldn't love him—she deserved better. Yet he would never allow her to go, not now—he was going to be selfish.

Touching his forehead to hers, he asked, "You mean it, don't you?"

"Yes." Her voice sounded so small, so forlorn.

"Don't do that—don't be sorry you told me." He brushed his lips over hers. "I've waited all my life to hear you say that."

Fresh tears slid down her cheeks.

"Don't cry, angel." He wiped his thumbs over her damp cheeks. Her silent tears ripped at his heart, until finally he'd had enough and pressed his mouth against hers.

During his entire life, he'd never thought this love he felt for Lilly could ever be his. In his time, this was never a possibility. UBF members didn't marry—it was against orders. Even a steady lover was frowned upon. He had to come to the past and found what he'd never been allowed. He was so damn lucky.

Slowly, he fed on her mouth, running his tongue along the soft contours, tracing her scar, and finally nipping gently, coaxing her mouth into opening for him. He loved her sweet, innocent taste—it made him want to devour her. Running his hands down her back, he cupped her behind and massaged, satisfied when she leaned in to him, sighing. She was lightly trailing her hands over his chest and arms, her need growing to match his own. He felt a light tug at his breeches, followed by the loosening of the drawstring. Lilly stroked his cock through the thin material and he groaned when the torment stopped.

Stepping back, Lilly gripped Gabe's hands and pulled him until he was standing. He stared down at her, desire etched into her lovely face, her eyes a beautiful rich chocolate brown. Closing the gap, she stroked his cheek and lightly ran her fingers over the bruise at the corner of his eye, then trailed her finger over his cheek to his mouth, where she traced his lips. She lightly scraped her nails down his chest, stopping to touch the hard muscles of his stomach. Then, pushing his breeches down, she clasped his thick erection in her hand. Pressing her mouth to his hot skin, she began kissing his chest as she started to stroke his shaft.

* * * *

He smelt so good, like the outdoors. She licked at his hard nipple and smiled when he sucked in a breath. She loved the feeling of power she had when she touched him, and Gabe was so patient with her, allowing her to explore his body and take her time. But this time it felt different — she wasn't nervous or afraid of her desire. She wanted him — all of him.

Squeezing his erection, she moved her hand down the length and watched as he closed his eyes.

All of him. She repeated the words to herself.

She kissed her way down his stomach, flicked her tongue around the outside of his navel to his lower belly, where she was kneeling in front of him. His thick shaft pulsed in her hand.

She looked up at him as she licked the tip of the sensitive head.

He slid his hand over the side of her face and tangled his fingers in her hair as she took him in her mouth and began a slow, rhythmic pace. She swirled her tongue over the head, smiling to herself when he sucked in a ragged breath. It was nice to know that she wasn't the only that had trouble breathing during sex.

Allowing his rich, male taste to fill her mouth, Lilly continued sliding her mouth up and down, taking him deeper and deeper into her mouth until she became almost lost in the heady, erotic sensation.

"Enough." Gabe's strong hands lifted her. His expression was dark, his mouth pulled into a straight line, his nostrils flared as he struggled to catch his breath. She smiled — she couldn't help it. His expression softened as he lowered his hand to the top of her breasts, hooking a finger around the neckline of her sheer gown. "This is the last time this will be in my way."

Before she had time to blink, Gabe withdrew a knife from his back and, holding the neckline, sliced through the thin fabric, straight to the bottom.

Lilly's mouth dropped open. Gabe watched her as he returned his knife to behind his back. A sexy smile curved up the corners of his mouth when the material slid off her shoulders and pooled around her feet.

Red-faced and still shocked, she blurted out, "Now I don't have a nightshirt."

Chuckling, he reached for her, gripping her waist. "You don't need one." He pulled her close, taking control of her mouth, sliding his tongue in deep, moving his hands over her body, finally stopping on her bottom. He kneaded the flesh as he kissed her neck, ran his tongue over her racing pulse. Bending her backwards, he kissed his way to her breasts. Lilly locked her hands in his hair to keep him close — she didn't want him to stop. His mouth on her skin, the licking and nibbling, was heavenly. She inhaled deeply when he drew her nipple into his warm mouth and sucked hard. A blast of euphoric heat flew through her body, causing a hot, relentless need.

Moving against him, Lilly arched her back, pressing her breast further into his mouth. She ached for him, wanted him so much she thought she would cry out if it didn't happen soon.

"Gabe." His name came out a husky plea.

"I know, angel." His hot breath burnt her skin. "I want you, too." He pulled her upright and said, "Lock your arms around my neck."

She didn't think she would have the strength — his kisses had left her body feeling rubbery. But as soon as she held on to him, Gabe lifted her until she felt his thick erection drive into her body.

Rolling her head to the side, Gabe traced his tongue along the side of her neck, leaving a warm wet trail to her ear. His breath was hot on her skin as he dug his hands into the backs of her thighs, driving into her again, the invasion pure ecstasy. Then, lifting her slowly, he allowed her to take control. He slid his tongue in her mouth as she moved against him. She whimpered into his mouth as her nipples brushed against his chest and her hips jerked against him, the steady pulsing in her core becoming almost unbearable. He gripped her tighter, pinned her against his chest and growled, "I want more."

Carrying her to the edge of the bed, he laid her down, his body deep in hers. Looking down, Gabe stopped, a puzzled frown on his face.

He traced the scar on her lip. "You love me."

Her heart melted when she heard the wonder in his voice. "Yes."

"Tell me again," he demanded, embedded deep within her. "Tell me you love me."

She covered his hand where it rested on the side of her face. "I love you, Gabe."

He closed his eyes and covered her mouth in a possessive kiss.

Gabe moved, then. Lifting her hips, he drove into her and began a hard, fast pace, so deep they were one. Her hands cupped his face, pulling him down. She tried to kiss him but his hard, forceful thrusts had her moaning against his mouth instead. It was too much. The touching, the kissing, his body moving deep in hers, the love she felt for him. It was all consuming, and she prayed it would never end.

Gabe eased back and moved his hand down between their joined bodies, gently stroking her sensitive clit while he drove into her in long, slow strokes. She covered his hand, holding it in place when the pulsing took over. A low groan rumbled in his chest and he quickened the pace just as her body shivered. Gabe captured her mouth just as she cried out his name.

Chapter Twenty-Seven

"Where's McGill?" Gabe asked, taking a seat next to Harry.

"I sent Charles to get him."

Gabe nodded at Edna as she placed a wooden plate in front of him, filled with salted meat, hard cheese and chunks of bread. He slid the food into the centre of the small, round table.

Gabe looked up at George and Marc, who sat across from him. "How long has he been here?"

"Two days." George replied, clasping his hands together. "And I don't mind telling you, he gave us quite a fright. He painted a very grim picture."

"Yeah!" Marc mumbled, a piece of food in his mouth. "Especially Lilly—she was really scared." A playful smirk came to his young face. "But don't worry. I took care of her for you."

Gabe turned to Harry, struggling not to smile, then back to Marc. He raised an eyebrow. "You did, did you?"

"Marc," George warned. "Gabe just got back, don't wind him up."

Marc shoved a piece of cheese into his mouth. "What?" he grumbled. "It's the bloody truth. I was the one to tell her not to worry about Gabe—I said he would be fine." He looked Gabe in the eye and shrugged. "I was right."

Gabe gave up the struggle and smiled at the kid. Damn, he was happy to be back. He knew Lilly was the main reason, but Marc and George and, of course, Harry had a hand in his feeling of contentment. They were a strange family of sorts, all thrown together by death and a very odd little man. It was amazing the way life had changed.

Harry elbowed him in the side as McGill hurried across the great hall towards their table.

"I'm sorry to keep you waiting." He stopped, looked around the table, pulled his glasses from his pocket and pushed them up his nose. "Where's Lilly?"

"She's still sleeping." Gabe watched the nervous little man carefully.

"We should wait for Lilly, she should be here."

"No," Gabe said calmly. "We will have our talk, and I will fill her in later." He had spent most of the night making love to her, and had opted to let her sleep. He'd left her after giving her a light kiss on the forehead. "Apparently, you gave her quite a scare."

McGill grimaced. "It wasn't intentional. But I don't think she would have liked if I'd lied to her."

"No, she wouldn't have," Gabe agreed, then fixed his glare on McGill. "But I don't like her being scared. So don't do it again."

The man nodded nervously, sweat gathering on his brow. Damn, the man was skittish. Yet for some strange reason it didn't bother him like it usually did.

"Sit down, Professor. Tell me the reason behind this UBF team wanting me dead."

Gabe cocked his head to the side, trying to focus on the scent. It was the third time he'd smelt it since McGill had begun his story. It was light, with no strong emotional attachment, and somewhat familiar — yet he couldn't place it. He had got used to the different scents in the keep and surrounding area, and this scent didn't belong to the UBF soldiers he and Harry had dealt with in the forest. Of course, he hadn't picked up all their scents.

"That team must have fucked up big time if they got posted on guard duty," Harry commented. "Why wouldn't they just have done their time, then moved on?" Harry shook his head. "On the bright side" — he slapped Gabe on the shoulder — "it's good to know Gabe is considered a celebrity of sorts and my time wasn't a complete waste." Harry turned to Marc and George. "I taught him everything he knows."

Gabe snorted. "The only thing you taught me was where the mess hall was. The rest was entirely me."

The four men laughed, but McGill didn't. "You're taking this lightly. Aren't there still two members of this team out there" — he waved his hand — "somewhere? Ready to kill you?"

"Yes, there are, and Harry and I have already put a plan into place."

"Which is?" George asked.

"We wait for them to come to us," Harry announced.

"Huh?" Marc choked on the piece of bread in his mouth. George slapped him on the back, until he could clear his throat. "What?" he croaked.

"Why would you do that?" McGill asked curiously, the scientist in him coming to the surface.

"When they come, they'll be in our home. And nobody knows this keep better than Gabe and I."

McGill leant forward. "A mouse, trapped in a maze?"

"That's the idea..." Gabe trailed off. A fresh scent swept into the room, it was familiar, with a hint of rose. The four men stood and Gabe turned, coming to his feet just as Lilly reached his side.

"Good morning." She smiled at the men, her gaze stopping on him last. She looked so pretty this morning, wearing a soft blue dress that gave her a fresh appearance—or maybe it was the flush mixed with her freckles that did that. He wasn't sure, but he liked how her dark hair was pulled back at the sides, giving him a clear view of her pretty face.

Stepping past him, she stopped in front of Harry and gave him a quick hug. "I'm so glad you're back." She patted his shoulder and stood back, smiling at him.

Gabe tensed, ready for a possessive feeling to take hold, but it didn't come. Lilly cared for Harry and the others—he could see that—but that look of love she gave him wasn't there when she looked at the others. Her love was his, and his alone.

Harry smiled. "Thank you, Lilly." He said warmly. "That's very nice to hear."

Gabe raised his eyebrows, surprised by the comment. Never, in all the time Gabe had known Harry, had he ever spoken so...kindly.

Gabe shot him a questioning look, but the only explanation he received was a shrug. He grabbed a stool for Lilly and placed it next to his, but she stepped back.

"It's very grey today and will probably rain soon. I wanted to go for a quick walk into the village and back."

Gabe tensed. It wasn't safe. Not with Eric and the team's leader running around out there. When he had spoken with George late the night before, he had explained that Lilly had gone for a walk every day since he'd left. Sometimes she'd gone two or three times a day. George believed that because her brain was constantly in motion and she was lacking her normal daily stimulation, the physical activity was a way for her to compensate.

How could he stop her from doing something that was essential for her well-being?

The answer was simple. He couldn't.

Later on, he would sit down with George and come up with ways to keep her mind active and healthy — beside the physical, more intimate activities that would benefit them both.

"Okay." He nodded, but added for his own peace of mind, "Can you make it a quick one? Charles will escort you and there will be others close by." He angled her mouth up to his and kissed her. "Take my cloak. It's cold."

He probably shouldn't have done that. To show any sort of affection was unusual for him, but when it came to Lilly, it seemed to be in overdrive. Had he kissed Lilly in front of the other men to show she belonged to him? Probably.

Harry, George and Marc were smiling approvingly. McGill didn't look happy, but to be honest he didn't care. He sat and turned his attention back to the professor. "What else can you tell me about these men?"

* * * *

Lilly wrapped Gabe's cloak more tightly around her. The wind had picked up and a cold drizzle accompanied it.

As usual, when she passed the last cottage before the end of the village, the elderly man who lived there gave her a wave as he tended to his ever-growing flock of chickens. She returned the wave and continued on her way. The grey clouds moved quickly overhead and Lilly decided to pick up the pace before the weather turned worse. The rain never bothered her, but she wasn't alone. She looked behind her at the three men escorting her. They would probably disagree.

At the edge of the village, she heard what sounded like a child whimpering. She stopped and looked into the forest. With no sun to light the forest, it was too dark to see clearly, the grey clouds causing deeper than normal shadows. She stepped closer to the forest. Nothing. Taking another step, Lilly struggled to see into the thick foliage.

"My lady? It is not safe." Charles appeared at her side, the others close behind.

"Didn't you hear that?" she asked.

Charles stepped ahead of her, listening, when she heard the cry for a second time.

Charles looked back at her, holding out his arm when she tried to pass him.

"We can't just stand here. That's a child—we have to help!" The soft cry reached them again. "Charles, she sounds so scared. What if she's hurt?" She pushed past him and followed the cry.

"Wait, my lady!" Lilly heard Charles curse, then order, "Inform Lord Sutherland there may be an injured child in the forest."

The crying became louder, more urgent, and Lilly followed the sound until she spotted a little girl next to a large tree. She had seen the little girl before, running around the village with a few of the other children. She was sweet-looking, with white-blonde hair and big, blue eyes.

"Hello." Lilly stopped a few feet from the child, not wanting to scare her any more than she already was. "What's your name?"

Charles stepped up to her side as the child answered, "Isabelle." The girl sniffed and wiped at her tears with the back of her hand then, looking up at the tree, asked, "Can I go home and see Mama now?"

Charles suddenly pushed Lilly behind his back, the other soldier moving to join him as the man stepped out from behind the tree. The sound of the gun firing was no more than a whisper, yet Lilly still jumped at the sound. The soldier next to her fell to the ground, blood slowly seeping from the small hole in his heart.

Dragging her eyes away from the dead body, she looked at the little girl, who seemed confused by the scene. Then she looked at the blond with the gun.

This was not the man she had dreamt about—this was not Eric. There was hate in his ice blue eyes, and the smile on his thin face was cruel when the little girl started to cry.

"Shut up," he hissed, towering over the small child.

"Don't even think about it, John," said a calm, deep voice from behind another tree.

Lilly looked in the direction of the familiar voice and watched as Eric stepped out into the open. He crossed to the little girl and smiled down as he touched her soft hair. "Go home to your mama. Quickly now." And he gave her a gentle shove.

With his larger frame still protectively in front of her, Charles demanded, "What do you want?"

Instead of answering the question, John, the one with the blond hair, simply raised his gun and, without blinking, fired.

* * * *

Gabe bolted for the door the moment Lilly's cry reached him. The cry wasn't piercing, but more of a muted sob. It was faint, giving the impression Lilly was on the far side of the village, maybe in the forest. That sound of fear and shock drove him hard. He didn't have to be next to her to know she was terrified.

With fear and adrenaline pumping through his body, he drew his gun, not caring about the shocked expressions of the villagers he passed, and ran full speed through the courtyard.

An out-of-breath soldier came running towards him. "My lord, in the forest, there's a—"

That was all Gabe caught as he ran past. A heavy pounding from behind told him he wasn't alone, and

Harry appeared at his side as he sprinted through the village.

"It's them." Harry pulled his gun from his under his shirt.

"I know."

"They have her," Harry growled.

"I know."

Gun raised and ready, Gabe slowed his pace and, hunching slightly, made himself a smaller target as he stepped into the forest. He inhaled slowly, deeply. There was no way he would miss any possible targets. He inhaled a second time and stopped.

Lilly.

The muscles in his back and shoulders tightened as the scent of her fear filled his chest.

Closing his eyes, he inhaled again and focused. Two scents. The first reeked of hate, excitement and sweat. The other was that same, subtle scent he had picked up earlier today while in the keep. Gabe's jaw clenched tight, pulling at the muscles in his temples.

Eric.

The bastard had been in his home, close to *his* family, close to *his* Lilly.

Making eye contact with Harry, Gabe raised two fingers and pointed in their direction. Harry nodded and moved to the right, disappearing into the thick brush.

Slowly pressing forward, Gabe blocked out the scent of Lilly's fear and focused on the scents of the two men he was going to kill.

* * * *

"He's coming." Eric crossed his arms.

"Yes. Thanks," John hissed.

Raising an eyebrow, Eric regarded his team leader steadily. What a fool. John was about to die and he didn't even have enough sense to realise it. He was so consumed with revenge it blocked out all sane thought. In all fairness, Sutherland was reacting the same way. He didn't understand why these two soldiers were allowing their emotions to rule their actions, when they had been trained not to.

He looked over at Lilly. He could see why Sutherland wanted her. But he could fight his desires, his needs. Why couldn't Sutherland? What had changed? What was it about this woman that made him react this way?

John pulled a tracker from his pack, along with the piece of paper with the information Dr Penner had given him, and began punching in longitude and latitude, the time and date.

The situation was getting out of his control — it was time to rein John back in.

"Do you really think shifting her will help your little mission?" he said. "He's going to kill you for this, and bury your body where no one will ever find it."

John finished entering the arrival date into the tracker. "You sound scared, Eric," he mocked. "Though I'm not sure why. You're the only one ever to test as high as Sutherland. You stand a better chance than me."

Eric lost emotion.

"What?" John asked, straight-faced. "You seem surprised that I know your test scores." He laughed. "Why do you think you were transferred onto my team? I wanted the best, and with your scores it seemed guaranteed. Until that bitch Kim. All she had to do was stay low and let us protect her until she testified in court, and she would have been free to go. But she had to skip out on us to see her rebel boyfriend, and get herself shot. That bitch screwed us over. All of us."

Eric stepped closer. "She was a task. Nothing more."

John's finger rested on the track button. As soon as he pushed the blinking green light, there would be no way to stop the TSIS from tracking Lilly.

He would have to kill John. There was no other way.

Fuck. It shouldn't have come down to this. Killing a UBF member was like killing a brother. In this case it was an evil, vengeful brother — but a brother all the same.

Slowing his breathing, Eric watched John closely. It would have to be quick and without any warning, because even with his erratic behaviour, John was still a UBF soldier and trained to pick up any unfriendly movements.

Inhaling one last time, Eric stopped smiling. He shifted his gaze to Lilly. Apparently, he wasn't the only one who wouldn't allow this to happen.

Chapter Twenty-Eight

Lilly stared wide-eyed at Eric—she couldn't help herself. When he'd turned and looked at her, she could have sworn she was looking at Gabe. But it wasn't Gabe. It was Eric.

Wait...

Her brain went into overdrive. She quickly pulled away into her own memories and replayed the conversation she'd had with Gabe.

How many women were you matched with? Even though the conversation had already taken place, her stomach still rolled when he answered.

I was matched with fifty different women.

Do you have any children with any of these women? She paused the scene and studied Gabe. His green eyes and his naturally intense stare. The shape of his chin and the bone structure of his cheeks...

Eric's mouth curled into an evil smile before he turned his attention back to John.

John glared at Eric. "You seem to think I'm the only one he'll kill. You're part of this team too, Eric."

"Not by choice." Lilly watched as Eric took another step closer to John.

"I told you, I wanted the best."

Eric smiled that wicked smile again. "Yes, you did. Now I'm going to tell you the real reason I was transferred onto your team."

"What the fuck are you talking about?" John snarled.

In a calm, emotionless voice, Eric explained. "Your leadership was in question and I was added to your team to report any misconduct. Your request for my transfer just happened at the same time. So we used it." Eric shrugged his broad shoulders.

"Misconduct? That's bullshit. I've never done..." John trailed off, staring at Eric. "Jill?" the blond asked quietly. "This is because of Jill?"

"No. This is because you and Jill were lovers. That's against regulations. And you know it. Kim Rivers was your responsibility to protect. She wouldn't have made it out of the safe house and been shot if you two had been doing your jobs like you were supposed to. It's a classic example of *why* we're not allowed to marry, not allowed to get attached. It interferes with the job."

There was a brief pause as the men eyed one another. Lilly became a statue, too scared to even move and, without any choice, absorbed the scene before her.

The cool air around them became still and heavy.

Eric raised his rifle at the same moment John raised his handgun.

Lilly held her breath.

"I don't get it," Eric said, his eyes never leaving John. "You were screwed the second Colonel Spencer found out about Jill. How could you let it happen?"

John shook his head, his gun pointing at Eric. "Things were fine when the others were around, but when they left and it was just the two of us... I couldn't always control myself. And nothing mattered then. Nothing but Jill."

Eric's accusing look turned to one of puzzlement.

John laughed bitterly. "You have no idea what it's like. To have someone. That need to hear her voice, to be near her, to touch her, to keep her safe. And then knowing she feels the way you do..." His voice turned cold, as he bit out, "But it doesn't matter now, does it? Because she's dead. He killed her. And I won't stop until he feels *this*." John's face turned into a mask of grief and rage. "This hollow pain. Why couldn't he just die like we planned —"

John stopped, realisation crossing his slender face. "You helped him, didn't you?"

"No," Eric said, his finger hovering above the trigger. "I didn't. I just didn't help you."

"At the edge of the forest, when we launched the arrows. We followed your lead."

"Yes, you did," Eric agreed.

"You hesitated on purpose," John accused.

"Even if I hadn't, it wouldn't have made a difference. Sutherland would still have survived."

"You fucking traitor," John snarled.

Eric lowered his head slightly and glared up from under dark, slashing brows. "The feeling's mutual."

The two men glared at each other. Lilly had listened quietly while they spoke, absorbing every word. John was going to kill her to get revenge on Gabe, because he had killed John's lover. A woman named Jill.

She frowned, a heart-sick feeling growing in her stomach.

A woman. A shiver ran down her spine at the thought but she quickly blocked out the idea, refusing to believe Gabe, the man she loved, would do such a thing. Shaking her head, she focused on the tracker in John's hand.

"I'm sorry all this happened. Gabe would never hurt—"

John's dry laugh cut her off. "How long have you known Sutherland? Two minutes." "We"—he nodded at Eric—"had to study him, the battles he was in and how he made his kills. All his kills—both men and women. Your Gabe is just as guilty as the rest of us. Maybe more."

Lilly struggled to absorb the new information.

Oh, God.

She took a breath, hoping it would calm her. She wasn't stupid—she'd always known Gabe had killed—he'd told her he'd killed Harry's would-be assassins. But a woman was different, wasn't it? Maybe on some level she'd already known what he was capable of—it would explain why, at first, she had reacted to him with such visceral fear. Until they had become lovers. Had gaining her trust just been part of his training? A way to control the people around him, to utilise every asset given to him?

No. She fought her conscience. Gabe wouldn't do that. Would he?

She was so confused her head was spinning in circles.

Tears pooled, but she fought hard to keep them from spilling over. Swallowing, she asked, "But how will killing me make everything right?"

"It won't. It will, however, give me a great deal of satisfaction knowing the 'perfect soldier' can't save the one person he loves. And technically, I'm not going to kill you." He gave her a sympathetic smile. "The tower will."

Her entire body seized up. *The tower.* He was going to send her back. To work, where the CN Tower would crush her. She shook her head.

"That can't... But how...? It's impossible." Terror at the mere idea had her stumbling over her words.

"With these little trackers" — he waved the tracker for her to see — "and the right time and date, anything is possible." He pressed the button.

"Damn it, John." The words mixed with what sounded like a low growl as Eric pushed forward with his rifle, eyes locked onto his target.

Oh, God! Eric was going to shoot John. Lilly prepared herself for the violence. Seconds passed without a sound. Eric appeared frozen in place, until he suddenly lowered his gun and backed away from John.

"Well, now, this is a pleasant surprise." John smirked, his gun still aimed at Eric.

What was happening? Why was Eric backing away?

Then she saw it. In the trees behind John. A large, dark shadow, moving steadily towards the clearing. It reached the edge of the clearing, just behind John. Dried leaves crackled as Gabe stepped out from the shadows.

All of a sudden the scene before her sped up. John turned at the noise, his gun swinging wide, looking for a target. Gabe, standing close behind John, grabbed the short barrel, stopping the movement. With a speed she would never have thought possible, Gabe had wrapped his other arm around John's neck, his fingers digging in to the tender skin on the man's throat.

John fought hard, thrashing his body around in effort to free himself, clawing at Gabe with his one free hand.

Lilly stared in horrified silence as John's face went purple. Dropping the gun, he tried to prise Gabe's hand off him. It proved to be a fatal move. Gabe quickly took advantage and, grabbing his head in a death grip, twisted it violently to the side. She twitched as the loud crack echoed around them and the limp body fell to the ground.

A creepy silence surrounded the clearing, as though the forest was in shock at the violence that had just taken place.

She stared at the body, his eyes wide, mouth—

"Lilly." Gabe's soft command caused her to blink, but she still couldn't look away. One minute, John had been fighting to live and the next…

"Lilly," Gabe snapped, stepping over the body. "Look at me."

She obeyed and saw him moving slowly towards her, but he stopped, his hands clenched into fists. He was studying her again, not with his normal curiosity, but with concern.

"Don't." He shook his head.

"Don't what?"

"You're scared."

"Yes," she admitted.

She could see his nostrils flare before he asked, "Of me?"

Was she scared of Gabe, or the acts he was capable of? The actions of a trained soldier.

"You told me about your training. I knew you were capable of... It's just that..." She stopped, tripping over her words.

Gabe could smell the fear pouring off her and he needed to make sure he wasn't the cause—well, at least not the entire cause.

"Lilly," he began slowly. "I've killed before. It was what I was trained to do. I'm sorry you had to see that. It's not the part of me I wanted you to see."

"It's easy for you, isn't it?"

He gave her a roundabout answer. "I don't tolerate those who would try to kill innocent people."

"Was...was Jill one of those people?"

She knew. That sickening feeling he'd had when he'd killed the woman twisted in his gut. But he told Lilly the truth. "Yes, she was."

"You killed her."

He nodded as she struggled to keep eye contact with him.

"Okay." She finally looked away, confusion and pain in her eyes.

"She was a fully trained UBF soldier, and she did what any soldier would have done, she followed an order. She would have kept trying until she killed me, and she would have killed anybody who stood in her way—including you."

Lilly turned to Eric, asking without words if what Gabe said was true. Gabe saw Eric nod his head in agreement.

Anger flared in him. "No. Don't look at him—you look at me," Gabe snapped. Lilly looked to a stranger for the truth. A stranger who, up until five minutes before, Gabe had thought wanted to kill him.

"Lilly," he stressed. "I would never, never kill a woman unless she was a direct threat to me or the people I love. A deadly threat. I don't like the idea of killing a woman, much less actually killing one. A woman can bring a life into the world. How could I want to kill something that..." He stopped, unable to continue, and bit out, "It left me feeling sick and angry when it happened."

He caught her gaze. "How many times do I have to tell you not to be afraid of me? I could never hurt you," he pleaded. "Haven't I proved it time and time again? Have you ever had a reason to fear me?"

"All right." He sighed when she didn't answer. "Are you afraid now because of what you saw or because of what you know?"

"It scares me to think about you hurting a woman, but I understand she wasn't a normal woman." She stared him in the eye. She had no idea how telling the simple act was—if she was scared of him she wouldn't be able to look at him at all. "I've never seen you mistreat anyone and you have never given me a reason to be afraid of you." Then she admitted, "It's your intensity, I think, that frightens me."

"I'll try to tone that down at bit." He inhaled. The fear was all but gone—he was proud of her for standing her ground and facing her fear. "Still trust me, angel?"

* * * *

322

Lilly let her love for him run through her. His honesty, though scary, made her love him all the more. There would always be areas of Gabe's life she would find startling, but this was who he was, and she would love all of him.

They moved towards each other. All she wanted was to throw herself at him, feel his arms around her, but she stopped, staring at the trees. Another large, dark shadow was moving in the forest, and her relief was quickly replaced with fear as Harry stepped out of the trees with his gun aimed at the back of Eric's head.

"No, Harry, don't!" she called, as the first stirrings of the wind began to move around her.

The tracking system. Lilly shivered. The tracker was trying to locate her. She stepped to the side. Maybe if she kept moving it would take longer to find her. She needed the time to tell Gabe about Eric. Time, sadly, was now hunting her. She couldn't afford to waste this moment, so she blurted it out. "You can't kill him. He's Gabe's son."

All three men looked at her.

"You know?" Eric asked, a slow smirk pulling at his mouth. "How?"

The wind stirred again and she stepped back the other way. Her hands began to shake nervously.

"I wasn't sure until you looked at me just a moment ago. Your eyes. They…" She was going to say they glowed like Gabe's. But Gabe's eyes only did that when he looked at her, and she wanted to keep that for herself. "They're similar to Gabe's. The rest just fell into place. You're both the same height and build. You both have this…evil smile. The only differences are the dimples and black hair."

She wanted to kick herself for not realising it sooner. Her mind had known all along and her dreams had been trying to convince her of the truth. But she had been so concerned with Gabe's safety she had only seen Eric as a threat.

Harry, still pointing his gun at Eric, stepped around him and looked from Gabe to Eric and back.

"I'm right?" She asked, breathing faster, a heavy nauseous lump sitting in her stomach. The wind was getting stronger as it swirled around her, and again she stepped away, avoiding it.

"Yes. My mother was Sarah—"

Gabe cut him off. "Graves." He nodded. "I remember. Short, dark hair and she had dimples when she smiled." Eric nodded and smiled, showing Gabe his mother's dimples.

Lilly watched as Gabe studied Eric and nodded, an accepting look on his face. Gabe had a son, a family — this was wonderful. She swallowed the lump that had moved into her throat. The wind tugged at Gabe's cloak, forcing her to step back. What she wouldn't give to be a part of it. To be a part of Gabe's family.

* * * *

Gabe turned to Lilly and watched her pull his cloak close around her. She was terrified, and sad. He couldn't just smell it, he could feel it.

He reached down and picked up the tracker the blond had dropped. McGill would need it once he reached them. He held the tracker tightly in his grip and stepped closer to Lilly. Then he realised what was happening.

He fought the vortex, but the force and speed of the wind was increasing, keeping him away from her.

Her gaze was on the ground at his feet when he called to her. "Lilly!"

She stood unmoving in the centre of the spinning debris.

He hardened his voice and snapped out the command he had used earlier. "Lilly, look at me!"

She raised her sad eyes and stared into his face. His stomach clenched. The look was so accepting.

Emotions he had never experienced filled him. Fear of not being able to save Lilly, fury over her being taken away from him and his love. A love so deep, he knew no other would be able to fill the space in his chest when his heart was ripped out...because she *was* his heart.

He shook his head. "No. Lilly, no!" He would not allow this. He would not lose her. He would not let her go.

McGill arrived with Marc and George, and he whirled to face them.

"What's happening?" Marc asked, coming to an abrupt halt. Then he stared in shock. "No. Lilly!"

George stopped next to Marc. "Is everything all right...? No," he breathed.

Gabe thrust the tracker at McGill. "Stop it *now*," he ordered. "Right *now*!"

Eric stepped forward with a sympathetic look. "It can't be stopped once the tracker has locked on to the target."

Gabe turned his gaze on the man who was his son. The son he'd never known he had. A man he didn't know. Glaring into familiar green eyes, he ordered, "Harry, if he moves again, shoot him."

"Easy, Gabe," Harry warned, shaking his head.

Dismissing Harry, Gabe turned his attention back to McGill. He was studying the tracker, shaking his head, and explained, "This is a remote unit. You can only enter destination coordinates into it. It can take you from one location to another but," — he nodded at Eric — "he's right. Once the destination has been entered and the track button pressed, there is no way to stop it."

Gabe reached out and grabbed the man by the neck, squeezing. "Don't lie to me," he growled. He felt the wind pick up even more and he let go of McGill and turned to Lilly.

McGill coughed behind him. "Gabe, I'm sorry, there's nothing I can do from here. If I was back in the lab, I could override it through the main system. These remote units just don't have that capability."

Gabe stepped towards Lilly, into the vortex. He leaned into it, the invisible wall easily holding his weight in place. He needed to be close to her, as close as possible. His heart stopped as he locked eyes with her. His dark cloak was pinned against her body, flashes of her blue dress peeking out between the dark wool, her hair flying out in all directions. She looked like the stone carving of an angel bound for heaven.

He clenched his jaw tight. There was nothing he could do. He couldn't save her. The only person who had ever loved him, the only person he had ever loved, was slipping away from him. Going back to her own time, where she would die. He could not lose her, he would find a way to get her back. "Trust me," he called to her.

She blinked rapidly as tears streamed down her cheeks. Gabe felt his eyes begin to burn, as he mouthed the words, *I'll bring you back.*

He watched helplessly as the vortex closed above Lilly's head, roaring with rage when it lifted her off the ground and pulled her away.

Chapter Twenty-Nine

Silence.

Not even the birds made a sound. Gabe stared at the spot where Lilly had stood. He walked over and looked around. Nothing. The wind had erased all traces of her—he couldn't even smell her scent. It was as if she had never been.

Turning to look into the dense forest, hiding his rage from the others, he slowly closed his hands into fists. An unfamiliar force pulled at his insides, twisting his stomach into shaky knots. He suddenly felt restless, anxious, even agitated. Emotions he had never felt before crowded him. He was surrounded and completely unprepared to handle it.

Someone stepped up behind him and he knew it was Harry. Harry was the only person stupid enough to try to console him. Harry was the only person he would *allow* to console him. Harry placed a hand on his shoulder, squeezing gently.

"Gabe." His Scottish accent was thick. "What do you want us to do?"

"Yeah, Gabe," Marc sniffed. "Anything. We love Lilly, too."

"Easy, Marc," George said calmly. "Gabe knows that."

Gabe clenched his jaw. They all loved Lilly. He knew it, he just hadn't realised how much until now. His stomach squeezed, the urgent need beginning to eat away at him.

His abrupt turn caused Harry to drop his hand and step aside. He nodded his thanks as he stalked towards McGill.

He stopped an arm's length away—he didn't want to frighten McGill, and he didn't want to waste time chasing the man. Crossing his arms, he glared down at the professor. McGill stared back, pushing his glasses up his nose.

"Give it to me," Gabe ordered.

"Pardon?" said McGill, but his fingers tightened on the tracker.

"Don't fuck with me, Professor." The words were hard, and meant as a warning.

"I only have one tracker." McGill hesitated briefly, sweat collecting on his forehead. "I... I don't think it would be a good idea if you went to my time. You see—"

"I don't care what you think," Gabe growled. "Give me your tracker."

"You don't need him," Eric commented stepping forward.

Gabe eyed Eric. His son. He had so many questions to ask, but he couldn't afford to waste the time right now. The need was twisting him from the inside out—he needed to get to Lilly. He knew with his entire being he wouldn't stop feeling this way until she was safely back with him.

"Why's that?" Harry asked

Eric walked over to his dead team leader's body. "Because John, here, has the rest of the team's trackers." Pulling a knife from his boot, Eric cut John's pack free and stood, opening the pack to pull out a tracker. "Use these to get Lilly back. I would."

Gabe nodded at Eric.

"Now, just wait a minute." McGill spoke up, sounding alarmed. "You don't even know how to use it."

"I'll show them. It's surprisingly easy," Eric offered.

"What?" McGill shouted nervously. "No, no. You can't go back. It is out of the question. I will not allow it. I... I'll figure out a way to get Lilly back."

Marc stepped up next to Gabe. "Why so worked up, Professor? Afraid you might get caught?"

Gabe looked at Marc, puzzled, then back at McGill, who had begun to sweat. "What exactly will you get caught at?"

McGill didn't answer, he just stood there sweating.

Gabe looked at Marc and ordered, "Explain."

"He brought us here without anyone else knowing. We were a side project of his. If he shifts you or any of us to his time, people, i.e. his bosses, will find out what he was doing in his off-hours. And I'm guessing they won't be pleased."

McGill's face was very white. "Is that correct, McGill?"

The professor shook his head. "Will you at least let me try to get her back first?"

"No," Gabe snapped. Then he turned to Eric. "Can these trackers be reset for another destination? Or are they pre-programmed?"

"They can be reset," Eric confirmed.

"Good." Gabe stepped towards McGill, holding out his hand. "I will not ask you again."

Defeated, McGill pulled the tracker from his belt and placed it in Gabe's hand.

Gabe gave McGill's tracker to Eric. "Programme two of the trackers to McGill's destination. Harry and I are going to accompany the professor back to his time."

Eric nodded, looking thoughtful, then asked, "Why two? There are six trackers here—you all can go. Why stay here? You'll both be welcomed back into the UBF and those two"—Eric nodded, indicating Marc and George—"will be accepted in their fields. You can have a better life in my time. And enjoy the simple things, like indoor plumbing and hot and cold running water."

Gabe smiled. Was Eric hinting at something else besides indoor plumbing? Friends, or a family, maybe? How could he have that? His son looked to be the same age as him. And though the thought did appeal to him, he couldn't focus on that now—he needed to get to Lilly.

"One thing at a time. Will you programme the new destinations?"

Eric nodded. "No problem."

Gabe and Harry raced to the keep to collect their weapons and kit and headed back to the forest minutes later. Eric was holding out the trackers to them as they arrived back at the clearing.

"Both are programmed to the professor's destination. You want to have a look?" He offered one to Gabe.

"No." Gabe shook his head. "I trust you."

Eric smiled, showing off his mother's dimples, reminding Gabe of Sarah Graves. He had been so young then—a rookie—and Sarah had been nice. Both had been naïve.

He shook off the past. There was nothing he could fix now. He looked at Eric. Not that he would want to. The idea of having children had never bothered him—it was the reasons they were created that bothered him.

"I'm going to leave first and give my colonel the heads-up. I wrote down the professor's coordinates, so we'll be waiting for you at McGill's end." Eric stepped away, the wind whipping around him, and Gabe realised he had already pressed his tracking button.

Eric stepped into the clearing and waited for the vortex to close over the top of his head.

Gabe watched as his son was lifted into the air and disappeared from sight.

Next up was Harry, followed by McGill. Gabe stood next to George and spoke to him as they watched the professor vanish. "I'm sorry I'm leaving you with all this, but I have to go."

"I understand. We'll take care of it." A groan caught their attention and they turned to see Charles struggling to get up. George ran to the soldier's side calling, "Go, Gabe! Bring our Lilly back."

Pressing the tracking button, Gabe stepped into the clearing, stopping in the centre. A sensation of weight pressed down on his shoulders as his feet rose slightly off the ground. As weightlessness took over, he closed his eyes.

* * * *

Lilly's feet hit the pavement so hard, pain vibrated up her legs. The wind was still whipping around her. The tears were still falling. But her heart was gone. She had left it with Gabe. She didn't need it here. What would be the point? She was about to die.

Her body was released from the weighted sensation and she was free to move. She just didn't want to. She replayed his last words *I'll bring you back.* She inhaled. Would he try? She saw the resolve on his face. *Trust me.* She did trust him. He had never broken a promise to her, and he had never lied to her.

The rush of air from the falling tower was whirling around her and chunks of cement were fragmenting into hundreds of pieces around her, stinging as they hit her exposed skin. Her eyes felt raw from the tears and floating debris.

How could he do it? How could Gabe get to her? She knew so little about shifting or how the trackers worked. However, she did know that even though she'd been in 1503 for over a month, in her time, in 2012, she'd been gone only seconds. That left a non-existent window in which she could escape.

Looking up, she saw the tip of the antenna pointing towards her as it fell, silently claiming her as its victim.

* * * *

Gabe landed hard, his bent legs absorbing the sudden jolt to his body. He straightened slowly and his body tensed as a colonel stepped towards him. "Captain Sutherland."

"Sir." He kept his eyes on the soldiers that stood behind the colonel. The soldiers with the rifles fixed on him.

"Stand down," the colonel called over his shoulder. They did.

Gabe nodded and stood to full attention. The older man smiled and returned the salute, then held out his hand. "Colonel James Spencer, Commanding Officer of the UBF."

Gabe shook the CO's hand. "Colonel."

"I understand from Captain Graves you may need some help?"

Gabe eyed Eric, who was next to the CO. The look on his face was grim to say the least.

"Yes, sir. I need any file footage you have of the CN Tower collapsed by a terrorist bomb in June 2012."

"CN Tower? I'm not sure what that is, but Professor McGill has agreed to help in any way he can. Isn't that right, Professor?" Colonel Spencer asked, turning towards McGill.

"Yes." McGill was facing a screen, furiously punching at a keyboard. "I'm looking for the footage right now."

"There you are, Captain. Whatever you need," Spencer announced, with a smile on his face.

Gabe nodded, waiting to hear the rest. He had been 'in' too long not to know that a favour asked would mean another asked in return.

"And while you're waiting for Professor McGill to gather information, I wonder if you would be willing to assist in a few tasks that have been put into my charge." Spencer clasped his hands behind his back, rocking back onto his heels, waiting for an answer.

"Colonel, I was killed in action." Gabe felt the pull in his chest. He didn't have time for this shit right now.

"Yes, yes." Spencer waved his hand. "I know all that. I remember hearing about it. You had quite the reputation. I was a rookie when you were killed." He began a slow pace around the room. "I had asked to be transferred onto your team." He stopped and looked Gabe in the eye. "But I was told no." He moved again, slowly pacing. "I was disappointed. I wanted to learn as much as I could from you before I was to take command of my own team, and you were the best. Unfortunately, you were killed shortly after. I was... We were all surprised by what had happened." He stopped in front of Gabe. "But, as fate would have it, I now have my chance to learn from you, and so will my teams."

Gabe gazed over at Eric. He raised his eyebrows slightly, expressing his dislike.

"Colonel, are you asking me to train your teams?"

"That and lend your expertise on the tasks I have already mentioned."

Frowning, Gabe asked. "You don't trust your soldiers?"

"I have good men and women under my command. They are well trained—I have made sure of that. I want them to be better. I want them to be as good as you."

Gabe exhaled. "Colonel," he began clearly. "We're here because we require information on the attack on the CN Tower. We want to help—"He chose his words carefully. This man didn't need to know how deep his feelings were for Lilly—it could be used against him and could potentially put Lilly in danger. "We want to help our friend."

The colonel studied him. "You're referring to Lilly Marten, I presume." He inclined his head towards Eric. "I was under the impression there was more of an...attraction."

"That is what I observed, sir."

"Then why is he giving the impression there isn't?"

"He's being cautious, sir," Eric answered, staring at Gabe.

"Understood." Spencer nodded. "We will help in any way we can with your rescue of Lilly. All I ask is that you help me with my requests."

Gabe controlled the build-up of frustration. "Professor. How much time do you need?" Gabe demanded, keeping eye contact with Spencer.

"I'm not sure yet. I'm still trying to access the Canadian archives."

Gabe studied the colonel. He did not trust this man—rank had no impact on his judgement. Lilly was the only reason he was here. He didn't care about anything else. But if he didn't give a little, Spencer might close him down.

"I'll give you four hours a day. When McGill has all the intel I need to safely get to Lilly, I'm gone."

"Understood." Spencer nodded. "Eric will show you your rooms and where you can collect new kit. You'll have a training schedule tonight."

Gabe nodded. The colonel left, his escort following.

Gabe walked over to where McGill was searching through files.

"Do you think that was a good idea, agreeing to train men who could possibly want to kill you?" Harry asked.

Gabe shrugged. "If it gets me what I want, then so be it. Lilly is all that matters."

"You'd better watch the colonel. He seems a bit dodgy."

Gabe looked back at the door. "I noticed."

Chapter Thirty

Gabe threw open the door to McGill's lab and stalked into the room.

"No more."

The heavy, reinforced metal door echoed as it bounced off the wall.

"We've gone over every possible scenario, and some not so possible." He pulled his rifle over his head and slammed it onto the table. "Between you and those fucking ops Spencer had us do, we've wasted enough time." He ran his hand through his sweat-soaked hair.

They had wasted months running through each and every scenario from beginning to end, with every known element factored in, and after all this wasted time, his first plan was still the best option.

"We have lots of time," McGill pointed out. "No matter how long it takes us to decide how to save Lilly, it will be only a matter of seconds to her."

That was not the answer he wanted to hear. Body still tense and ready to do battle, Gabe stalked across the room towards McGill. Dirt mixed with blood and small pieces of debris fell from his gear.

"Terrifying seconds, Professor."

He had seen the old file footage of the tower falling. Every time he watched it, he knew Lilly was standing at the base, scared and alone. And every one of those times, he had to fight the urge to ram his fist into something. Those images and the thought of Lilly terrified and alone kept him awake at night.

God damn it. He should be with her, protecting her. He felt a rumble deep in his chest, and only then heard the growl. Frustration over having to wait to save the one person he loved was pushing him beyond his normal sense of control.

He was within arm's length of McGill when Harry stepped in front of him, blocking his view of the professor.

Harry shook his head, "We need him to get Lilly." Then he glared over his shoulder. "You do have the option of coming back afterwards, to pay him a visit."

Gabe glared at McGill, an evil smile pulling at his lips. "That thought alone should keep me going." He pointed at McGill from Harry's side. "No more fucking about. We go with my first plan. And we go tonight."

McGill stepped forward. "You can't go tonight. Spencer will not approve it. You still have another operation to go on."

"I reminded Spencer today what my main priority is."

"Lilly," McGill said.

"Yes, Lilly. Why the hell do you *think* I'm here?"

"If you don't make it, she'll die," McGill said with more emotion than Gabe had expected from a scientist. Gabe studied him. There was more to McGill's running over every option than being thorough. There was more there than just concern, there was pain. Gabe raised his eyebrows. Ah, shit! McGill was in love with Lilly.

Gabe exhaled, forcing his body to relax. How could he fault McGill for trying to protect Lilly? It was the very thing he was trying to do—their methods were just different.

"If she does die, which is unlikely, she'll die with the man she loves."

McGill turned back to the computer screen, the emotion wiped from his face. Gabe looked at Harry and shook his head. Damn it. Since when had he started feeling compassion for people? Especially McGill.

He walked over to the man and spoke as gently as his mood would allow. "I won't allow her to die and neither will you. So between the two of us, she will have a long, happy life."

"How can you know she'll be happy with you?" McGill asked. His voice held traces of bitterness.

"I don't know." Gabe shrugged, holding on to his temper. "But I can promise you I'll spend the rest of my life trying."

McGill stopped typing and faced him. "I hope so." He stood, walked over to a printer and withdrew the pages that had just emerged from it. He held them out for Gabe. "She deserves to be happy."

Gabe took the pages.

"All her information. Home address, work address, phone numbers, maps of Toronto, layout of her university and work. Information on the group responsible and their preferred method of building bombs. Detonation times... Everything you will need."

Gabe flipped through the pages. McGill was very thorough—every detail about Lilly's life and the attack on the CN Tower was there. McGill was doing the only thing he knew how, and his scientific approach would make saving Lilly almost a guarantee.

"There are a few concerns you need to be aware of," McGill said, pushing his glasses up his nose.

Gabe caught McGill's stare and frowned. "Go ahead."

"First off is the arrival day. I'm going to send you back three days instead of five."

"Why?"

"It will give you less of a chance of running into her. And there is still plenty of time to study the tower."

"It would be bad if I met her before she's shifted?" Gabe scowled, looking up from the pages McGill had given him.

"Lilly has a photographic memory. If she sees you before I first shift her, she will remember you when she arrives in 1503. You cannot come into contact with her on any level."

"So, what if he does?" Harry asked.

"What if he does?" McGill dramatically threw his hands into the air. "If Gabe meets her before she's shifted and she remembers it in 1503 that entire time might change. I don't know if it would be a good change or a bad change. And it might or might not alter what is happening now," McGill stressed. "Right now, we have a chance to save her. If the time we spent in 1503 alters, we might not get another chance."

"I'm hearing a lot of 'mights' and 'maybes'," Harry muttered.

McGill sighed. "There are so many possibilities. Who knows what could happen." He focused on Gabe. "Do you really want to take that chance?"

Chapter Thirty-One

Exiting Lilly's small apartment building, Gabe walked back down the dimly lit street to the waiting, dark blue SUV.

"Feel better?" Harry asked, handing him a bottle of water.

Gabe opened the bottle and raised his eyebrows before taking a long swallow.

"I'll take that as a 'yes'."

They both watched as a car approached and then slowly passed.

"How's her apartment? Secure?" Harry stared into the side mirror, following the car's progress.

"Not enough to keep me out, but not bad, considering." He could still smell her. Still feel her skin on his fingertips.

"Then we can go and find a hotel for the night?"

Gabe slowly turned to Harry, a you'd-better-be-joking look on his face.

Harry chuckled. "It was a thought."

"Think about something else," Gabe mumbled.

"She'll be fine. She did survive on her own before she met you."

"Mmm."

She was on her own right now. But once tomorrow was over and Lilly was back with him, Gabe would make sure she wasn't alone again.

The two men sat in silence for the rest of the night, watching the city move around them. Three days passed quickly, and Gabe watched from a distance as Lilly went about her life. Home. School. Work. She didn't go out, she hardly socialised, her 'hellos' were quick and made on the run, so she wouldn't have to stop and talk. She wasn't living. She was only going through the motions. He knew why. Self-preservation. Lilly was doing what she had to do to fit in without making close ties. She was more alone than he could imagine.

Looking down at his watch, Gabe waited inside the base of the tower, his shoulder resting against a wall next to a row of windows. Lilly should be arriving at any second…and she did. His chest tightened as she came around the corner on her bike. He watched through the reflective glass as she stopped and had a conversation with a woman — McGill's report said it was her manager, Stacey. He smiled as he watched Lilly chat with the woman. She liked the woman — he could tell by her smile. He straightened as he saw her look down at her feet, then step to the side. Seconds later, she repeated the process.

It had started. She was being tracked. He looked down at his watch. Less than a minute to go before the tower blew.

The two women said their goodbyes and Lilly waved as her friend ran for the bus.

Hands clenched into fists, Gabe checked his watch again. Ten seconds.

He fought the need to run to her. To pull her away before the tower fell.

The floor and walls shook as the top of the tower exploded.

Glass shattered, lights fell from the ceiling, display shelves and other furniture toppled to the ground, people screamed and ran in fear.

Gabe remained still, hands clenched tight at his sides, watching. The muscles in his neck and shoulders tensed to the point of pain. Still, he watched. He watched Lilly. He watched as she became still, frozen in place. He watched as the chunks of cement shattered around her, the fragments striking her face and neck. He watched as she looked up in fear, only to see the expression vanish and acceptance appear in her dark eyes.

With his heart racing, Gabe began to move steadily along the wall of windows, his eyes never leaving Lilly.

What was she still doing here? Why was it taking so long to shift her? Another large chunk of cement landed close to her. He was going to kill McGill for making her wait so long. She was being beaten to a pulp by flying cement.

Just as he reached the exit, he forced himself to stop. No matter how long it took to shift her, he had to wait. He couldn't go to her, not yet.

Gabe opened the door and stepped outside just as the spinning debris closed over her head and Lilly vanished.

* * * *

The crunch of a large piece of cement landed less than a foot away. The force of the impact sent fragments smashing into her. Closing her eyes, Lilly winced as her face and body were hit by the flying debris. The pain was minor in comparison to the deep sense of loss she felt. The ground rumbled as the sky deck and antenna rushed towards her, the sound almost deafening. Pulling Gabe's cloak tighter around her, she waited.

Gabe. God, she loved him. She replayed the last time he had made love to her and the words he had whispered against her mouth. *I love you, angel.*

His face appeared on the light grey cement that made up the base of the giant tower. His features were sharp and solely focused on her, his arms and shoulders moving back and forth. Sadness, sharp and deep, caused her chest to heave. Now, more than ever, she truly hated her ability. Closing her eyes didn't help. The memory of Gabe floating around in her mind was so painful, but she couldn't stop herself from replaying their time together.

So she stood there, with her eyes closed, and replayed the time she had spent with him.

Her heart was pounding in her chest, so loud she could hear it. A steady pounding that grew louder by the second—and she squeezed her eyes tight as she realised it wasn't her heart, but the tower closing in. She choked back a sob when the pounding was a breath away.

A blow to her side slammed her to the ground. The heartache, thankfully, disappeared when her world went black.

Chapter Thirty-Two

Keeping her eyes closed, Lilly took a slow breath, shifting her body, and her head throbbed in response to the slight movement. The dark room span for a moment when she opened her eyes, then stopped, coming into focus. The street light filtered through the new curtains on her bedroom windows. The curtains matched the new sheet set she had bought the week before. White cotton, with—she took another breath—small red roses. She blinked hard.

She was home. In her apartment, lying on her bed, with her new sheets covering her.

"Oh, God," she whispered, placing a hand over her mouth.

Had it just been a dream? All of it, a dream?

No, it couldn't be. She frowned. Her imagination was non-existent. She couldn't have been here the whole time. She had gone to work, almost been squashed by the tower, and then she'd been shifted back to...

Shifted. Time travel.

She looked around her room. Everything was exactly the way she'd left it before she went to sleep.

A soft whimper escaped as she sucked in air.

Gabe.

Her heart dropped into her stomach. Had she created Gabe to fill the void in her life? Her heart ached for a man who might be a fantasy.

She covered her face with her hands. "He was real, I know he was. I'm not crazy," she pleaded aloud.

Running her hand over her face and into her hairline, she suddenly stopped. Lightly, as though it might disappear, she traced the raised outline of a scar on her forehead.

The scar she had got when a chunk of cement had hit her. George had sewn it up. George had sewn up her head in 1503. Medieval England. Hope pounded in her chest.

"I'm not crazy. It happened," she whispered. "I know it did."

Sitting up slowly, she threw the covers off and slipped off the bed, keeping her fingers pressed against the scar, praying it would be there when she looked in the bathroom mirror. The room was dark, but she knew four steps would have her entering the small bathroom attached to her bedroom.

She reached out in the dark when she should have arrived at the door to the bathroom, and instead of touching a cool wall, she touched a warm, solid chest.

Shocked, she stepped back quickly, causing her head to spin. As she swayed, firm hands grabbed her by the shoulders and forced her backwards, those few steps, onto the edge of the bed.

With her eyes closed, she felt the strong hands release her and lightly trace the side of her face. Lilly sat there on the edge of her bed, scared to open her eyes. Was she dreaming now, or was this real?

"Lilly." The deep voice had her catching her breath.

Holding her breath, she listened for the familiar voice. She needed to know her mind wasn't playing tricks on her.

"Lilly. Breathe." Hearing the commanding tone, she did as he asked, keeping her eyes tightly closed.

Gabe.

There were so many emotions inside, flooding her heart and mind and body — too many to even count.

Gabe. Tears filled her closed eyes. He was here. Was he real?

"Gabe?" Her voice was so low she could barely hear it herself.

"I'm here, angel," he whispered back.

Angel.

That was her undoing. The tears slid down her cheeks as she opened her eyes. She needed to see his perfect face, his glowing green eyes. He stood before her, his broad shoulders blocking the bathroom door. He looked different, but it was Gabe. His light brown hair was cut short, the soft gold streaks gone. Her eyes drifted down the length of him. No cotton shirt or breeches, like she was used to seeing him in. He was now wearing clothing appropriate for her time. A white, fitted T-shirt that clung to his arms and chest, and a pair of loose-fitting jeans. She looked up, meeting his eyes. Hungry eyes.

"Gabe." Abruptly jerking up, she flung herself at him, burying her face in his neck. "Please be real," she pleaded into the side of his neck. "I don't want to be alone." She took another shuddering breath, the tears still falling.

* * * *

"You're not alone." He dug his hands into her hair, pinned her body against his. "I'm here." He breathed in her scent again. Lilly.

She trembled again.

"Don't cry," he whispered into her hair.

"You're real. Aren't you? Please tell me you are."

Her plea melted his heart. Pulling back, he cradled her face between his hands. Her eyes were squeezed shut. He smiled and wiped her tear-stained cheeks. "Open your eyes, angel."

He waited.

"Look at me, Lilly."

Her dark brown eyes opened, the exotic sweep causing his gut to tighten like it always did.

"This isn't a dream. I'm real. You're real. This is all real." She blinked rapidly, her eyes searching his face.

"You told me you trusted me. You haven't changed your mind, have you?" he asked, holding her gaze.

She shook her head. "I felt like I was going crazy. I woke up here, in my room and thought... I thought what happened with..." She put her hand on his chest, over his heart. "I thought everything was just a dream."

"It wasn't a dream."

She touched his face, her eyes filling with tears again.

He couldn't stand it anymore. He pressed his mouth to hers, tasting her tears. She relaxed against him and, wrapping his arms tightly around her, he deepened the kiss, digging his fingers into her skin, allowing the need for her to consume him. His eyes snapped open at her soft whimper and he pulled back, noticed her swollen mouth. The need to devour her pulsed hot through his veins, burning him from the inside out. He breathed, taking the time to control his body, but when he exhaled it came out closer to a growl.

Space.

Stepping back, he fought to get his hunger under control. The need for Lilly had been strong from the moment he saw her, but right now it was out of his control. It was the reason behind his present state. He hadn't been in control of a situation since the tracker was activated, and with that lack of control came the fear.

The one emotion he had trained himself to ignore filled every cell in his body. It consumed him. Fear for Lilly. Fear of not being able to save her. Fear of what his life would be like without her love.

"Gabe?" She stepped towards him, her dark eyes wide and full of concern. He could see the love on her face. A love he was never supposed to have, but would fight to keep. Gabe froze, the breath almost driven from his lungs. "You love me?" he asked harshly.

"Yes. I do love you." The declaration was soft but clear.

"Again," he ordered.

"I love you." This time she spoke with more force.

She did love him—and he had no idea why.

Exhaling, he fell to his knees, pulling her close. Pressing his face into her stomach, he circled her with his arms.

"Gabe?" Gentle hands cradled his head. She whispered. "What's wrong?"

He tightened his grip on her, her scent filling his lungs.

"Do you know how long it's been since I've seen you?" His words were rough, raw, mirroring his emotions. "Or since I touched you or tasted you? How long it has been since I held you while you slept?" He pushed up her T-shirt and kissed her stomach. "Four months. Four months of hell," he gritted out.

"I'm sorry." She ran her fingers into his short hair, trying to draw him closer. "I'm so sorry."

"I need you. Need you loving me." He squeezed his teeth together. "But I... It's so strong... I have no control."

She lifted his face, love in her dark eyes. "I trust you."

He closed his eyes and pressed his mouth to her stomach. He just wasn't strong enough to fight it. He didn't want to fight it.

Gabe curled his arms around her, his body crowding hers as he pushed her down onto the floor.

Gabe removed only the most basic of clothing before he took her. Their loving was fast and heated. He couldn't do slow—not right now. He needed to give in to his hunger and, once sated, he would take his time with her and give her everything she deserved.

God, he must have pictured this moment a thousand times. The moment he would have her back and he could make love to her. To be surrounded by her hot, tight body, to see the love on her face. Yet, lying with her under him, his body deep in hers, seeing the love on her face, was better than any dream. He kissed her soft, upturned mouth as she took him to heaven. Lilly was heaven. His own personal heaven.

Chapter Thirty-Three

"I can't believe you got to me."

Gabe rubbed his chin on top of her head. They were lying on her bed, covered by sheets with small red roses. Just yesterday he had stood next to her, while she slept covered by the same sheets. "I told you I would bring you back."

Her hand was resting on his chest. "I know. But you could have been killed."

"But I wasn't. So don't think about it."

"Where did you come from? How did you get to me so fast?"

"I was just inside the main entrance when you were first shifted. I had to wait for you to arrive back again, from 1503, before I started towards you."

She nodded. "It's strange. I know I was in England for a long period, but when I came back, it was right where I left off. I wonder how long I was actually gone."

"You were gone for four seconds."

She raised her head to look at him.

"Four seconds?" Her head filled with questions. "It's incredible! I was shifted back so close to the time I was first taken. How did you figure it out?"

Gabe kissed her forehead and said, "McGill's the one who figured out all the shifting times. I planned the rest."

"Did four months really pass by for you?"

The soft smile drifted from his face.

The way he had dropped to his knees and held her was still fresh in her mind. Gabe had tight control over his emotions, so it had alarmed her to hear the anguish in his voice.

He rolled onto his side pulling her to face him. "Yes." He stroked her cheek. "It took time for McGill to extract the information entered into the tracker used to shift you. Then we went over every scenario to get you out from under the tower. The rest of the time I was...working."

"Working? Where?"

He pulled her closer, pinning her against him. "I was working with Eric and other UBF teams."

Remaining silent, Lilly waited for him to continue.

"I was asked to help train the teams in Eric and McGill's time, in exchange for the UBF helping me get to you."

"Exchange. Is that a nice way of saying blackmail?"

"Yes, it is." He rubbed his hands up and down her back, soothing her sudden tension. "I agreed, though. I didn't want to run the chance of the CO getting in my way and trying to stop me. It did help take my mind off you." He shook his head when he saw her frown. "I didn't like having to wait to get to you. You needed me and I wasn't able to get to you as fast as I wanted. So while I waited for McGill, I directed my aggression at training and operations."

"Oh." She looked down, puzzled. "McGill said the UBF soldiers who came after you were constantly compared to your skills."

"It would piss me off if I was constantly compared to a dead man. But I straightened that out—it won't happen again."

She wondered what he had done to change the misunderstanding.

"Lilly." His tone demanded attention, and she raised her head. "I have been offered a position with the UBF in Eric's time."

"Okay." The questions didn't have time to form in her head before Gabe continued.

"I didn't accept or commit to anything. Actually, I'm still surprised Colonel Spencer offered it to me."

"Why?"

"Because I openly threatened him in front of a few of his officers. I told him I was done training his teams and if he didn't like it, I would drag his ass back with me and toss him under the tower when it fell."

Lilly felt her mouth drop open. "Would you really do that?"

"Yes." He answered the question without any hesitation.

Gabe stroked the scar on her lip. "We need to start thinking about when and where we want to live."

Gabe clearly saw her sad expression.

"But I thought we were going back? Marc and George are still there. And what about all those people who depend on you…?" She trailed off.

"We *are* going back to 1503." He quickly relieved her fears. "I gave my word to Thomas I would look after his holding until his younger brother could travel north. Angel," he said, "I won't leave those people to fend for themselves. We'll stay until Edmund arrives. But I have no idea when that will be, so we need to be prepared."

Gabe watched as a sweet smile spread across her face. He couldn't resist kissing her mouth, tracing her lips with his tongue and drinking in her sweet, heavenly taste. How was it that, just by being with her, it felt as though his sins, which were dark and plentiful, were washed away? She made him a different man. He pulled her onto his chest and wrapped his arms around her.

"We can't stay here," she said, resting her head on his chest. "And we can't stay in 1503 either, can we?"

Lilly knew the answer—he'd just wanted her to acknowledge it.

"No," he answered honestly.

"Is McGill's time our only option? That's why you told me about the UBF job?"

"All our basic survival needs would be met," he admitted. "But it's not our only option. If you don't want to go, then we don't go, and we find another time and place. I won't risk losing you for anything. It's that simple."

"But it does make the most sense."

As she lay on top of him, Gabe could feel her heart pound in her chest before she blurted out, "What about Harry and Marc and George? Will they come with us? Marc has the ability to go back home and so does George."

"Harry has been offered his own team with the UBF and a promotion. He's still considering it. As for Marc and George, if they choose to come, they'll be accepted into the UBF, working in their specialised fields."

"Do you think they'll come?"

"I don't know. George made it clear he has no desire to go back to 1940. Marc..." He shook his head. "I don't know. In the end, the decision is theirs. I won't force them." Gabe squeezed her tight. "There's one more thing I need you to think about."

"Okay...?"

"When we go back to the keep, there are certain events that will have to take place in order to keep up appearances."

"Like what?"

"We'll be getting married, Lilly and when it's over, you will be my wife."

"Marriages then aren't the same as now—they weren't a legal contract like in my time. And who knows what they're like in your time," she answered seriously.

He laughed—he couldn't help it. It wasn't the response he'd been expecting.

"We will follow the local customs and, when the time comes and we relocate, we'll do it again. But all nice and legal."

He ran his finger along her bottom lip and asked, "Do you want to go back to 1503 and become my wife?"

"Yes. But..."

"But?" He slid his fingers into her dark hair, holding her face to his.

"But what if we do marry, what about the UBF rule of no spouses? You can't be my lover, let alone my husband. And it sounds like they take the rule very seriously," she pointed out.

He shook his head. "The colonel knows what my priority is — he'll make an exception if he wants me to train his teams."

"But, Gabe…"

He stopped her when he heard the worry in her voice.

"Lilly, I love you. Do you really think I could just let you go because of a regulation? I never knew what I was missing before I met you, but I do now. There's no way I'll go back to that. You're worth the risk. Now, answer my question again." He locked eyes with her.

Lilly squeezed her eyes shut and slowly opened them. He was still there. She could still feel the warmth of his body. Still feel his arms wrapped around her.

"Lilly?"

This wasn't a dream. Gabe was real. Her heart pounded in her chest as she nodded up at him. "Yes." The word came out a soft whisper. Gabe tightened his hold, rolling her onto her back, pushing between her thighs, his throbbing shaft slowly entering her.

Trailing his fingers over her cheek, Gabe repeated the words he had said hundreds of years before. "You're mine, angel."

The words sparked a memory. The whisper of his voice, the light touch to her cheek, the smell of the room. Her eyes opened. The familiar feeling was too strong to ignore. Had Gabe been here, in her room...before she was shifted? Framing his face, she looked up. "Were you here...before?"

With a soft smile, he nodded. "I had to see you." He lowered his face, kissing her racing pulse. "Make sure you were safe."

The overwhelming feeling of love filled her. Before she had even met him, Gabe had been protecting and caring for her. With her heart bursting, Lilly tightened her hold on him, wanting him close, needing him as much as he needed her.

"Don't ever let me go." She repeated his words as they became one.

Breathless, Gabe whispered against her mouth, "Never."

Epilogue

England, 2111

"Well, Captain?" Colonel Spencer leant back in his leather chair, fingertips pressed together. "Can I assume he is back, playing lord of the castle?"

Eric nodded. "Yes, sir."

"And you spoke with him about the offer I made?"

"I did, sir." Eric stood with his legs apart, gripping his beret behind his back.

"And?" Spencer pressed.

"He said, 'Not yet.'" Eric repeated the exact words Gabe had used.

"Not yet? Then when?" Spencer asked

"He's waiting for the brother of the former lord to arrive and claim the holding."

"He's making me wait." Spencer smiled. "What about York?"

Eric smothered a smile. "Sergeant York has also decided to wait until the brother has arrived."

Actually, Harry had told him clearly where he could stick Spencer's offer, then said in a rough growl that he was still thinking it over.

"I can't fault him for being loyal." Spencer sat forward, resting his elbows on his desk. "And the girl? Is Sutherland still going to marry her?"

Eric looked at his colonel. For once, he wasn't sure what his commanding officer would do with this information. "Yes, I believe he is."

Spencer sighed deeply. "That does make my life difficult. Does she have any skills we can use?"

"Not that I'm aware of, sir." That wasn't a lie. Eric didn't really know much about Lilly, except that Gabe was very protective of her, not leaving her side whenever he was near. In addition, when he approached Professor McGill, the man became tight-lipped when questions about Lilly were asked.

There was something different about her, uniquely so. He just had to figure out what that was. He was, however, astute enough to recognise that if Spencer was to find out that Lilly had some kind of hidden talent he would take advantage of it and use it for his own cause.

"Then we'll have to find a way of keeping her busy and away from Sutherland while he's training my teams."

Eric stepped forward, placing his hands on the colonel's desk. "Sir," he began. "He won't allow you to send Lilly away. And if you try, he will tear this place apart."

Spencer raised his eyebrows as Eric finished the warning. "I've seen him with her. Taking her off this base, away from him, or even touching her will be the fastest way to get yourself killed."

Spencer stared up at him with an arrogant smile. "Thank you for the warning, Eric, but I do know who we're talking about here. Having her removed from the base was not my intention. Sutherland made it very clear he would not come without her, which is why I am willing to allow her presence. I only meant we must find her something to do during the day, so she's out of his way."

"I'm sure we can find something for her to do."

"I agree." Spencer dismissed the subject and moved on to the next. "Now." He opened a red folder sitting in front of him. "How is it going with Beth in weapons research? Any problems?"

"No." Eric clasped his hands behind his back, giving the impression his new detail was working well, when in fact it was the opposite. Dealing with Beth had become a daily battle, and for the first time in his life as a soldier, it was a battle he wasn't sure he could win.

Beth's bright smile suddenly pushed past the barriers he had built in his head, and he fought like a soldier about to be overrun by the enemy to push them back.

He finished answering his colonel. "No problems at all."

Now, that was a lie.

About the Author

Nancy's addiction for a good trash novel began in her late-teens when her grandmother gave her a bag of Harlequin Romance books. She was hooked and spent the next few years lurking in the dark corners of used bookstores searching for her next fix. Until, one marriage and two kids later, her own ideas had her jumping up at 3am (much to her husband's annoyance) and typing them into her laptop. Beside her husband and children, Nancy has three passions, rearranging furniture, buying bed linens and, of course, writing. Nancy lives in Eastern Ontario with her family and two over sized lap dogs.

Nancy Adams loves to hear from readers.

You can find her contact information, website details and author profile page at http://www.total-e-bound.com

Total-E-Bound Publishing

www.total-e-bound.com

Take a look at our exciting range of literagasmic™
erotic romance titles and discover pure quality
at Total-E-Bound.

CPSIA information can be obtained at www.ICGtesting.com
Printed in the USA
LVOW06s1157031213

3636893LV00001B/43/P